As tired as ~~she was~~ **a spent long** ~~minutes~~ ~~staring at~~ **ceiling and picturing Hunter's tall, muscular body squeezing into the small antique bed in the guest room.**

She imagined his long legs hanging off the end of the mattress, his wide shoulders filling the width of the bed and his chiseled face nestled on the pillow. Did he snore? Did he sleep in the buff? What would it be like to curl against his strength and sleep wrapped in his arms? To kiss him goodnight, feel his skin against hers, have his hands

Brianna scrubbed both hands over her face and stopped the daydream in its erotic tracks. Her skin tingled from her scalp to her toes, and a pleasant heat had curled in her belly. *Dream all you want, but don't get any ideas about acting on the fantasy.* Hunter wasn't hers to claim.

PROTECTING HER ROYAL BABY

BY
BETH CORNELISON

Published in Great Britain 2014
by Mills & Boon, an imprint of Harlequin (UK) Limited,
Eton House, 18-24 Paradise Road, Richmond, Surrey, TW9 1SR

© 2014 Beth Cornelison

ISBN: 978-0-263-91422-1

18-0614

Harlequin (UK) Limited's policy is to use papers that are natural, renewable and recyclable products and made from wood grown in sustainable forests. The logging and manufacturing processes conform to the legal environmental regulations of the country of origin.

Printed and bound in Spain
by Blackprint CPI, Barcelona

Beth Cornelison started writing stories as a child when she penned a tale about the adventures of her cat, Ajax. A Georgia native, she received her bachelor's degree in public relations from the University of Georgia. After working in public relations for a little more than a year, she moved with her husband to Louisiana, where she decided to pursue her love of writing fiction.

Since that first time, Beth has written many more stories of adventure and romantic suspense and has won numerous honors for her work, including a coveted Golden Heart Award in romantic suspense from Romance Writers of America. She is active on the board of directors for the North Louisiana Storytellers and Authors of Romance (NOLA STARS) and loves reading, traveling, *Peanuts'* Snoopy and spending downtime with her family.

She writes from her home in Louisiana, where she lives with her husband, one son and two cats who think they are people. Beth loves to hear from her readers. You can write to her at PO Box 5418, Bossier City, LA 71171, USA, or visit her website, www.bethcornelison.com.

To my prince—I love you, Paul!

Thank you to Mackenzie Walton for sharing her beautiful cat Sorsha for this story, and to Julie Sieger for sharing Cinderella and Sebastian. Look for all three of these kitties to appear again in Grant's book! Julie and Mackenzie won the bid to have their kitties featured through Brenda Novak's Auction for the Cure of Diabetes.

Thank you to Robyn Elyse Rosenberg for allowing me to use her name for Brianna's aunt. Robyn, also, won the bid for this opportunity through Brenda Novak's Auction for the Cure of Diabetes.

Chapter 1

She stared in stunned silence at the man standing in her living room, a man she'd once trusted. Working to shake herself from the numb shock that locked her throat, she blinked hard and scrubbed her hands over her face. "Why didn't you tell me any of this last winter? Don't you think I had a right to know what…*who* I was involved with?"

He had the decency to look guilty. "I'm sorry. I didn't tell you for this very reason. I knew this was how you'd react."

She exhaled harshly. "Well, it is rather…*startling* news, wouldn't you say?"

"I know. But we'd agreed what we had was a vacation fling. I didn't think I'd ever see you again. I didn't think I'd…develop feelings for you. And I never thought you'd—"

"Get pregnant?" She rubbed her hand over her nine-months-swollen belly and grunted. "Well, neither did I. But here's the proof that condoms aren't one hundred percent fail-safe."

"Indeed." He gave her a worried grimace. "The question now is, how do we hide the baby? How do we protect him?"

"Protect him?"

He took a step toward her, his hands spread. "If anyone finds out he's my child, my bloodline, they'll want to kill him like they've tried to kill me."

A thread of fear tugged inside her. "But if I don't tell anyone who his father is—"

A shattering of glass at her back door cut her off. He cursed in a foreign language she didn't recognize.

"It's too late," he said, his voice tight, panicked. His eyes were round with alarm and apology. "They're here. They know." He shook his head. "I'm so sorry. I didn't think anyone had followed me."

Adrenaline spiked inside her, and she sidled closer to him as crashing sounds filtered from the back of her house. "I don't understand. Who—"

"There's no time! You have to go! Run!"

"But you—"

"You can't worry about me. You have to save our child!" He pushed her toward the front door. "Hurry! They'll try to kill you, try to kill him."

A dark-clad figure appeared from her kitchen and raised a long-muzzled gun. Fired.

The father of her baby pushed her to the floor as the bullets whizzed over them. The jolt as she hit the floor sent a sharp pain through her belly, and a warm gush of fluid trickled down her leg. She clutched her middle, worried for her baby.

In the next second, he was shoving her up and to-ward the front door. "Go! Hide! Don't come back here!"

Bullets pelted the wall near her, and she screamed. How had her life become such a nightmare?

Snatching the keys to her old car from the peg by the door, she raced out to her front driveway as fast as a pregnant woman could run. The pain in her midsec-tion grew, and she nearly doubled over. With a quick glance over her shoulder as she tumbled into the driver's seat, she saw three men now in her living room with her baby's father. They held him by the arms, restraining him, a gun at his temple.

Nausea swamped her. They would kill him, she was sure. But why? What was their motive?

One of the men burst through the front door, fol-lowing her. He raised his weapon, and she gunned the engine. The *thunk* of bullets hitting the rear of her car spiked her fear. She gasped and scrunched as low as she could in the seat as she sped away. Tears blinded her as she raced down the street. She didn't know where she was going. Away. To hide. To—

Another sharp pain gripped her stomach. More warm fluid puddled beneath her. Oh, dear God! Her water had broken. The fall in her living room must have started her labor!

She held her belly and cried out as the contraction tightened. Forget hiding. Her baby was coming. Dou-bling over in pain, she raced down the highway, pray-ing she could reach the hospital in Lagniappe in time.

The car was coming right at him. Weaving. Speed-ing. With him at twelve o'clock.

Adrenaline shot through Hunter Mansfield. Irritation and alarm nipping the back of his neck, he slowed to a stop along the rural Louisiana road where he jogged every Sunday afternoon. He assumed a ready stance on the balls of his feet, prepared to jump out of the way of the erratically lurching vehicle as it neared. The glare of sunlight reflected off the windshield, preventing him from seeing the driver. A drunk? A distracted teenager?

The small blue Honda's engine roared, and the car lurched forward, its wheels kicking up gravel as the passenger-side tires moved from the pavement onto the narrow shoulder. Hunter braced himself, rapidly weighing whether to dive for the four-foot ditch to his left or feint right into the road, assuming the car wouldn't correct its path in time. Both posed risk.

The ditch.

Just as he shifted his weight to spring to his left, the sun slipped behind a cloud. He caught a glimpse of a face behind the steering wheel. A woman. A startled, frightened look. A last-second swerve, tires squealing.

He jumped aside but not fast enough. The sedan clipped his hip as he launched himself toward the ditch. He landed with a tooth-jarring thump. Rolled. Pain streaked from his shoulder down his arm.

He twisted to watch the Honda rocket past, grumbling an invective under his breath.

Still traveling at a high speed, the car overcorrected from the swerve to miss him and fishtailed. In seconds, the driver had lost control. The sedan careened off the road at high speed, flipped and rolled into the ditch.

Horror punched him in the gut. Scrambling to his feet, Hunter ran down the road to the inverted car and crouched at the broken driver's window. "Hey, are you okay?"

A pained and panicked cry came from inside.

Unable to see the front seat even from a squat, he got on his stomach and peered inside. The sight that greeted him backed his breath into his throat.

The woman lay crumpled on the roof of the sedan, which was now below her. Her forehead was bleeding. Her face was wrenched in a mask of agony. And she clutched her...*rounded belly.*

Hunter's anxiety ratcheted up a notch. She was *pregnant.* And judging from the pool of bloody fluid under her hips, her water had broken in the crash.

Another wail of pain from her confirmed it. She was in labor.

"Damn," he muttered as a chill slid through him, despite the warm autumn sun. "Ma'am, are you hurt anywhere other than your head?" He reached in far enough to put the car in Park and turn off the engine.

She turned wild blue eyes toward him. Frightened eyes. "Don't hurt me!"

He raised his palms. "I won't. Calm down."

"Please! Don't hurt me. I'm not—" She stopped with a gasp and a moan, holding her stomach.

Hurt her? What the—

"I'm not going to hurt you, ma'am. Why would you think—"

"My baby!" she gasped between shallow pants. "It's coming!"

"Yeah. I see that." He jerked at the Velcro strap that held his cell phone strapped to an armband while he jogged, and dialed 911. "I'm calling an ambulance now. Try to slow your breathing. You're hyperventilating."

Another frightened groan answered him, and she cast a nervous glance around her. "Where am I? What happened?"

Hunter arched an eyebrow. "You don't remember?"

Her brow puckered, and her eyes reflected anxiety, confusion. "Something's wrong. I can't..."

He frowned. How hard had she hit her head? Was she a meth user? Mentally unstable? He studied her face, but her smooth, unblemished skin and her white teeth didn't show any telltale signs of drug use. She was, in fact, strikingly beautiful, with a youthful oval face, thick golden-blond hair, clear blue eyes and lush red lips.

"Try to calm down. Take slow, deep breaths. No one is trying to hurt you." When the emergency operator came on the line, Hunter quickly gave the man the bullet points of the situation. Location. One-car accident. Woman in labor. Bleeding forehead. Possible delusions.

When he'd been assured an ambulance and police were on the way, Hunter switched the call to speaker setting and put his phone on the ground by the car, leaving the line connected as instructed.

"Ma'am, I'm going to try to open the door so I can help you." Crawling onto his knees, he pulled at the crushed door. Though it gave a little, the bent frame was jammed. Hunter rose to his feet for better leverage and tried again. The shoulder he'd landed on when he dived into the ditch throbbed, and he paused long enough to roll his arms and loosen the muscles.

"Ow!" The fear behind the woman's cry spurred him to act faster, put everything behind getting the door open.

"Hang on, ma'am. I'm coming." Propping a foot against the dented frame, Hunter pulled on the door with all his strength. Sweat streamed down his already damp back and brow, but with a creak of straining metal, the door finally gave way. Getting on his belly again, Hunter crawled inside the flipped car and sidled up to the injured woman. "Okay, ma'am. Help is on the way, and I'm going to do what I can until they get here."

Instead of the relief or gratitude he expected, the woman's expression reflected terror as he drew closer. "No! Don't hurt me!"

That again? Hunter huffed. She was the one who'd almost killed him with her erratic driving! He took a deep breath and touched her arm lightly. "I'm not going to hurt you. I want to help."

"But someone was… I think, someone was coming after me. I feel… I can't remember…" She seemed so distraught that Hunter paused.

"Who's coming after you? Why were you in such a hurry?" An abusive husband maybe?

She swallowed hard, and her brow furrowed. "I…I don't know." She tipped her head and gave him a funny look. "Wh-who are you?"

"My name's Hunter. I saw you crash, and I'm here to help you. Do you remember anything about the accident or why you were driving so fast?"

"I…" She closed her eyes, wincing, then gave him a frightened look. "I had a contraction…and then I was upside down, and my water had broken and…you looked in the window…and—" She cried out in pain, drawing her shoulders in and cradling her belly again.

Hunter took her hand in his and patted her wrist.

"You're okay. Take a deep breath and blow it out through your mouth."

He racked his brain for what he could remember about childbirth from when his nieces had been born. Darby Kent, the mother of one of his nieces, had been one of his closest friends since college, and he'd stood by her through her pregnancy, practicing breathing techniques with her and coaching her on the way to the hospital for her delivery. Though the specifics of the labor breathing weren't coming back to him at the moment, he knew hyperventilating was not good. Which was what the woman was currently doing.

"Hey, look at me." He moved a hand to her cheek and angled her face toward him. Her wide, fearful eyes latched on to his. Their piercing blue hue and vulnerability socked Hunter in the solar plexus, grabbed him and held on tight. "I'm not going to leave you. We're going to get you through this. I know you're scared, but you need to calm down. Take slower, deeper breaths or you're going to pass out."

She closed her eyes once, then refocused on him. Some of the panic in her gaze eased, and she slowed her breathing. She inhaled deeply, if shakily, and blew it out with a whimper.

"That's my girl." He gave her a warm smile and squeezed her fingers. "Now…what's your name?"

She stared at him blankly for a moment, then frowned. "I…don't know."

Hunter drew his eyebrows together, an uneasy stir in his gut. "You don't know your name?"

She blinked, clearly confused, and panic edged back into her eyes. "I don't know! How could I not know?"

He shifted his gaze to the gash on her forehead. "That

cut on your temple says you hit your head in the crash. Do you remember anything about who you are or where you live? Are you married?"

The pregnancy suggested she might have a husband somewhere who'd be worried about her, but her left hand had no rings. Although…his sister-in-law had stopped wearing her wedding ring during her last pregnancy because her hands had swelled.

Tears filled her eyes, and a visible tremor shook her. "No. It's all a blank. I just…have this feeling…something bad happened. That someone wants to hurt me…"

He dabbed at the bleeding gash, where a goose egg was now swelling, with the hem of his shirt. "Okay, memory loss happens sometimes after you hit your head. Clearly that's what's happened, so…let's see what clues we have in the car. Do you have a purse? A wallet with your driver's license?"

"I don't knooooow…." The word evolved into another wail of agony, and with a grimace of misery, she gripped her stomach. "It hurts so much. Oh, God, don't let anything happen to my baby!"

"Breathe through the pain, honey." Hunter stroked her hair with one hand and squeezed her fingers with his other. "Did you take a Lamaze class or anything?"

Her blank gaze flicked to him. "I don't—"

"You don't remember. Right." He exhaled through pursed lips. Memory loss meant she wouldn't remember who from her family or friends to call to be with her. He needed to find her wallet or her cell phone or something that would give them some helpful information. But at that moment, his first priority was keeping her calm. Delivering the baby, if it came to that. Damn! Where was that ambulance?

A cold sweat popped out on his lip, but he swallowed the nausea that rose in him at the thought of delivering her baby. He had to keep it together for her sake. "All right. We can do this. You're gonna be fine."

When she squeezed his hand back, he met her teary gaze.

"Thank you, Hunter." She raised her free hand to wipe her face and flicked him an attempt at smiling. "For staying. I'm scared, and I don't want to be alone."

Hunter's heart cracked, and he wiped the moisture from her cheeks with a crooked finger. "I won't leave you alone. I promise."

His assurance seemed to relieve her mind, and she drew a slow, deep breath. When her next contraction hit, he coached her through the pain, reminding her to breathe deeply and slowly. She squeezed his hand with amazing strength, and when her pain eased, he dropped a light kiss on her forehead. "That's it. You're doing great."

Come on, ambulance! Anytime now!

Between her contractions, Hunter searched the tumbled sedan, an older Honda Civic that reminded him of the jalopies Grant used to tinker with in their driveway when they were younger. The car was made pre–air bags…a safety feature that would have served the woman well today, judging from the growing bump on her head and her memory loss. There was nothing in the glove box that told him who she was or where she lived. No registration papers or car title. Odd. She didn't seem to have a purse or wallet with her, either. Also strange based on the habits of the women he knew. And no cell phone? What was up with that? What woman in this day and age went anywhere without her cell phone?

Hunter kept his frustration with her curious lack of identification to himself, not wanting to upset her further. Another contraction gripped her, and he shifted his attention to her again. She was bearing down, her teeth gritted, her forehead creased with effort.

"Oh, hey, no!" Hearing his panic in his tone, he paused a moment and forced a smile. "Try not to push... yet. The ambulance is bound to be here soon. Just...hold on a little longer." He dabbed again at the bleeding cut on her head and the perspiration rolling into her eyes. "Why don't we focus on something else?"

"Like wh-what?"

He glanced around for an object that might hold some interest or personal meaning to her. Darby had called it a "focal point" when she'd had her daughter four years ago. Hunter had been charged with making sure the picture of his brother Connor, the baby's father, whom they'd believed at the time was dead, made it to the hospital.

He saw nothing but broken glass and crumpled metal—neither were images she needed to fix in her head. Then he spotted her keys, still dangling from the steering column. He slid the keys out of the ignition and found them hooked to a ring with two decorative additions—one was a metal crab that read *I ♥ Cape Cod,* and the other was a small wooden piece carved to spell out *Brianna*.

"Brianna?" He jerked his gaze to her and held up the key chain. "Does that ring a bell? Is your name Brianna?"

She stared at the key chain, a knit in her brow and a desperate look in her eyes that wrenched his heart.

"I don't know. Maybe? Why else would I have that on my keys?"

"*If* they're your keys," he said, and the despondent look that crossed her face made him immediately regret voicing his doubt. "Forget I said that. I'm sure they are." He forced a grin to his mouth. "So…Brianna. That's a pretty name. For a pretty lady."

Her cheek twitched in a weak smile of acknowledgment. Clearly she wasn't in the mood for compliments, no matter how well intended.

Another contraction seized her, and he held the keys in front of her. "Focus on the keys. Think about tranquil walks on Cape Cod. The soothing sound of the ocean."

She gave him a dubious, uncertain look as she struggled to breathe deeply.

"Well, the key ring says you love Cape Cod. I figured it was worth a shot." He rubbed her arm and crooned, "That's it, Brianna. You're doing great. Deep breath in, and blow it out through your mouth."

She followed his coaching like a champion, and pride tugged in Hunter's chest.

The distant wail of a siren filtered through the autumn air, and relief loosened anxiety's grip on his gut. "Hey, hear that? The cavalry is coming."

Rather than happiness, concern darkened her eyes, and she gripped his hand tighter. "Don't go. You said you'd stay with me. Please?"

Her plea tangled in the deepest part of him, and warmth filled his veins. "I won't leave. I just have to make way for the EMTs to help you. They'll take you to the hospital, where the doctors and nurses can give you and your baby the care you need."

A tear dripped onto her cheek, and her sweaty grip

tightened on his hand again. "I don't want to be alone. I'm scared, Hunter. I know it sounds crazy, but I have this feeling…someone wants to hurt me. Hurt my baby."

"That's probably just part of the disorientation because of your amnesia."

She glanced away, hurt dimming her eyes. "Maybe. But…with you here, I…feel safe."

Well, damn. What could he say to that? All he had on his schedule for the rest of the day was a postjog shower and watching the Saints game with his brother Grant.

"Be right back." He flashed her a reassuring smile as he shimmied out of the car to flag down the EMTs and tell the 911 operator the ambulance had arrived. As the emergency techs approached the flipped car, Hunter gave them a quick rundown of Brianna's condition.

After placing a neck brace on her, the EMTs eased her out of the jimmied door. Despite her protests that it was unnecessary, they strapped her on a backboard until they could confirm at the hospital whether she had any spinal injuries. Hunter clutched her hand and murmured soothing words while one EMT checked the progress of her labor.

"The baby's head has crowned. We need to hurry. Lights and sirens," he told the driver as they pushed Hunter aside and slid the stretcher into the back of the ambulance.

Hunter stepped back, giving the men room to work, and turned his attention back to the overturned sedan. All in all, Brianna was lucky not to have been hurt far worse. Why hadn't she been wearing a seat belt? Why was she on this rural road outside the city limits? Why—

His gaze snagged on the trunk of the sedan. Were those…*bullet holes?* He moved closer for a better look, a tingle of apprehension scraping his nape. He rubbed his finger across the bullet-size holes and bit out a curse. Someone had shot at the back of Brianna's car. But how recently? She'd said she had a feeling someone was trying to hurt her.

Maybe she'd been right.

Chapter 2

A chill totally incongruous with the warm autumn afternoon slithered through Hunter. The bullet holes could be old. But based on the way Brianna had been driving, the fear that gripped her even after losing her memory, his guess was someone had been shooting at her *today*. Minutes ago. And whatever danger had sent her speeding down this highway was still out there, still a threat.

"Hunter!"

Her cry pulled his attention back to the open patient bay of the ambulance. Her hand stretched toward him, and fear flashed in her eyes. "Don't go!"

He set his jaw. He had promised to stay with her, and he was a man of his word. Not only was she frightened and alone, she was in labor. In pain. *In danger.* Her amnesia made her even more vulnerable to the person trying to hurt her.

He hurried back to the ambulance, but when he tried to climb in, one of the EMTs stopped him. "No passengers."

Hunter scowled at the medic, in no mood for rules. "She needs me. Can't you see how scared she is?"

"Sorry. You can meet us at the hospital." The EMT tried again to push Hunter aside, and he pushed back.

"Meet you? With what? Look at her car!" He waved a hand at the overturned sedan. "Am I supposed to walk?"

The medic twisted his mouth, wavering. "Are you family?"

Hunter opened his mouth and caught the truth before it slipped out. He swallowed hard and silently begged his mother and God to forgive him for the lie that rose to his tongue. "I'm her husband. That's my baby she's having!"

The EMT eyed him suspiciously, clearly having picked up on his earlier hesitation.

Going with the story he'd presented, Hunter squared his shoulders. "You said the baby could come any minute. Don't make me miss the birth of my first child!"

Brianna wailed in pain at that moment, as if to punctuate his plea. The medic relented and stepped out of Hunter's way.

Brianna squeezed her eyes shut, gripped the edges of the stretcher and waited out the excruciating contraction. In addition to the wrenching pain in her belly, her head throbbed. She'd hit it on something when the car flipped, Hunter said. But everything prior to blinking Hunter's face into focus as he peered through the broken window was a frightening blur. A blank canvas, really. How could she have forgotten everything, even her own name?

She tried again to recall where she'd been going, who

she was, why she'd been on that road—and got nowhere. Panic fluttered in her chest, speeding her heart rate and her breathing.

The EMTs were at work, taking her vital signs, checking the baby's heart rate, starting an IV in her arm.

Hunter moved into view, smiling down at her and wrapping her hand in his. "You're okay, sweetie. Hang on. Deep breaths, remember?"

Remember deep breaths? Heck, she couldn't remember what she had for breakfast, but she nodded at him just the same. Struggled to slow her breathing. Truth was, when Hunter stroked her hand and smiled at her like that, breathing *at all* was difficult. The man was gorgeous, even rumpled and sweaty as he was. He had piercing blue eyes, thick black hair that curled against his neck and the sort of strong, rugged face you saw in outdoor-adventure magazines. His sleeveless T-shirt showed off impressive muscles in his arms, but it was his smile that held her attention. His broad, gentle smile had the power to calm and excite her at the same time. Her pulse did a happy jig when he grinned, while a peace filled her, despite her scary circumstances. Hunter's presence made her feel safe.

Impossible as it seemed, considering she didn't know him, didn't know *anyone or anything* at the moment, Hunter kept her from flying apart. He reassured her and soothed her. His eyes, his smile, spoke softly to her soul. As if—

Another blinding pain ripped through her torso, obliterating the crazy poetic thoughts. "Oooh!"

Again Hunter stroked her hair, patted her hand, coached her through the contraction. "That's it, Brianna. You're a champion. Keep breathing."

She gobbled up the inane words as if they were manna from heaven. Hunter and his encouragement were all she had at that moment, and she clung to his hand, clung to the support he gave her like a lifeline.

"You don't appear to have any bleeding that would indicate a placental abruption, and the baby's heart rate is within range." The EMT beside her started pelting her with questions as he worked. "We need to get some medical history and personal information. Are you allergic to any medications? Latex or iodine?"

"I…" She swallowed hard. The panic swelled again. "I don't know."

"She hit her head," Hunter explained. "She can't remember anything. Not even her name."

"Okay," the EMT said, turning his attention to Hunter. "Do you know if she has allergies?"

Brianna knitted her brow. Why would Hunter know that about her?

"I, uh…don't…" he stammered. "I'm not sure."

"Does she have a Do Not Resuscitate order or living will on file?"

Hunter's gaze flicked to her as if she could answer. Brianna could only stare back at him in confusion.

"Don't know."

"Her blood type?"

Hunter shook his head.

"Name of her ob-gyn?"

"Uh…"

The EMT arched an eyebrow. "Kinda important stuff to know about your wife. Your *pregnant* wife."

Brianna gasped. *Wife?* What—

Another pain tightened her belly, and both Hunter

and the EMT turned to her. She gripped Hunter's hand, squeezing hard as the wave of pain racked her. "Hunter!"

"I'm here, hon. You're okay." He turned to the EMT, his face stern. "Can't you give her anything for the pain?"

"Not without knowing her history or allergies. And we have to be careful not to send the baby into distress."

"I'm…okay," she lied. "Don't put the…baby at risk."

Hunter gave her a worried look and stroked her hair gently.

After finishing his physical checks, the EMT pulled out a clipboard and shot a narrow-eyed glance at Hunter.

"I'm gonna guess here and say you don't have any of her personal info, either. Address, phone number, insurance or Social Security number?" The EMT flipped up a palm, giving Hunter the opportunity to deny his assertion.

A guilty look crossed Hunter's face. He licked his lips and blew out a sigh. "No."

The EMT grunted, tossed the clipboard aside and busied himself taking her blood pressure, checking the progress of the delivery.

Clearly Hunter had lied about his relationship to her in order to stay with her. Knowing that stirred a mix of feelings in her. While she hated that she'd led him to fib, she was grateful for his willingness to stay with her and allay her fears. Brianna tugged on Hunter's hand, and when he met her eyes, she flashed him a brief grin of appreciation for his efforts. In response, he trapped her hand between his two larger ones and rode in silence, until the ambulance bumped over the curb of the hospital driveway.

The EMT rallied, pushing Hunter aside as the ambulance jerked to a stop and the back doors flew open. Brianna was jostled as her stretcher was rolled out and the legs unfolded for the ride into the hospital. As she was whisked away, Hunter disappeared from her field of vision. A clawing sense of agitation raked through her. "Hunter!"

"Don't be scared!" she heard him call as the order-lies rolled her into a back hall, taking her away from her anchor, her protector. But she was frightened. Without Hunter, the eerie sense of danger crowded her again. Someone had tried to hurt her. She was sure of it.

And now she was in labor. Her memory gone. A deep sense of loneliness and foreboding closed around her like a smothering cloak.

Hunter tried to bat away the hands that blocked him from following Brianna into the E.R. "I want to go with her. That's my wife!" he said, sticking to the lie he'd already committed to. "Come on. She's scared, and I promised I'd stay with her."

"You can be with her in a minute," a woman in scrubs told him, leading him by the arm to an office. "We just need a little information for billing purposes."

He raked his hair with his fingers and exhaled a frustrated sigh. "Fine. What do you need?"

"Take a seat over there. I just have a form for you to fill out."

The fear in Brianna's voice as they took her away echoed in his mind. Poor thing. She had to be terri-fied. He thought of the EMT's questions as they rode in from the accident scene. He had no idea what to tell them about Brianna's medical history or family or bill-ing information.

Crud. He glanced over the form, and his gut rolled. Well, he'd come this far. Might as well lean into it.

Name—Brianna Mansfield. Marital status—married. He gave them his address as hers, his phone number…his name as her spouse and emergency contact. He plowed on, filling out the form, giving the hospital the information they'd expect if he were in fact Brianna's husband. For just an instant, he imagined that scenario. Coming home at the end of a long day to her warm embrace. Waking up to her pretty face. Having a child with her…

His heart thumped. The medical staff would assume he was the father of Brianna's baby. He'd told the EMT as much. Though he'd savored his role as uncle to his brother's kids, had been a father figure to his niece Savannah for the first four years of her life, the thought of being a father still gave him pause.

Of course, he wasn't the baby's father. He shook off the tangential thoughts and focused on the papers in front of him. This was all a ruse for Brianna's sake… until her real family could be found and brought to the hospital. At the bottom of the sheet, he signed and dated the form, then handed the clipboard back to the admissions clerk. "Can I see Brianna now?"

"Sure. This way."

Hunter wiped his palms on the seat of his running shorts, wishing he didn't look and smell like a gym rat, and followed the woman to the nurses' desk.

When a nurse finally breezed past them, Hunter grabbed her arm to catch her attention. "I'm looking for my wife, Brianna. She's in labor."

The nurse nodded to him without stopping. "She's delivering the baby now. Susan, will you show him where to scrub up and find him a sterile gown?"

The admissions clerk opened her mouth to respond, but the nurse hurried off and disappeared into an exam room. By the time the admissions clerk had located the sterile head-to-toe garb and Hunter felt he'd sufficiently washed his arms, hands and face, Brianna was already cradling a red-faced baby and crying tears of joy over her new arrival.

"Better late than never, Dad," the E.R. doctor said, waving him in. "We're just finishing up here, but everyone's doing fine."

He stepped over to the side of the surgical table where Brianna lay and, behind the sterile mask covering his mouth and nose, he smiled. Realizing she couldn't see the gesture meant to congratulate and comfort her, he winked, as well. "Sorry to be so long. Hospital business…then they made me put all this stuff on." He tugged at the sleeve of the sterile gown.

"It's all right." She grinned at her baby, then angled her arms to show Hunter. "I have a son. Seven pounds, seven ounces. A healthy baby boy. Thanks to you."

Hunter gazed at the puffy-faced bundle and felt a tug in his chest. Newborns generally weren't what he'd call cute. Even his nieces had needed a few days to register on the cute scale for him. But somehow, knowing he'd helped ensure this baby arrived safely, he felt a little connection to Brianna's son that put the swollen cheeks and pointy head in perspective.

"Hey, little guy. Welcome to the world." He crooked a finger and ran it along the baby's chin. "So what are you naming him?"

She shook her head tiredly. "I don't know. Surely I had a name picked out, but…I don't remember it. I can't give him a name until I get my memory back." She glanced up at him, and her blue eyes were dark with anxiety. "If I get it back."

He put a hand on her arm and gave her a supportive squeeze. "What have the doctors said about your head injury? Your amnesia?"

"Not much yet. Delivering Little One here was their first priority. But they are setting up for me to get a CT scan now." She gave her son's head a kiss and closed her eyes. "This is crazy. I don't even know if my son's father is at home waiting for me, worrying. There must be someone. I didn't get pregnant on my own."

A funny gnawing filled Hunter's gut—maybe because he'd been playing the role of her husband, and hearing her talk of someone else having the rightful place in her life felt off. "You're not wearing a ring."

She raised her left hand and stared at her naked fingers. "No. But someone meant enough to me nine months ago that I got pregnant. Where is that man? He should know his son has been born." Her breathing grew shallow and rapid again. Her brow furrowed, and lines of distress crinkled around her eyes. "I'm scared, Hunter. Without any memory, I'm all alone. I have no home. I have no money. I have no identity or history or—"

"Hey." He cut her off as the desperation in her voice rose. "You have me. I'm gonna help you figure out who you are and where your family is. Okay?"

A tremor shook her, and when she blinked at him, a fat tear broke free of her eyelashes. "Why? You don't know me."

"Yeah, well, the hospital thinks I'm your husband."

"You told them that…for me? So you could stay with me?"

"Yeah." He caught her tear with his thumb. "I guess I'm a sucker for blue eyes and a damsel in distress."

The E.R. nurse came back into the room and raised the railing on the other side of her surgical table. "They're ready for you in radiology. If you'll give Dad the baby to hold for a moment, a nurse from the nursery will be down in a minute to take him upstairs for more health checks."

Brianna's eyes met Hunter's. "Is that all right?"

His gut pitched. He'd held babies this small when his nieces had been born, but somehow this felt different. He was being entrusted with a child not even twenty minutes old, given the responsibility of a father's care and protection. He swallowed hard, hesitating.

"It's okay, Dad," the nurse said, chuckling. "Baby won't break."

Hunter pushed out a cleansing breath and slipped his hands around the tightly wrapped bundle lying against Brianna's chest. In the process of gathering the baby into his arms, he brushed intimately against her breasts. When her breath caught and her gaze darted to his, heat spread through him and raised a flushed prickling in his cheeks. "Sorry."

In response, she twitched her lips in a brief, nervous grin as she released the baby to him. He could feel the heavy throb of her heartbeat against the back of his hand as he adjusted his grip on her son. His pulse drummed in his ears as he pulled the tiny life close to his chest and cradled the baby's head in the crook of his arm.

"Hey, sport," he crooned to the puffy-faced baby, who wrinkled his face and whimpered pitifully like a puppy. "No, no. Don't cry. Mom will be right back." As Brianna was wheeled out for her CT scan, her troubled gaze lingered on him. Hunter gave her a nod and a wink. "I got this. Don't worry."

But as soon as Brianna and the nurse disappeared, the baby loosed a plaintive wail. A bubble of panic swelled inside him. A crying baby was usually his cue to pass a baby back to mom or dad. But he was supposed to be playing the dad role for the next few hours. *Yikes.*

"Shh. Easy, fella." He gave Brianna's son a little bounce and patted the baby's bottom the way he'd seen his brother Grant do with his daughters when they were infants. "You're okay, dude. I'm gonna help your mom out, and everything's going to be just fine."

He paced the small room, trying to comfort the crying baby, wishing the nursery staff would hurry and take the baby upstairs. As he cradled the infant, rocking his arms from side to side, he flashed back on the accident that had brought him here. Brianna racing down the highway, losing control of her car. *Bullet holes in the back of her flipped sedan.*

A chill rippled through Hunter. Who had fired at Brianna, and why? Was she still in danger, or had she been victim to a random crime? He recalled her fear of someone hurting her when he'd first tried to help her, and uneasiness scraped through him.

No matter how he looked at it, the cards were stacked against Brianna. Amnesia, a new baby…and some unknown threat to her safety. He may have known her for only an hour, but she had no one else. She and her baby needed him, needed his support, his friendship…and his protection.

He gazed down at the new life in his arms. So tiny. So fragile. So…vulnerable.

"Don't worry, sport. I'm going to take care of you

and your mom," he promised Brianna's son. "I'll help her remember who she is, where your dad is. And I will make sure both of you stay safe."

"Where the hell are you, man? You've been gone for three hours!" Hunter's older brother Grant said the minute he answered Hunter's call.

Pinching the bridge of his nose, Hunter cut his brother a lot of slack for his sharp tone, and a stab of guilt also poked him for worrying Grant. His brother had been through hell in recent months, having tragically lost his wife in May. Grant was now a single father, raising his two young daughters alone, and didn't need any extra grief on his plate. Considering the tumult of the spring and the circumstances surrounding Tracy's death, Hunter should have called sooner so Grant wouldn't worry.

He'd left for his jog from Grant's country home after Sunday lunch with the Mansfield clan. He'd been expected back inside an hour to shower and watch the Saints game with their dad. Since Tracy's death, the family had been spending a lot more time with Grant, helping with the kids and hoping to lift his spirits.

"Sorry about the radio silence." Hunter could imagine Grant—and their mother—pacing the hardwood floors of Grant's farmhouse, fretting about him. "I've been… distracted. I'm at the hospital with—"

"The *hospital!*"

Hunter winced. He should have led with a disclaimer. "I'm fine! Really. But I witnessed a car accident, and I rode in the ambulance to the E.R. with the woman whose car flipped."

"Aw, skunk." Grant mumbled the kid-safe curse he

and his wife had invented when their oldest started re-
peating everything she heard. "Is the woman okay?"

"She hit her head pretty hard and has no memory
of who she is at the moment. That's why I'm here. She
was pretty scared, but she and the baby are okay other
than that, I think."

"She had a baby with her?" Grant's tone ratcheted up
a degree on the worry scale.

Hunter raked his fingers through his sweaty hair. He
really needed a shower, but wouldn't leave the hospital
until he knew Brianna was all right. "She was in labor.
She just had the baby a few minutes ago."

"Skunk," Grant repeated. "No wonder you stayed
with her. So…when do you think you'll get back here?"

"No telling. Go on and eat dinner without me. I may
swing by my apartment for a shower later, but I doubt
I'll make it back out to your place today." He remembered then that his truck was sitting in Grant's driveway.
"Wait, my truck's out there, and I need it." He winced,
hating to beg a favor from Grant, who had two small
kids to deal with. Maybe his parents could bring him
a vehicle. "Are Mom and Dad still there? Could one of
them bring my truck to the hospital when they head
back into town?"

"I think we can work something out between the three
of us." He heard Grant sigh. "So this woman has no idea
who she is? There was nothing with her that identified
her? A wallet or cell phone or piece of mail?"

"Not that I found with my preliminary search, but I
plan to go back out to the car and look again." Hunter
glanced up to see Brianna being wheeled out of the radiology department. "Text me when you get here with
my truck, okay? I gotta go."

"Sure. Love ya, bro."

"Back atcha." Hunter tugged a sad grin, wanting to tease his brother about unmanly professions of feelings. But knowing why his brother had started telling him he loved him at the end of phone calls and visits made teasing impossible. The suddenness of Tracy's death had shaken the whole family. Factor into that the third Mansfield brother, Connor, returning to WitSec with his wife and daughter, and the family had plenty of reasons to be particularly mindful of family bonds. They all hugged more, said frequent "I love yous" and didn't take their time together for granted.

As the hospital aides rolled Brianna's stretcher closer, he couldn't help but wonder about her family. Did she have anyone looking for her? Was someone, even now, pacing the floor and waiting for her to call? A pang of sympathy prodded him and fired a sense of urgency inside him to find out who she was and where she lived.

Her eyes found his as she neared him, and he sent her an encouraging smile. "They took your son upstairs to be checked more thoroughly by the staff pediatrician. And they're getting a room ready for you on the maternity floor."

She nodded, then winced, her hand lifting to her temple, where her head had a new bandage.

"Any news from the CT scan?" he asked.

"Not yet." Her sky-blue eyes clouded with worry. "The doctor is reading it now."

"The CT scan and MRI both show what we suspected," the staff neurologist said, his hands shoved in the pockets of his white lab coat. "You have a significant concussion, which has caused swelling in the brain. That swelling is what has caused the memory loss. I have every reason to believe that as the swelling goes down, you should get most, if not all, of your memory back."

"Most?" Brianna gaped at the silver-haired doctor, stricken cold by the idea of losing any part of her history to permanent brain damage.

When she'd finished in radiology, Hunter had followed her up to the room where she'd been admitted to the maternity ward. He sat beside her bed now, leaning forward in the chair, eagerly taking in every word the doctor shared about her condition. As any good husband would. Except he wasn't her husband. Before today, he hadn't even been an acquaintance. Why was he so willing to help her, to pretend they had a relationship? Was it just so that she didn't face her amnesia alone?

Hunter frowned. "Do you mean some of her memory loss could be permanent?"

"It is possible. The brain is a tricky and mysterious thing. But I wouldn't worry too much about that. All indicators are you'll be good as new in a couple of weeks."

A couple of weeks? She swallowed the dismay that choked her. Even if two or more weeks without her memory seemed like an eternity, she needed to count her blessings. She had a healthy son, the hope of recovering her past, her identity…and Hunter. She had Hunter to help her through the scariness of amnesia. But how long would he stay? She couldn't ask him to give up his life, his commitments, in order to babysit her. He'd already gone way above and beyond the call of duty, pretending to be her husband in order to stay beside her, allay her fears, give her moral support. All too soon she'd have to face the void of her unknown life alone. That thought brought back the chill, the prickling sense that someone wanted to hurt her. What had put her on that road where her car flipped today? Who was after her, and why?

Chapter 3

Hunter turned to her with that knock-'em-dead smile of his, pulling her out of her worrisome musings, and gave her wrist a squeeze. "That's great news, huh? That you should recover all your memories, given time?"

Threading the sheet of her hospital bed through her fingers, she worked up a smile for him. "Yeah. Great news."

"So how will it work?" Hunter asked. "Is there something I can do to help prod her memories?"

"Generally, no. The swelling needs to go down before the process of memory recall can happen. When it does happen, it won't be a sudden info dump. Things will return slowly, a piece at a time. Prepare yourself to feel frustrated by the puzzlelike feel of the bits and pieces coming together, but try not to stress too much over the seemingly scattershot return of the memories."

"So photos and bits of memorabilia won't trigger recall?" she asked, disappointment weighting her chest. Her head chose that moment to give an almost symbolic throb. She'd refused the painkiller they'd offered her, knowing she'd be nursing her baby boy soon.

"They might serve as a prompt. But not before the swelling has decreased sufficiently. The key is going to be patience. Give your focus where it belongs. Building new, precious memories with that baby of yours."

Thoughts of her son brought a genuine smile to Brianna's lips. "Thank you, Doctor."

The neurologist pulled a pen from his pocket and signed a chart that he stuck in the file holder on her door. "Now get some rest, and I'll check in on you again at the end of my rounds."

The doctor pulled her door almost closed to give her and Hunter privacy, and being alone with her rescuer suddenly became awkward. She glanced at him as he shifted to a more comfortable position in the bedside chair. He flicked a smile at her and drew a deep breath.

"So…" he said.

"Hunter…" she said at the same time.

His grin stretched, and he waved a hand toward her. "Go on."

"What were you—" she said on top of him again. Now she chuckled stiffly. "Sorry."

He shook his head. "No. Ladies first."

She took a slow breath and untangled her fingers from the knots she'd been winding in the sheets. "You don't have to stay. I know I asked you not to leave before, but…I was scared and hurting and—"

His warm hand wrapped around her cool fingers, and her gaze darted up to his. His dark blue eyes were full of compassion and crinkled slightly as he grinned. "I'm not going anywhere. I made you a promise, and I intend to keep it."

She squeezed his fingers, relishing the connection to him. Not only did his warm grip feel good around her chilly hands, but his loyalty and friendship touched a place deep inside her that she had an odd sense had been empty and cold for a long time. "I release you from that promise. I have no right to hold you here. You don't know me. You have no responsibility for me. You've already done so much, and I'll always be grateful. But I don't want you to feel obligated to me."

He gave her a dismissive raspberry. "I'm your husband, remember? Of course I'll stay."

Brianna sighed and shook her head. "We both know you're not. That's just the lie you told the EMT so you could ride with me when I was panicking."

His brow furrowed, and when he stroked her knuckles with his thumb, a pleasant tingle spun through her. "Yeah, well…maybe I'm getting into the role. Maybe I want to hang around for a while to make sure you're okay." He cocked his head. "Would that be okay? I could help you start figuring out who you are and if you have family somewhere that should be called."

Her heart pattered. She wanted desperately to accept his offer, but how could she impose on his kindness that way? "You heard the doctor. It could be weeks before I remember everything." She frowned and dropped her gaze to her lap. "If I remember."

He untangled his fingers from hers and nudged her chin up. "Hey, stay positive." His palm cupped her cheek, and she couldn't help but lean into his touch, his buoying comfort and encouragement. "I was thinking

I might do a little investigative work. I can go back to your car and see what, if anything, I can find that would help us solve some of the mystery surrounding you."

She raised her chin, hope lifting her spirits. "Good idea."

"For starters, I'll take down your license-plate number and see if the DMV will tell me who the number is registered to."

She nodded, feeling a surge of energy in light of Hunter's idea and optimism. "Of course! Why didn't I think of that?"

He shot her a wickedly handsome lopsided grin. "You were a little preoccupied having the world's cutest little boy."

A knock on the door heralded the arrival of a nurse rolling a bassinet in from the nursery. "Mrs. Mansfield?"

She blinked, confused by the name until Hunter winked at her and said, "Speak of the devil. Here's our boy now."

Mansfield. Hunter Mansfield. She let the name roll through her mind, testing it, savoring it. Funny to think she knew more about Hunter than she did about herself. A last name, for instance.

The nurse parked the bassinet beside her bed and scooped up the baby, swaddled tightly in a blue blanket. "Here you go, Mama. He's been asking for you. I think he's ready to nurse."

Brianna's breath caught, and her gaze darted to Hunter. Nurse? "Um...I—"

Hunter's cheeks flushed a bit, and he met her uneasy glance with his own.

"It helps if you massage the breast first to increase

the milk flow," the nurse said as she settled the baby in Brianna's arms.

Hunter shot out of his chair and hustled toward the door. "Honey, I just remembered a phone call I need to make. I'll just be out here in the hall, okay?"

She released the breath she'd been holding and nodded. "Sure."

As Hunter slipped out of the room, the nurse helped Brianna get situated, propping pillows under the baby and her arm so that she could hold her son more comfortably. The baby latched on after a few tries and suckled greedily. Brianna stared down at the tiny face, marveling at the miracle she held and swamped by a love so strong and pure it brought tears to her eyes. Of course, some of the tears could be the product of the crazy cocktail of hormones, her frustration with her amnesia and the throbbing pain in her skull.

"That's the way. You've got it," her nurse said. "I'm going to go, but if you need me, just push the button on that cord there." She pointed to the nurse call. "Or get that nervous daddy in the hall to help." She sent a wry look to the door. "He's got to get over those new-father nerves before you go home. You're gonna need a lot of help with the baby while you recover from that concussion."

Brianna swallowed hard. "Right. Thanks."

She might need a lot of help, but she couldn't ask Hunter. Surely she had family or a friend, a neighbor… *someone* who could help her with the baby. The baby gazed up at her with his blue eyes as he nursed, and she was washed anew with overwhelming awe and love. Maybe it wasn't hormones. Maybe this was the deep maternal bond that women had known for centuries.

"Oh, sweetie, you are so precious to me. We're going to be okay. I promise."

Her son's eyes closed, then fluttered open again.

"It's okay. You can sleep. I'll be right here." Her reassurance to her baby boy reminded her of Hunter's pledge to stay with her, to work with her to piece together her identity and lost memories. As she watched her baby suckle, an overwhelming need to name her son roared through her. She might have no identity, no past to draw from, but she could give her son a name. A name with meaning and significance.

"Hunter?" she called. "Hunter, are you there?"

He burst through the door, his expression worried. "I'm here. What's wrong?"

"What's your full name?"

He blinked. "Huh?"

"Your full name? Do you have a middle name?"

His attention shifted to where her baby still nuzzled her breast, and his Adam's apple bobbed as he swallowed. "Um…"

Oops. Heat prickling her cheeks, she tugged the receiving blanket up to cover the baby's head.

He scratched the stubble on his chin, his brow puckering in thought as if trying to remember what she'd asked. "Oh, uh…Benjamin. Why?"

"Hunter Benjamin Mansfield," she said, liking the sound of it. "A strong, noble-sounding name."

He shrugged. "If you say so."

She smiled. "I do. Would you mind if I named my son Benjamin…after you?"

Shock froze his features for a moment before his mouth twitched in a lopsided grin and his eyes lit with wonder. "Seriously?"

"He needs a name. I may not be able to fill out all the blanks on his birth certificate yet, but I can give him a first name. Seems fitting, you being the man who came to our rescue." She paused. "If that's all right with you."

He chuckled and swiped a hand over his face. "I'm... honored! Yeah."

She smiled and peeked under the blanket at her son. "Then Benjamin it is."

Naming her baby was a small thing in the big picture, but at least one thing in her blank-slate life had been settled. A disproportionately large swell of relief filled her.

"Was that it? You need anything?" Hunter asked.

Fatigue pulled at her, weighting her limbs. "A nap. But first this guy—" she tipped her head toward the baby "—needs to fall asleep."

He sent her a commiserative nod. "Yeah, you've had a busy day." Sliding his hands down his backside, as if searching for back pockets that the running shorts he wore didn't have, Hunter edged back toward the door. "Well, then...I'll let you finish feeding him. In fact, I'm thinking I'll go scare up a sandwich or something. You sure you don't want a snack or a soda?"

"No thanks. Just sleep." As if hearing her request, her son's eyes—*Benjamin's eyes*—closed groggily, and she stroked a finger along his silky-soft cheek. "That's a good boy. Sweet dreams, Ben." She raised her head. "Could you help me move him to the bassinet?"

Tugging the bedsheet up, she kept herself covered as she held Ben out from her body enough for Hunter to slide his hands under the blue bundle. When he splayed his fingers, Hunter's hands were large enough to ably cradle her son's head and bottom securely. The sight of those masculine hands against the soft blanket that swaddled her child sent a ripple of awareness through her. Those same strong hands had held hers with gentle warmth, had comforted her with tender care…and had pulled open the crumpled door of her wrecked car with brute power. How would those amazing hands feel caressing her skin? Exploring her body? Her pulse kicked, and her mouth dried.

What was she doing letting her thoughts stray down that path just hours after childbirth? Sure, Hunter was drop-dead handsome and kind to a fault, but talk about bad timing! She didn't even know if she had someone at home waiting for her, worrying about where she was. And because Hunter had told the hospital she was his wife, if someone *did* call looking for her, they wouldn't know she was here, even as a Jane Doe.

"Hunter? What if my family is looking for me? The hospital thinks my last name is Mansfield."

He cut a side glance to her from the bassinet, where he watched Ben settling in to sleep. "Huh, I hadn't thought about that." He frowned and rubbed his chin. "But before we backpedal on that story, we need to consider all the angles of this."

Under the sheet, she adjusted her clothes, post-nursing, and snuggled down on the bed, completely wiped-out by the delivery. "What angles?"

"Well, like your safety."

She lowered her eyebrows, a niggling sense biting the back of her neck. "My safety?"

"You don't remember? When I first got to your car, you were sure someone was trying to hurt you." He moved to the chair by her bed and sat on the edge, leaning toward her with an anxious look on his face. He knew something he wasn't telling her. "Are you sure you don't remember anything from right before the accident? Why were you racing down that road so fast?"

"I was in labor. I—" She stopped, knowing somehow there was more to it. She sank back against her pillow, shut her eyes. Behind closed eyes images and sounds of the day's trauma replayed in her head. Lying in the overturned car. The blinding pain in her head. The blood. The ambulance sirens. She took a deep breath and tried to push the swirl of confusion over the accident and tangled feelings toward Hunter out of her mind. The nagging sense of disquiet sorted itself out from the other memories. A fear that stole through her like a wraith, chilling her to the bone. Someone had wanted to hurt her. She was sure of it.

Brianna's eyes flew open, and she gasped. Her gaze darted around the hospital room as if expecting to find someone standing over her, ready to snuff the life from her.

Hunter scooted the chair closer, took her hand. "What? What do you remember?"

"Nothing…specific. Just this ominous, oppressive feeling of danger. I can't explain it, but…"

"I think I can." Hunter's expression darkened, and his gaze dropped to the floor, his forehead lined with deep furrows of concern.

Brianna's gut flinched, rebelled. A sour taste filled her mouth. "What?"

"When we were leaving the accident scene, I got a good look at the back of your car." He met her eyes, and the intensity in his blue gaze rocked her to her core. "Someone had shot at the back of your car. Maybe not today, but at some point. That's one of the reasons I want to go back out and look at the car before the po-

lice impound it. I'm sure the officer who responded to
the accident would have seen the bullet holes and will
be investigating, but I want to know all I can. So I can
protect you."

She tried to swallow, but her mouth had gone dry.
"Are…are you sure they were bullet holes? Maybe a
rock—"

"I'm sure." He sandwiched her hand between hers and
stroked her wrist with his thumb. "I served a few years
in the Army Reserves and have hunted with my brothers for years. I know guns, and I know bullet holes. The
ones in your car looked to be in the .38- to .44-caliber
range. The kind of weapon that has stopping power."

Her breath shuddered from her, and she stared at
Hunter, stunned by what she was hearing.

His hand caressed her cheek, cupped her face. "Brianna, I'm sorry to dump this on you. I don't mean to
scare you with this, but I thought you needed to know. So
you could take precautions. Be alert to possible threats."

"But…why…? I don't…" She wet her lips and tried to
slow her racing thoughts. "They weren't just trying to
hurt me, then. Whoever shot at the car was trying to…"
She gulped. "To kill me?"

Apprehension dented his brow. "That's how it looks
to me."

Her bottom lip trembled, and she caught it with her
teeth. Nausea roiled in her belly, and her aching head
pounded with fresh ferocity.

His grip on her cheek tightened, and he tipped her
face toward him. "But listen to me, Brianna. I'm not
going to let that happen. I'm going to help you get to
the bottom of this. We'll figure out who was trying to
hurt you and why. We'll find something to tell us who

you are and where your family is. I promise. I won't let anyone harm you or Ben."

Tears prickled her eyes. She had too much to process. An attempt on her life, the car accident, her lost memory. In the midst of so much turmoil, Hunter was a beacon to her. A safe harbor. She might not know him, but her instincts told her to trust him. Gratitude was an understatement of how she welcomed and cherished his offer of help and protection. Without her memory, with her body weakened from injury and a painful delivery, with a new baby to consider, she was vulnerable with a capital *V*.

She covered his hand with hers, and when she blinked, a tear tracked down her cheek. "Thank you, Hunter. So much."

Hunter's phone buzzed, and he checked the screen. "That's my dad. My ride is here, so I need to go." He leaned close and kissed her forehead. The chaste kiss sent ribbons of honeyed warmth through her. "I hate to leave you, but I feel like there are answers we need at your car. I need to get out there before the police haul it away."

A shiver raced over her skin at the thought of being left alone. But Hunter was right. They needed answers, and her car was the place to start. The only clue they had. "Okay."

He winked at her and rose from the chair.

"If you need anything, anything at all, I've got my cell phone with me. Call me." He wrote his number on the whiteboard the nurses and hospital staff used to leave the patient notes and reminders. "I'll be back in a couple of hours. Try to rest. I'll ask the nurses' desk to keep an eye on your room. No visitors until I get back. Okay?"

She nodded, but knew she wouldn't get to sleep, no matter how much she needed a nap. She had too much swirling through her thoughts, too much weighting her heart. She had a new baby to protect. *Benjamin.*

The door clicked closed as Hunter left, and she glanced at her sleeping son. So tiny. So innocent. So dependent on her.

The dark suspicion that had hovered over her since the accident pressed down and crowded her until she couldn't breathe. Hunter had found bullet holes in her car. Somewhere beyond the hospital walls, someone was waiting to kill her.

Chapter 4

Three hours later, Hunter returned to the hospital and knocked quietly on Brianna's door before entering, just in case she was the with the doctor…or nursing. He was no lech, but the idea of her baring her breast, even to feed her son, was fodder for vivid images in his mind's eye. He could too easily imagine her curves bared for his exploration, their bodies tangling in the sheets. Considering Brianna was a new mother, those tantalizing fantasies left him feeling uneasy and guilty. Was he wrong to feel this attraction to her? She was a beautiful woman, and every time their eyes met, he experienced a sense of connection, a crackling energy and deep stirring in both his body and his soul.

Hearing no response to his knock, he cracked the door open and peeked inside. "Brianna?"

Brianna sat propped up in the bed, the baby in her arms, her gaze latched firmly on her son. His pulse tripped at the sight of her, and he took a moment to simply drink in the poignant image.

She'd gotten cleaned up, as he had, and someone had found her a brush for her hair. It shone in glossy gold waves that framed her face and spilled over her shoulders. Her cheeks had more color now, and her skin had a fresh-scrubbed glow. The love in her expression as she gazed at her son was so pure and peaceful, his breath stilled in his lungs. He'd seen that same expression before…on his sisters-in-law's faces when they'd rocked his nieces. A mother's love. Maternal awe and wonder. Raw, unfiltered affection.

Watching her hold her baby, Hunter, too, felt a stir deep inside, but of a harder-edged emotion—a fierce determination to protect Brianna and her child. The clawing need to defend her was tangled with a sense of possessiveness and responsibility. She was *his* to care for, *his* to guard and provide for. *His.*

Except she wasn't. He shook his head briskly. Somewhere out there, the father of Brianna's baby was likely waiting for her. A man she'd cared enough for that she'd made love to him, carried his child. A man who had prior claim to her.

Hunter shoved down the stab of jealousy that thought fired inside him and stepped farther into the room.

Brianna raised her head, clearly startled, when he moved to the foot of her bed. "Oh, hi."

He aimed a thumb at the door. "I knocked, but…"

"Sorry. My head was somewhere else. I didn't hear you." She wiggled her fingers in invitation. "Come in. Sit down."

He didn't like the idea that she'd been so unaware of her surroundings that he'd made it to her bed before she noticed him. With someone gunning for her, literally, she needed to be more alert, more careful. He made a mental note to talk with her about that.

"What did you find out?" she asked as he took a seat beside her.

"Not much yet. I didn't find anything in the car that was helpful, but I took down your tag number and brought my laptop with me from my apartment." He patted the computer bag slung over his shoulder. "We can do an online search for your tag number and see what comes up."

She nodded. "A police officer stopped by after you left, wanting my statement about the accident. I couldn't tell him much, obviously."

A prickle of unease chased down his back. "Did he show you his badge? Was he in uniform?"

She frowned at his question. "Yes to both. And he left a card—" she motioned to her tray table "—and said they'd need a statement from you."

"Okay. Am I supposed to call him?" Hunter picked up the card and read it. *Sergeant Mark Wallace, Lagniappe Police Department.*

"I told him you'd be back in a little while. I think he was going to come back up here after he got dinner."

He nodded, and setting his computer bag aside, he leaned forward for a better look at her son. *Benjamin.* A curl of warmth rolled through his midsection. To say he was flattered she'd named her son after him would be an understatement. He'd helped her because it was what any decent person in his situation would have done. Maybe committing himself to helping her discover who she was and protecting her from the person responsible for shooting at her car was more than others would do.

But something inside him compelled him to look after Brianna.

"Did he nap?" he asked now, gazing down at Benjamin's bright blue eyes. The baby's eyes shifted slightly toward him. He remembered his sister-in-law telling him a baby's distance vision was unfocused early on, but Benjamin looked straight at him, perhaps drawn by the sound of his voice. Holding the baby's gaze, Hunter felt a stir of emotion deep inside, a softening at his core.

"He did. He's eaten a little more, too."

Hunter smiled at Benjamin, even though he knew the baby was still too nearsighted to see it. "Hey, sport. How ya doin'?"

"Would you like to hold him?" Brianna asked.

Hunter shifted his attention to her. "Um, maybe later. Right now, I think we should do some research." He opened his laptop and logged on to the internet. "The sooner we figure out who you are, the better. My family was going nuts looking for me after just a couple of hours this afternoon. I can imagine yours is especially worried, given your pregnancy and all."

"You have family in town? A wife?"

He jerked his gaze up from his keyboard, and she blinked at him with wide, startled eyes. "No. I'm not married. I meant my brother and parents. I'd gone out for a jog when you wrecked your car."

She released a deep breath, visibly relieved that he wasn't married. And wasn't that interesting?

Hunter glanced at the results of his browser search for Brianna's car tag number. After scrolling a few pages, he found nothing helpful. A visit to the state's DMV web page gave him little, as well. A few sites promised to conduct a search of private records for a fee, but he ignored those. Buzzing his lips in frustration, Hunter sat back in the chair. "Well, I'm not getting far here. Have you remembered anything else, no matter how small, that might help us with this puzzle?"

"No. Just this weird sense of danger. Of panic." She bit her bottom lip and furrowed her brow. "I wouldn't even know my first name if not for that key ring."

"What about the other key chain that was on your car keys? The one that said 'I Heart Cape Cod.' Cape Cod ring any bells now?"

She closed her eyes for a moment, then sighed. "Nothing."

"Well, it's early. The doctor said to give your swelling a chance to recede."

A knock sounded at the door, and a uniformed officer poked his head in the room. "Excuse me."

Hunter stood and greeted the policeman. "Are you Sergeant Wallace?"

"I am. Would you be Hunter Mansfield?"

"Yours truly. I understand you need a statement about her accident." Hunter waved the officer toward the only chair in the room, but Sergeant Wallace declined with a shake of his head.

"This shouldn't take long. I just need your account of what happened to confirm what Ms. Coleman told us."

"Ms. Coleman?" Hunter tipped his head. "Is that her name? Brianna Coleman?"

The policeman looked confused for a moment, then arched an eyebrow. "That's right. You have no memory from before the accident?"

Brianna shook her head. "Nothing. Can you tell us anything? Did you run my license plate? Who is the car registered to? Where do I live?"

Sergeant Wallace flipped open a small notepad and read, "Your tag was registered to Brianna Coleman, home address 443 Cypress Creek Lane, Lagniappe."

Wallace rattled off a phone number and Social Security number as well, and Hunter pulled a scrap of paper from his computer bag and jotted the information down.

"What did the tag registration say about my marital status? Was there anyone else listed as co-owner or my spouse?" Brianna asked, her expression full of hope.

The sergeant consulted his notes. "Not that I see." Wallace raised his gaze to Hunter. "Want to tell me what you saw this afternoon? Did you see the car crash happen?"

Hunter flexed the fingers of one hand with the other and gave the officer a recap of what happened from the time Brianna drove toward him to the moment they left in the ambulance.

Her eyes widened as she listened. "Oh, my God. I almost hit you?"

He jerked a small nod, and seeing the guilt that crossed her face, he quickly added, "But you didn't. That's what counts."

"So you didn't see who might have fired at the car?" Sergeant Wallace asked.

"No." Hunter rubbed his hands on his jeans. "If you find any more information that will help Brianna locate her family, will you call us? I'm planning to stay with her, help her out for a while. You can call my cell." He gave the officer that phone number, and Sergeant Wallace jotted it in his notes.

"Will do." As the police officer took his leave, he added, "Congratulations on the new baby, Ms. Coleman. Hope you'll feel better soon."

"Thanks." Brianna flashed him a muted smile. Clearly she was anxious over the lingering questions about her family, Benjamin's father and the lurking danger. As he was.

He eyed Brianna after the policeman left. "So...Brianna Coleman. That name ringing bells for you?"

She chewed her bottom lip and stared across the room, her nose wrinkled in thought. "Well, yes and no. It doesn't feel wrong. It's...comfortable. But I can't say it's bringing anything back or screaming, 'That's me!'" Her shoulders dropped, and she frowned. "If that's my name, why don't I just *know* it? It should be organic. Part of my cells. Instinctive."

Connor shook his head and scooted toward her. "Not necessarily." He unclipped his cell phone from the case at his hip. "Look, we have a home phone number now. I'll call it and see if anyone is there. Okay?"

Her eyes rounded. "Yeah." She sat taller in the bed, watching him anxiously as he dialed. The phone rang four times before an answering machine picked up. A mechanical voice repeated the number he'd dialed and told him to leave a message.

"I got a machine," he told her, and her expression deflated. When the beep sounded, Hunter said, "Hi, my name is Hunter Mansfield, and I'm looking for the family of Brianna Coleman. Brianna is safe but needs to be in contact with her relatives. If anyone gets this message, please call me." He left his number in case she didn't have caller ID.

"No one answered," she said and sighed. "Maybe I have no family."

"We don't know that. They could be in the shower. Or, more likely, out looking for you." He returned his phone to the holder at his hip and rubbed the beard stubble on his chin. "Later on, I'll drive by your house and knock on the front door. We will find your family, Brianna. Have faith."

She flashed her a half smile and nodded. "Aye, Captain."

An idea came to Hunter, and he flipped a page on the notepad he'd used to take down her information from Sergeant Wallace. He extended it and the pen toward her. "Let's try something. Take these."

She glanced down at Ben. "Okay, but you'll have to hold him."

He set the notepad down and held his arms out to receive the baby. Ben gave a disgruntled whine but soon settled in Hunter's arms.

She lifted the pen and paper. "What do you want me to do with these?"

"Sign your name."

She puckered her brow. "But…"

"You know your name now. So write it. Like you're signing a document. Don't think too hard about it. Just write."

She bent her head over the pad and slowly wrote out her name. "There." She held the pad out to him.

"Do it again. Faster." Hunter gave Ben's swaddled bottom a soft pat when he gurgled.

"Why?"

"An experiment. Just work with me."

She sighed and wrote her name again. Then blinked. "Hmm."

"What?"

"I…did that without really thinking about it. I was still thinking about how silly your experiment sounded."

He flashed her a cocky grin. "Not so silly now, huh?"

Lifting one eyebrow, she wrote her name again, even faster. And again. "I'll be darned."

"Did it feel natural? Like muscle memory?"

She raised her head, and her face lit with wonder. "It did." Taking a deep breath, she wrote her name again and again, filling the page with her loopy signature. She chuckled. "I know this. It feels right."

"Some people learn better by hearing, others by sight, others by doing. It makes sense to me that maybe your memories will come back more with certain triggers than others. I learned that in high school. My grades were suffering, and my parents hired me a tutor. Turns out my teachers' style of issuing reading assignments didn't match my auditory learning style. I needed to hear it explained to me to make it stick." Hunter walked around to the bassinet and set Ben down in the small bed. "I have something else we can try."

Returning to the bedside chair, Hunter tapped on his laptop keys. He pulled up a satellite ground-level-view website and typed in the address Sergeant Wallace had given them. The picture of a small gray-siding-and-red-brick house with a neat yard came up. He moved the laptop so that Brianna could see the image.

"According to the address Wallace gave us, this is your house. Do you recognize it? Does it feel right?"

Brianna squinted at the screen, studying it. The eagerness and expectation in her eyes was heartbreaking, especially when that hope faded and moisture filled her eyes. "No. I don't feel any tugs of recognition. Damn it!"

Hunter closed the top of the laptop, set it aside and moved to sit on the edge of her bed. "It was just an idea. Maybe seeing it for real will be different. Maybe seeing the inside, your furnishings and pictures, will be the trigger you need. And time."

She nodded slowly, touching the bandage on her forehead. "Time for the swelling to recede."

"Exactly." He took her hand in his and kissed her fingers. "To me, the fact that your signature felt natural is a good sign. I bet you get all of your memories back real soon."

She nibbled her bottom lip again. "Maybe. I... Hunter, what if the reason I can't remember is because I'm blocking a bad event? I can't get past the fact that there are bullet holes in the back of the car I was driving. The one thing I did sense or know after the accident was that I was in danger. What does that say?"

His grip on her hand tightened. "I haven't forgotten that. I don't know what it means, but I do know this— whoever shot at you isn't going to get a second chance. I'll make sure of that."

Hunter spent a long, restless night in the chair next to Brianna. Though the chair folded out into a bed of sorts, the contraption was the epitome of discomfort, and every noise from the hall woke him. His brain was wired to be on guard, to listen for intruders, to be alert to changes in his environment, even while resting. He'd served one tour in Afghanistan during his five years with the Army Reserves and learned the meaning of the term *combat nap*. That past spring, he'd helped guard his niece's hospital room when men connected to organized crime had threatened his brother Connor and his family. Because of that experience, he considered himself qualified to guard Brianna and Ben.

Morning came early, as it did in a hospital, the maternity nurse waking Brianna to feed Ben at four forty-five. She gave him a groggy glance as Ben was settled in her arms, and Hunter took his cue.

"I'm going to rustle up some coffee. Is the cafeteria open?" he asked the nurse.

"It will be at five."

Brianna sent him an appreciative smile. Her hair was mussed from sleep, and as she raked the gold wisps back with her fingers, Hunter's pulse kicked. Brianna Coleman was the sexiest thing he'd seen in a long time, and she managed to be sexy without trying. Her natural, early-morning rumpled state charmed him. The glow that shone from her eyes and her smile as she greeted her son and settled him in her arms was more striking than any makeup she could ever put on.

Hunter swallowed hard. It was dangerous to have such strong feelings for her when they didn't know yet whether Ben's father was still in the picture. She could be married, damn it!

He gave his head a little shake as he shuffled out of the room. For probably the hundredth time in the past few weeks, he wished he could call Darby Kent, whose friendship and advice had always been spot-on. As much as he admired his older brothers and valued their input on business matters, Darby, with her female point of view and common sense, had always been the one he turned to for advice concerning matters of the heart. She would be able to put his fascination and obligation to Brianna in perspective. But Darby and her daughter, Hunter's niece, had recently joined his brother Connor in Witness Security. He'd likely never talk to Darby or Connor ever again, and he felt the loss to his marrow.

With the morning staff making rounds, Hunter figured Brianna was safe enough until he came back with his breakfast. Just in case, though, he'd stopped at the nurses' station and asked them to keep a watch out for strangers entering Brianna's room.

That done, Hunter walked down the stairs and exited the hospital to get a breath of fresh air. The dark autumn morning still held a chilly nip, though he knew the Louisiana sun would quickly warm things up after daybreak. He started around the perimeter of the parking lot at a slow jog to work the kinks out of his muscles and get his blood pumping. Immediately his brain began to click through the same questions that had plagued him since the car accident.

How was he supposed to help Brianna figure out the source of the danger to her? Now that he had her name, home phone number and address, he could be more thorough with his quest for information. He could call the courthouse and see if there was a marriage certificate on file for her. He could stop by her house and see if anyone was home, if her purse was there. He heaved a deep sigh, feeling better for having an action plan for the day. He finished the circuit of the parking lot and reentered the hospital, heading straight for the cafeteria, which was just opening.

He bought himself a large coffee and an egg-and-bacon breakfast sandwich to take upstairs. It was still too early to call Grant or his parents and check in with them. He needed to let someone know he'd be taking the day off from work, though he'd make an effort to stop by the construction sites he was managing later in the day. Working for the family business had its perks, and a flexible schedule was one of the better benefits. He couldn't ignore his responsibilities as site manager for

Mansfield Construction, but his father and Grant would always cover for him when he needed personal time off. In fact, Grant, the accountant and business manager for the office, enjoyed having an excuse to get out of the office and be at the work sites every now and then.

When he got back to Brianna's room with his breakfast, Brianna was still nursing Ben, with a baby blanket draped over her shoulder and the baby. The television played quietly from the mount on the wall, and her food sat uneaten on her tray table. She glanced up at him as he walked in, and her expression was an odd combination of concern and joy.

"I have a cat," she said without preamble.

"Excuse me?"

"I was sitting here with Ben, thinking about what mornings would be like from here on, taking care of Ben and getting ready for work, whatever that job may be, and I had this overwhelming feeling that I was neglecting something important. Then it just came to me. I have a cat that I always feed in the morning. Sorsha. She's black with long hair and a white spot on her tummy. She's always right there in my face when I wake up every morning, demanding pats and ear scratches along with her breakfast. She's like my furry child, my first baby. I can't believe I would forget her!"

Hunter grinned as he took his seat. "Any more unbelievable than that you'd forget your own name?"

She pulled her mouth into a slant. "Touché."

"Still, you remembered something about yourself, your life, your home. That's progress."

She gave him a small smile. "Yeah. I guess. The thing is, she needs to be fed. What if there is no one else there to feed her? Hunter, will you—"

"Yes."

She flashed him a lopsided grin.

"I'm already planning to stop by your house later today, with your permission, and check it out, see if anyone besides the cat is home. I'll feed Sorsha while I'm there."

"Thank you." Her smile brightened, and his body temperature rose a couple of degrees. Damn, but she was beautiful.

"Now—" Hunter frowned at the untouched breakfast "—you need to eat."

Brianna grinned at him. "I will. Soon. But my hands are a little full here, and Ben's breakfast comes first."

He opened the sack with his breakfast sandwich. "But your food's getting cold."

"I imagine in the coming years, I'll eat a lot of cold meals." She bent her head to peek under the blanket. "Isn't that right, Ben?"

Hunter unwrapped his food, feeling a bit guilty eating while his food was hot, then nodded toward the television, where a car dealer was raving about his crazy prices. "So what are we watching?"

"Local news. I was thinking if my family reported me missing, there might be a story about it."

"Good thinking."

"Yeah, but so far all they've shown are national news stories." Brianna picked up a piece of her toast and took a bite.

On the TV, the commercials ended, and a serious-faced newscaster reported on a dip in the stock market.

"Has the doctor been by this morning? Has anyone told you yet when you can get out of here and go home?"

"No on the doctor, but my nurse thinks they'll let me

go home tomorrow morning if I don't show any complications." She twisted her mouth in consternation. "I hate to say it, but…I'm a little nervous about going home, taking care of Ben by myself. Especially when we don't know who shot at me or why."

"You won't be going home alone. I told you, I'm going to help you. I'll protect you until we know the danger to you is past. Until we find your family. I'm not going to abandon you, Bri."

She scowled at him. "I can't ask you to do that. I'm not your responsibility."

"Maybe not. But I'm volunteering. I can't in good conscience leave you with a new baby, a concussion and some unknown threat out there."

"Hunter," she said on a groan and peeked under the blanket at Ben again, "I don't feel right imposing on you."

"And I don't feel right turning my back on you when you're alone." He paused. "If you don't *want* my help, I guess I can't force my way into your life, but…"

She slanted a look at him. "I do want your help. I appreciate it. So much. I just feel guilty taking over your life this way."

"Well, stop feeling guilty. I'm happy to help." Hunter sat back in the chair and took another bite of his sandwich. "When I go by your house today, I can find your purse or phone or pictures that might—"

Brianna's gasp cut him off.

"Turn it up!" Gaping at the TV, she waved a hand at the remote control beside him.

"What?" He set his breakfast in his lap and grabbed the remote.

"Turn the volume up!"

He did and together they watched a news report about a coup attempt against the ruling monarch of Meridan, a small European island nation Hunter had never heard of.

Hunter frowned, puzzled why the story was so important to Brianna. "What's wrong? Why—"

She waved a hand, shushing him, and her face grew paler as the news report continued.

"Mourning citizens took to the streets, shocked by reports that King Mikhail had been assassinated," the reporter said. "Prince Cristoff, heir to the throne, has not been seen in public for several days, and rumors have circulated that the prince has also been assassinated."

Hunter turned to watch Brianna's odd reaction to the news story rather than the television. "Brianna?"

She gave him another hushing wave of her hand as the screen filled with file footage of a well-dressed man with dark hair waving to a crowd before climbing into the back of a limousine.

The reporter's face filled the screen again. "Palace officials deny the rumor of the crown prince's death but won't comment on Cristoff Hamill's whereabouts."

Brianna's expression leeched of color as she turned to Hunter. "I know him."

"What?" He wrinkled his brow and glanced back at the television. "Who? The reporter?"

She blinked, her expression stunned. "No. Cristoff."

A startled chuckle escaped Hunter before he could stop it. "The prince guy?" He aimed a finger at the TV. "That's in Europe somewhere. What makes you think you know the prince?"

"It's just a feeling…a flicker of something. An image. A memory. I…"

For the first time, Hunter began to doubt Brianna.

How could she remember some obscure prince from a tiny European country? It wasn't as if this Cristoff guy was often in the news the way Prince William of Great Britain was. But the recognition that filled Brianna's face seemed so real.

A tickle of unease started at the base of Hunter's neck. "Brianna, I don't know. Maybe you know someone who looks like him."

She drew a slow, deep breath and gawked at the television. "No, it's him. I'm sure of it. But I don't just *know* him, Hunter." She faced him, her eyes wide. "Prince Cristoff is Ben's father."

Chapter 5

Her head pounding, Brianna stared at the TV screen long after the news story about the unrest in the tiny country of Meridan ended and the announcer moved on to a report about the local city council. The pain from her concussion made it that much harder to concentrate and focus on the fuzzy memory that elbowed its way to her attention and wouldn't be ignored. As crazy as it sounded, even to her, she was certain she'd not only met the man identified as Prince Cristoff Hamill of Meridan, but she'd seen him recently. In her mind, a voice echoed, saying, *If the baby's mine, then he's my heir and next in line for the throne.*

Next in line for the *throne*? Brianna rewound the news story in her head. A coup attempt. An assassination of the king. A missing prince. She shivered as a cold certainty settled over her.

"It's not me they want to kill—it's Ben. He's the heir

to the Meridanian throne." She glanced toward Hunter and met a skeptical frown.

"Brianna, do you hear yourself? Why would a rebel faction in Meridan, wherever that is, want to kill your son? How would you know the prince?"

She sank back against her pillows and closed her eyes, wishing the throb under her skull would give her even a moment's peace. "I don't know, Hunter. I know it sounds crazy, but…the same way I just *knew* about Sorsha, I *know* Ben is Chris's baby."

"You mean Cristoff?"

She cracked open her eyes and cut a side glance to Hunter. "What did I say?"

"You called him Chris."

She pulled her brow down, letting the name replay in her mind. "It just rolled off my tongue. Like my signature was muscle memory last night. I know him as Chris. I'm sure of it."

Hunter swiped a hand over his mouth, his expression saying he was unconvinced. "Well, I can't disprove that theory, so we'll keep it as a possibility."

Her shoulders sagged. Did she really expect anyone to believe she'd had an affair with a prince and that her child was of royal lineage? It sounded improbable even to her own mind, but the certainty, the echo of a voice, the fear for Ben's life wouldn't let go. They gripped her heart and shook her, demanding that she pay attention.

She gave Hunter a level look, wanting desperately for him to believe her. "When I get home, I'll find proof."

Ben finished his breakfast and started wiggling and arching his back in discomfort. The night nurse had showed her how to burp him after a meal, and she shifted

him up on her shoulder now and patted his tiny back
with gentle thumps.

Hunter wadded up the paper wrapper from his breakfast sandwich and shot it at the trash can across the room.
The crumpled paper bounced off the rim and landed
on the floor. When he stood to retrieve the trash, he
stretched his back and gave her a considering glance.
"Tell ya what. I'll go to your house now, feed your cat
and have a look around for anything else that might jog
your memory or indicate where your family is. Assuming there's not an anxious roommate or husband at the
address the cop gave us, waiting for news of what happened to you."

She rested her cheek against Ben's tiny, warm head.
The milky, clean scent of him filled her senses and even
soothed the ache at her temple. Love for her baby swelled
bigger in her chest every time she looked at him, until
she thought she'd burst. Yet, impossibly, her heart grew
to hold even more awe and affection for the tiny life
she'd created.

But the limbo of her amnesia loomed over her. Not
having a full picture of who she was and what had happened in her past was a liability she couldn't afford if
someone was trying to hurt Ben. An urgency to fill in
the blanks raked through her, and she gave Hunter a
decisive nod.

"Yes. Break into the house if you have to. I have to
piece together my past, my relationships, and figure out
why Chris—Prince Cristoff—resonates so strongly for
me. I need information if I'm going to protect Ben."

"All right." From his pocket, Hunter pulled out the
keys he'd taken from her car's ignition the day before.

The I ♥ Cape Cod key ring dangled from his finger, taunted her. Why couldn't she remember Cape Cod?

"I'm guessing one of these keys is for your front door. I shouldn't have to break in." He gave her a wink as he left. "Back in about an hour."

An odd jittery sensation shuddered through her as he disappeared out her door. Hunter's presence gave her a reassurance she'd come to depend on in the short time she'd known him. From the scary moments after coming to in the wrecked car, through her delivery and confusing memory loss, Hunter had been a port in the storminess and uncertainty in her life.

But she knew she couldn't continue monopolizing Hunter's time and counting on his help indefinitely. Even if she didn't have any family and whether or not she regained her memory, soon she'd have to figure out how to take care of herself and Ben alone. Scary though that thought was, she had to face the truth.

She nestled her son under her cheek, and a fierce maternal instinct raked through her. If someone was trying to hurt Ben, they'd have to kill her to get to him, because she'd fight to her last breath to defend him.

Hunter used his phone's GPS program to find Brianna's house in a small subdivision on the outskirts of town. The quiet street of modest houses and grassy lawns looked like an idyllic place to raise a little boy. In his youth, he and his two older brothers had raced bikes and played hours of baseball in a neighborhood similar to this one. When he reached the address Sergeant Wallace had given them, Hunter eyed the house but saw no signs of life, no vehicle in the driveway, no glowing porch light waiting to welcome her home. Just

the same, he knocked loudly on the front door and listened for footsteps inside. No one came to the door, but
when he cupped his hands around his eyes to peer in
the glass panel beside the door, a fuzzy black cat stood
in the foyer swishing her tail impatiently.

Hunter keyed open the front door and gave Brianna's
living room a cursory glance. "Hello? Anyone home?"

Sorsha answered with a loud meow and trotted over
to rub against Hunter's legs. He squatted and held his
fingers out for the cat to sniff. "Well, some watchcat you
are. Are you this friendly with all strangers or just the
ones you hope will feed you?"

The cat answered with another loud meow, then
turned and headed to the next room, glancing back as
if to see whether Hunter was following.

He chuckled. "Your food bowl is this way, I take it?"

Sorsha led him to the pantry door, where she pawed
and meowed plaintively. When he opened the pantry,
the feline showed him which container to open by head-
butting the large storage bin and purring excitedly. He
dutifully scooped a large cupful and followed Sorsha,
who clearly had the routine down, across the kitchen to
an empty bowl. The cat gave a *merp* of thanks as she
started chowing greedily.

After giving the cat a few strokes and marveling at
the silky softness of her fur, Hunter left to investigate
the rest of the house. The first thing he spotted was a set
of papers on the kitchen table. He bent to read the page
on top with the heading Sales Agreement. The document spelled out the terms of the sale of Brianna's 1988
Honda Civic to someone named Phil Holtz. Phil had
yet to sign the sales agreement, and beneath the sales
agreement was the title, also waiting to be signed over

to Phil Holtz, and a file of maintenance records. On the other end of the table was a brochure for a new Honda minivan. Clearly Brianna was in the process of upgrading her vehicle in preparation for motherhood. Which explained why he hadn't found any identifying papers in the car at the accident scene.

As he walked through her living room, he scanned her bookshelf, trying to get a sense of who Brianna was, where her interests lay, what her tastes were. In a word, her shelf was eclectic. She had everything from old cookbooks to nature journals, romance novels and bestselling mysteries to scientific textbooks. Nonfiction works about the human genome, epidemiology and chemistry sat next to a tattered family Bible and biblical-study books.

Moving on to her bedroom, he found her purse with her cell phone and wallet inside. The fact that she'd left the house without her purse or phone told him she'd left in a hurry. The bullet holes in the back of her Civic flashed in his mind's eye.

Next, he checked her bathroom, including her medicine cabinet to determine if she was currently taking any prescriptions her doctor might need to know about. Other than a bottle of prenatal vitamins, some antacids and a bottle of acetaminophen, he saw nothing of note.

Beside her bed, her answering machine was blinking, indicating new messages. He punched the button to listen, then added the romance novel on the bedside stand to the items he would take back to the hospital.

"Ms. Coleman, this is Henry's Dry Cleaning," the female voice on the answering machine said. "Your clothes are ready for pickup at your earliest convenience. Thank you." A beep.

Hunter scanned the room and spotted an old family

portrait on her dresser. He walked closer to get a better look. Based on her parents' hairstyles and his estimate that Brianna was about twelve in the picture, he judged the photo to be approximately fifteen years old.

"Brianna, it's Aunt Robyn. Just checking to see how you are doing. Any more Braxton Hicks? Call me if I can do anything for you, honey. Bye."

Hunter jerked his attention to the answering machine. Aunt Robyn? So Brianna did have some family checking in on her. After getting a fresh set of clothes from her closet for her to wear home from the hospital, he took the family portrait from the dresser and stuck it in the top of her purse. An old picture and an aunt Robyn. Not much to go on, but maybe they'd be enough to trigger something in Brianna's memory.

Brianna studied the photograph Hunter handed her, and something warm and familiar tugged at her heart. "Obviously they're my parents. I mean, look at my dad. I'm a female version of him." She grinned, seeing the similarity in smiles beaming at her from the picture, but she still had so many blanks about her past. "It feels right. The picture seems familiar, but I still can't remember their names or specific events. Whether they're still alive or if they live across the country. Were they planning to come into town for the birth of their grandson? I need to call them and tell them I'm okay, but…" She shook her head.

"Oh, speaking of calls…" Hunter rubbed his hands on his jeans and gave her a guilty glance. "I listened to your phone messages. I hoped there'd be something useful there."

She turned her head and blinked at him. "Was there?"

"Well, sort of. Someone calling herself Aunt Robyn called to check on you. She didn't sound worried or upset to have missed you, though, and she didn't leave a call-back number."

"Aunt Robyn?" Brianna wrinkled her nose and bit her bottom lip as she thought about the name. Though it did resonate with her, it didn't have the sure, warm feeling that her parents' picture did. "Maybe. Something's there, but…"

"Oh, and your dry cleaning is ready at Henry's."

She quirked a half grin. "Thanks. Now if only I could remember where Henry's is."

He set her purse on the edge of her bed and scooped her phone out. "Maybe it's in your contacts list on your phone?"

She set the portrait aside and took her phone, grinning when she saw the screen saver photo of Sorsha. "And how was the warrior princess?"

"Who?"

"Sorsha. I named her after the warrior princess in the movie *Willow*."

Hunter gave her an odd look. "*That* you remember, but not your aunt Robyn?"

She paused, considering his question. "That does seem like an odd detail to recall when so much else is blank, but the doctor did say my memory would return in random pieces. No rhyme or reason."

He lifted a shoulder. "True. And Sorsha is fine. Grateful for her breakfast."

Brianna gave the screen saver another happy glance before swiping the screen to search her phone for contact names, photographs, messages, anything that would help her. As she scrolled her contacts, she found a listing for Robyn Elyse Rosenberg. Could that be the woman who identified herself as Aunt Robyn? Worth a shot.

She tapped the screen to call the woman, but the call went straight to voice mail. "Um, hi. It's Brianna Coleman," she said, feeling awkward. What if Robyn Elyse Rosenberg was a business contact, her ob-gyn or her real-estate agent? "I'll call again later. Bye." She disconnected the call and frowned at Hunter. "So do I just go through my contacts list and ask anyone who answers, 'Do you know me? Who am I?' That seems…weird."

He rolled up a palm and sent her a commiserative moue. "You have a better idea?"

She sighed. "No." Glancing back down at her phone, she noticed she had an alert indicating four messages were waiting for her. The first three were voice messages, one a repeat from the dry cleaner, another confirming her appointment for today with a Dr. Greene's office. Her ob-gyn? That'd be worth looking into later. The third message was from someone named Phil Holtz asking her to call him.

Frowning, she shook her head. "Phil Holtz. That name means nothing to me."

"Oh, that's the guy you were planning to sell your car to. Guess you should let him know it got totaled."

"I was selling my car?"

Hunter nodded. "Seems so. The paperwork was all on your kitchen table."

"Oh." She grunted and glanced at the phone again. The last message was a video sent via text message.

Curious, she opened the video, then gasped as a man filled the screen. *Chris.* Or rather, Prince Cristoff. "Oh, my God, it's him!"

She waved a hand at Hunter, motioning for him to come closer and watch with her.

"Who?" he asked as he leaned close to see her phone. When he recognized the face, he shifted closer still, his body bumping hers, his head so close she could smell the toothpaste on his breath. "Start it over and turn up the volume."

She did as Hunter suggested, and with him hovering next to her, they watched Prince Cristoff smile stiffly from the tiny screen.

"Hi, Brianna. It's Chris." He rolled his eyes. "Obviously." Pause. Deep sigh. "Let me start by apologizing for the scene at your house the other day. I know my news came as a big shock, and then to have those men storm in…well, I'm sure it was terrifying for you. I'm sorry."

On some level, Brianna acknowledged the apology, the admission that there had been an incident that precipitated her sense of danger, but at the moment, she was preoccupied with Hunter's nearness. The sound of his breathing beside her ear, his body heat wrapping around her, his wide chest nudging her arm as he leaned close to study the small phone screen. He had a raw sensuality about him that she shouldn't be noticing one day after giving birth. To another man's baby. A man still speaking to her from her phone…

"I never wanted you to be caught up in the politics of my life. That's one of the reasons I didn't tell you who I was." His gaze darted away from the camera briefly, then back. "Look, here's the thing. I know you've heard the reports by now about what's happened in Meridan. The men who came to your house were sent by the palace police to protect me. They misread the situation at your house and assumed you were a threat."

Hunter grunted, and she felt the vibration from his chest against her back. A heady tingle answered and reverberated through her, all the way to her toes. She drew a deep breath, hoping to clear her head and focus on the video, but the tantalizing woodsy scent that clung to Hunter filled her nose and upped the coil of awareness in her core.

"I set them straight," Chris was saying, "and I'm now under their protection. Because of the sensitive nature of the situation in my country, I'm asking you not to call the American police. Please. That's very important. This needs to stay quiet. I've…gone into hiding until further notice and…" Another sigh. "I want you to be safe. I want you to join me here, where my guards can help protect you. And our baby when he arrives."

A pang shot through her. So Chris knew about the baby, knew it was his. Now he should be told of the baby's arrival…if she could find him.

Chris's brow furrowed. "You'll both be taken care of, and we can be together again. As a family. Like we planned. Like we dreamed of that night at the coast. Remember? We had your favorite dinner—grilled shrimp and scallops."

Hunter shifted slightly, clearly unhappy with Chris's familiarity in his reminiscence. But why shouldn't Chris be nostalgic? They'd obviously cared about each other if they made a baby together. And according to Chris, they'd planned to have a family, to be together long-term.

"Think about that night, and then join me here in New Orleans." Chris gave the address of a hotel near the French Quarter, and Hunter wrote it down.

"That's all, Brianna. Take care, and I'll see you soon."

The video ended, and Brianna lowered her phone. Her head buzzed with all the tidbits the video added to the puzzle. First and foremost, confirmation that she'd remembered correctly her relationship with Prince Cristoff. Confirmation that she was embroiled in an international political intrigue. "Wow."

"Yeah. Wow." Hunter dragged a hand over his mouth and chin, and his palm made a light rasping sound as it scraped across his stubble.

The subtle noise skittered down her spine, and her skin tingled as if anticipating the sensation of that bristle brushing against her fingers, her cheek, her breasts. A steamy image followed the thought, and her mouth dried.

Stop it! She gritted her teeth and focused on the issue at hand. Prince Cristoff. Meeting in New Orleans.

"Do you think I should go? If I am in danger and he has guards who can protect me and Ben…" Her sentence trailed off when she raised her gaze to Hunter's and met his bright blue eyes. *Gracious, but he's handsome!*

"May I?" He reached for her phone, then sat on the edge of her bed, giving her a little more space, as he replayed the message from Chris.

"Well?" she prompted when he was silent for several seconds after the second viewing.

"I'm not sure you should race off to New Orleans quite yet."

"Why?"

"For starters, you just had a baby, you have a concussion with memory loss, and your body needs time to heal."

She gave a small nod of agreement, but inside, a flutter of expectation and longing stirred in her. If she didn't go to New Orleans to meet Chris, did that mean she'd have more time with Hunter? And why was it she preferred Hunter's company, Hunter's protection over what Chris was offering? Prince Cristoff had power and connections. Hunter had only his good intentions and personal strength.

"But beyond that," Hunter continued, "something about this video bothers me. I can't put my finger on it yet, but—" He twisted his mouth in consternation.

In the plastic hospital bassinet by her bed, Ben stirred, making a squeaky whining sound that arrowed straight to her heart. She glanced at her son, enamored with every wiggle and mewl. "And Ben's so small. I can't imagine traveling with a newborn is wise."

Hunter handed her back her phone and rose from the bed. "Want me to get him for you?"

She smiled and put the phone on her bed tray. "Would you?"

"Sure." He stepped around the end of the bed and smiled at Ben as he reached into the bassinet. "Hey, fella. Don't fuss. Mom's right here." He lifted her son without the awkwardness or hesitation she would have thought a bachelor would. His large hands skillfully splayed behind Ben's head and lower back, tucking him safely against his body to carry her son to her hospital bed. Hunter's grin lingered, and his eyes were bright as he studied Ben's face, which was red and scrunched up as he whined. Ben's crying didn't have Hunter panicking or irritated. He looked so at ease, so natural with Ben, that Brianna's throat tightened with awe and regret. What would her life be like if Hunter were the father of her child instead of some stranger who'd apparently abandoned her after their affair? And why was it she felt this longing and connection to Hunter, who was, in fact, a stranger to her, as well?

"You seem so comfortable with him," she said as Hunter settled Ben in her arms. "I'd have thought most men would hold a baby more like a dirty diaper or ticking time bomb."

A warm chuckle rumbled from his chest. "I used to. But in recent years, my brothers have given me three nieces to practice on, one of whom I helped with from the day she was born."

No sooner had Hunter arranged Ben in her arms than her cell phone began playing a perky country song. The caller ID read Robyn Elyse Rosenberg. As she carefully rearranged Ben to free one hand, Hunter pointed to the phone. "Want me to get that or take the baby?"

She shook her head. "I have to learn to juggle it all if I'm going to raise this rascal on my own." She thumbed the "Answer call" spot on the screen. "Hello?"

"Hi, darling. Sorry I missed your call earlier. I was with a patient. How are you feeling?"

She tried to decipher the nature of her relationship with the woman from context clues. *Darling* indicated a familial connection or close friend, but the comment about the patient could mean Ms. Rosenberg was her doctor. "Uh, pretty good. Sore." Brianna paused, then added, "I'm in the hospital. I had my baby."

Robyn Elyse Rosenberg gave a loud cry of delight. "Oh, Bri, darling, how wonderful! Are you both all right? Boy or girl? Details. I want details!"

Brianna filled the woman in on the birth, still feeling awkward about the blank in her memory about who the woman was.

"You had him yesterday? Why didn't you call my office? You know I'd have dropped everything to come be with you."

Brianna gave a wry grin she knew the woman couldn't see. "That's the thing. I didn't know that. I hit my head in a car accident. I don't remember anything about my life. I was brought to the hospital in labor from the car accident."

"Oh, my goodness! Brianna, how awful!"

"So…could you tell me who you are to me? How do we know each other?"

After a beat of stunned silence, Robyn said, "I'm your mother's only sister, your aunt Robyn, honey. You really don't remember anything?"

Brianna fingered the edge of the bedsheet. "I really don't."

"Well," Robyn said with purpose in her tone, "I'll fill in as many blanks for you as I can when I come see that precious baby. But not now. I have to go. Full schedule of surgeries this afternoon."

"So…you're a doctor?"

Her aunt chuckled. "You really have lost your memory. No. No *M.D.* after my name. I'm a surgical nurse. In Houston." She grunted. "Listen, sweetie, we'll cover it all when I get there. Take care and kiss that little boy for me. Bye!"

"I—" Her phone beeped and "Call ended" lit the screen. "Bye," Brianna said with a twitch of her lips. She glanced to Hunter. "So my mother's sister, Robyn Elyse Rosenberg, is a surgical nurse in Houston. She says she's coming to see the baby, but didn't say when."

Hunter's face brightened. "So you *do* have family, someone who can help you with the baby, help you remember your past. That's great!"

His wide smile and obvious relief caused a funny tug under her ribs. Though she, too, was pleased to learn she had family, she could tell Hunter saw Aunt Robyn as his escape hatch. He was loyal enough and compassionate enough to stay with her as long as she seemed to be alone in the world, but his kindness had to have its limits. Hunter couldn't stick around until Ben left for college. As much as she enjoyed Hunter's company, she had to let him go. She needed to stand on her own two feet, amnesia or not, and figure out how to care for and protect her son on her own.

The idea of protecting her son from political militants seesawed in her gut. She was out of her league there. Chris could help, but she was in no condition to travel alone with a small baby for several days. Maybe a couple of weeks.

She just prayed she could keep a low profile, regain her memories regarding Chris and figure out what to do about her royal baby before the people responsible for the bullet holes in her car caught up with her.

Chapter 6

The next afternoon, the staff doctor consulted her chart, then divided a look between Hunter and Brianna. "Obstetrically, I see no reason why you can't go home this evening, but I'm still concerned about that knock on your head. It will take a while to heal fully, but I'm willing to sign your release papers, provided you have someone stay with you around the clock for the first week or so." He looked straight at Hunter. "That means, if you don't get paternity leave, you'll need someone to cover for you when you go to work."

Paternity leave. Hunter swallowed hard, remembering he'd told the hospital he was Brianna's husband when she'd been brought in. And he'd been by her side since the baby was born. Of course, the doctor would assume he was Ben's daddy. Not for the first time, Hunter's gut somersaulted at the idea of being a father, even a pretend one. A doting uncle was one thing, but a dad?

"Oh. He's not—" Brianna started, and he jumped in.

"Not going to leave my wife unattended. No, sir." He shot Brianna an "I got this" smile and a silencing, raised-eyebrow stare.

"Good." The doctor checked his notes, then launched into an explanation of how to sterilize bottles and nipples for feeding Ben and the importance of keeping the baby in a germ-free environment for the first several weeks.

Brianna frowned and interrupted the man, "Um, sorry to stop you, but…you do remember from medical school that there isn't such a thing as a truly sanitary home environment, right? Microorganisms are everywhere, and not all of them are bad. A person's immunity is built because of the presence of microorganisms in the body."

"Uh…well, yes, but—"

"As far as sterilizing bottles…as soon as you remove the bottle from the sterilizing bath and it is exposed to the air, it will technically be unsterile again. And once it touches another surface—" She stopped midsentence, blinked and divided a glance between Hunter and the doctor, who'd folded his arms over his chest and now studied her with a cocked head.

She grimaced and sent the doctor a rueful look. "I'm sorry. I don't know where that came from. I'll be careful about germs, of course, but…NIH studies have shown that children overprotected from microbes have higher levels of IgE antibodies later in life and suffer more allergies. If children aren't exposed to common illnesses as children, they never develop an immunity to common germs and may be sicker as adults."

The doctor narrowed his eyes. "And you know this because…?"

Hunter was wondering the same thing. He remembered the scientific journals he'd seen at her house. Obviously they weren't just for show. She read those journals.

She sat back in the bed and stammered, "I…I don't know. It just…came to me as I listened to you."

The doctor twisted his mouth. "Interesting. Perhaps this is an indication that your memory is returning. And you're technically correct. But let's keep the little one healthy for the first couple of months until his body develops the strength to fight the bad germs. Deal?"

She nodded. "Right, of course."

"Okay, then, moving on." The doctor looked down as he scribbled his signature on Brianna's release form and continued with his checklist. "Mom, no driving for two weeks. No lifting anything heavier than the baby. No strenuous exercise until your regular doctor releases you for that, and—" he paused again and aimed his pen at Hunter "—no sex for at least six weeks."

Hunter blinked and shifted awkwardly on the chair. "I—"

"I mean it. I hear stories from new moms all the time about getting flak from their husbands, pressure to fudge on that six-week restriction." The doctor narrowed his gaze on Hunter. "No sex for six weeks. Got it?"

"Uh…" Just like that, an image of him tangling his naked body with Brianna's flashed in vibrant color and clarity in his mind's eye. Heat swept through him, and he cut a glance toward the bed, where Brianna gaped back at him. Her cheeks had flushed, and she nervously licked her lips, drawing his attention to their plump, bow-shaped perfection.

The doctor cleared his throat. "Do you understand?"

Hunter jerked his focus back to the man in the white

lab coat and raised his hands as if surrendering. "Yeah. Sure. Six weeks. Got it."

The doctor stepped closer to the side of the bed and, in a lower volume, addressed Brianna directly about medications, hygiene issues and follow-up appointments.

His head buzzing with adrenaline, Hunter leaned back in the chair and swiped a hand over his face. *Sex with Brianna? Thanks for putting* that *picture in my brain, Doc.* As if he wasn't having a hard enough time keeping his thoughts about the beautiful new mother on a gentlemanly track.

Hunter pinched the bridge of his nose and scoffed at himself. *Yeah, right. You didn't need the doctor's warning to push your mind into the bedroom.* His thoughts had never been far from that erotic path since he'd first looked in the window of her overturned car and had been poleaxed by her gorgeous eyes and stunning face. Knowing the gentle soul behind her appearance only made his attraction to her stronger. An attraction he needed to rein in and get over if he didn't want to get his heart squashed down the road.

Brianna's son was heir to the throne of Meridan, for cripes' sake. She'd had a relationship with a *prince*. She had a life in a palace waiting for her, with wealth and bodyguards and all the best life had to offer, thanks to Ben's royal heritage. He was crazy to think she'd ever settle for a construction foreman from Lagniappe, Louisiana. Disappointment plucked at him, but coming in second was nothing new for Hunter. Being the youngest brother to two high-achieving, good-looking Mansfield men often meant being overlooked or getting hand-me-downs.

"All right, then," the doctor said as he handed Brianna

her discharge paperwork. "The records department has the little guy's birth certificate ready for you to verify and sign, and then you're free to go. I'll send an orderly in with a wheelchair." He leaned over Ben's bassinet, and a grin curled his lips. "Take care of your mama, sport." As he slipped out the door, he gave a small wave to Brianna and Hunter. "Congratulations, you two."

Brianna slanted a glance toward Hunter. "Sorry about that."

"About what?" Hunter pushed out of the chair and started gathering the items the hospital was sending home for Ben. Hunter was well versed in hospital discharges, having helped Darby, his best friend and now his sister-in-law, with his niece's many stays in the hospital during her battle with cancer.

"The awkwardness when the doctor assumed you were my husband. The…sex stuff." Her cheeks turned an adorable shade of pink again.

A woman shuffled in, giving a sharp rap on the door, and she held a clipboard out to Brianna. "Ma'am, if you'll just read over this and sign at the bottom. Please check the spelling and dates for accuracy. I'll be back in a moment to collect it."

The woman breezed out again, and Brianna glanced down at the document. "Ben's birth certificate." A small smile tugged her mouth as she scanned the document. "Benjamin Coleman. Seven pounds seven ounces." Her brow twitched. "Uh-oh."

"What?" Hunter stepped closer to glance at the clipboard.

"'Father, Hunter Mansfield.' They listed you as his father."

He gave her foot a squeeze through the light blanket.

"That is what we told them when you were brought in. So I could stay with you."

"I can't say you're Ben's father on a legal document when you aren't. That's asking too much of you."

He winked. "I can think of a lot worse things than being assumed to be your husband."

"But this…" She tapped the clipboard with her pen. "This is big."

"Maybe. But you can't list Chris without leaving the kind of trail to Ben and evidence of his lineage you were wanting to avoid." He inhaled deeply, then blew it out through pursed lips. "Why don't you leave my name for now? Maybe you can amend the document later, when you know it is safe. I don't mind playing Ben's father awhile longer."

She flashed him a smile, then bent her head and beetled her brow. "Just the same, I'm going home now. The crisis has passed, and I know I have an aunt who can help me fill in the holes in my memory. I can't impose on you any longer."

An uneasy niggle scraped through Hunter. "Did I complain?"

"No. And it's not that I don't appreciate all you've done. I do, more than words can say!" Her eyes held a heartbreaking sadness and determination. "But I can't depend on your generosity forever." She squared her petite shoulders and firmed her full lips. "This pretend marriage needs to end. I want a divorce."

Hunter parked his truck on the driveway at Brianna's house and glanced at her across the front seat. He'd managed to convince her to hold off on their "divorce." He refused to leave her until he'd helped her settle back into her house and made sure she could handle her newborn on her own. For Ben's sake. Yes, he'd shamelessly played the baby card, knowing a mother's priority would always be her child.

"Home, sweet home. So do you recognize it? Any little tickles of memory?"

She sighed and stared hard at the house, her face lined in concentration, clearly willing her memory to return with every fiber of her being. If determination were the deciding factor in returning her memory, Brianna would be back in full form in no time. Unfortunately, she couldn't know if the rest of her memories would ever return.

"No." Her body sagged, her dejection palpable. "Nothing."

He patted her knee. "Give it time. The neurologist said the swelling could take days to recede."

The look she shot him echoed the doubts and questions that plagued him. What if the memories didn't come back? What if her past, her identity, her career, her family never returned?

"Are you sure you wouldn't rather go to a hotel or my apartment, just until we figure out the extent of the threat against you?" he asked.

She gnawed her bottom lip and dented her brow in thought. "I can't impose on you that way. Besides, Ben's nursery is here. And Sorsha. And I want to be surrounded by familiar things. If I'm in my own home, maybe my memory will return sooner."

"Maybe, but—"

"The sooner I regain my memory, the sooner I can figure out what I need to do about Prince Cristoff." She sent him a pleading look. "I *need* to be here."

Hunter disagreed, but for the time being, he let the issue drop. He could understand her desperate desire to regain her memory, and if she thought she'd recover her past surrounded by her possessions, he'd do his part by keeping vigil over her and her son.

Opening the back door of his extended cab, Hunter leaned in to unbuckle the baby seat Ben had ridden home in. "Welcome home, buddy!"

The baby's unfocused dark blue eyes blinked at him, and a bubble of spit popped at his lips. Hunter chuckled, feeling a tug of nostalgia. He remembered the family celebrations when his older brother Grant and his wife had brought their daughters home from the hospital. When he'd driven Darby home with his newborn niece to a surprise reception of Mansfield family and friends. Video cameras had rolled, joyful tears had flowed, sumptuous food had been shared. Laughter, toasts, family.

His chest tightened. None of that awaited Brianna. And that was just...*wrong.* He gritted his back teeth and glanced to the front seat, where Brianna was gingerly shifting her sore body to climb out of the truck. "No. Bri, sit tight. I'm coming."

"I don't need—"

He pulled his phone from his pocket and thumbed the camera app open. "We have to do this homecoming properly. Wait there." Switching his camera to video mode, he hit Play. "Here's baby Ben at two days old. He just arrived home from the hospital. Say hi, Ben."

Keeping the video trained on Ben, he lifted the carrier out of the truck and circled the fender to the passenger side. Raising the phone, he focused on Brianna. "Welcome home, Mom."

Brianna eyed the phone and gave a startled gasp. Patting her hair, she groaned, "Hunter, no. I look horrid. Turn that off!"

"Au contraire. You look beautiful, sweetheart. Doesn't she, Ben?" He focused the video on the baby, then set the car seat down so he'd have a free hand to help Brianna out of the truck's high front seat. A videographer would have been handy, but without any other help, Hunter juggled the role along with that of Brianna's escort, bellhop, baby carrier and welcome-committee chair. "It's not every day you bring your son home from the hospital, and this is one memory I don't want you to lose."

When he raised the camera to Brianna again, her eyes were full of tears. His pulse tripped, and he thumbed off the video. "Bri? Something wrong?"

"You're too good to be true."

"Because I'm filming Ben's homecoming?" He gave her a dismissive headshake.

"Because you thought of filming Ben's homecoming. Because you're trying in so many ways to make a horrible situation for me bearable. Even happy."

"Yes." He aimed a finger at her, choosing not to respond to her sentimentality. Experience had told him hormonal women, especially pregnant or postnatal women, were like quicksand. Better to not let them suck you into an emotional jag. "Happy. So no more tears. Give me a smile for this happy day." He raised the camera again and waited for her to wipe her cheeks and twitch a half grin. He started filming again and held out a hand to her.

Despite the warm autumn air, Brianna's hand was cold, heightening his perception of her vulnerability. His grip swallowed her slim fingers, and a protective instinct in him charged from its cave, roaring. He might not be

Ben's father, and maybe Brianna thought she needed to go it alone, but he'd formed a bond with this mother and her child in the past couple of days. He'd be damned if he'd cut and run, leave them to fend for themselves.

Down, boy, he told the testosterone-pumped beast snarling inside him. *Give her space. You can't force yourself on her if she doesn't want your protection.*

Brianna slid off the truck seat and leaned over Ben's carrier. Hunter kept filming.

"This is our home, sweet boy. What do you think?" She lifted him out of the car seat and cradled him in her arms, positioning him so that the camera could see his face. She gazed down at her son, and the tremulous smile she'd pasted on for the camera blossomed to full flower.

The joy and love that lit her face as she beamed at Ben hit Hunter between the ribs. Like a breath-stealing fist to the chest. He may have actually staggered back a step. His phone sagged so that his subject wasn't centered as he blinked at the scene in front of him, reeling.

He'd been at his brother's house when his children were brought home, shared the happiness of the event, seen the dorky, slaphappy look on Grant's face, even teased his brother about it. But like a bolt from the blue, now he got it. He understood the primal, gut-wrenching, heart-squeezing desire for a family. His own family.

Sure, he loved his brothers and parents, would die for his precious and precocious nieces. But watching Brianna cuddle her son, seeing her radiant joy, feeling that clawing he-man need to defend her and make her happy… Hunter drew a deep breath and recentered his subject in the video frame.

His gut pitched with recognition. He wanted *this*. Milestone happy memories with his own wife. Children. A house. A dog or cat, maybe both. Little League. Junior ballet.

He swallowed the knot of trepidation that climbed his throat. Where had this notion of settling down and committing to domestic life come from?

Sure, several years ago he'd offered to marry Darby, his best friend, after she found out she was pregnant with his dead brother's baby. But she'd turned him down. He'd been a little hurt and a lot relieved. She'd loved Connor and couldn't justify settling for his brother, preventing Hunter from finding true love. Darby's refusal had been a good choice, since Connor had proved to be alive after all and was now married to Darby and in WitSec with their daughter.

Since his well-intended proposal to Darby, he hadn't given marriage a second thought. Until now. Until Brianna. And once again, the woman who had him thinking of settling down had another man in her life, a man who, by all accounts, was the better option. An honest-to-God prince.

"Oops," Brianna said and chuckled, drawing him out of his thoughts. "Maybe that could be edited out?" She dug a burp cloth out of the diaper bag and wiped Ben's mouth where he'd spit up a little milk. After tucking the dirty cloth in the bag again, she faced Hunter and the camera. "Say cheese, Ben."

She flashed him a big smile, and Hunter felt the earth tilt a little. Jeez, he had it bad.

Get over it, Mansfield. You can't stand in the way of the royal life she has a right to.

He finished filming and pulled out the house key he'd used yesterday. After unlocking the door, Hunter stood back so that Brianna could enter first. Baby carrier in one hand, Ben in the crook of her other arm, she moved past him, trailing the scent of baby powder, an olfactive reminder of her vulnerability. She stopped short before she'd even cleared the doorway.

"Oh, my God," she whispered.

"What? Do you remember the—" Hunter noticed the condition of the living room and fell silent for a moment. The room had been tossed.

Sofa cushions were upended, drawers left open with papers spilled onto the floor, books pulled from shelves, furniture askew. After a moment of surveying the damage, Hunter took Brianna's arm and tugged her back, stepping in front of her. "Maybe you should go back out to my truck with Ben. I'll check the house and make sure whoever did this is gone."

"You mean it wasn't like this yesterday when you were here?"

"No. I'd have told you if I'd found this yesterday. This is new. This is…disturbing."

Brianna stared past him at the destruction to her living room. "It's like they were looking for something, but…what could I have that was so important?"

Hunter set the diaper bag on the floor and frowned. "Maybe a clue to where the prince is hiding."

She frowned. "The video message?"

"Maybe. We don't know if he's really in New Orleans or not. I still think something in the video was off."

"But if he's not there, I don't know—"

"You don't *remember*. Because of the accident. That's not to say you didn't have important information before your concussion, that you won't remember something as you heal and the swelling goes down."

Brianna's face, already pale with fright, leeched of even more color. "Hunter, I—"

"Hey, I'm not going to let anything happen to you. That's a promise." He pulled her into a lopsided bear hug, careful not to squash Ben, and stroked a hand down her back. He absorbed her tremors, even as his resolve to protect her ratcheted up. "Take Ben back to my truck. Lock the doors."

She pulled back and met his gaze with a troubled expression denting her brow. The turmoil in her eyes wrenched inside him.

After escorting her back to his pickup, he searched everywhere in the house he thought an intruder could hide. He checked closets and looked under beds—which was where he found a disgruntled Sorsha hiding. He coaxed the cat out with soothing tones and scratched Sorsha behind the ears when she crept out to him, meowing her complaint about the ruffians who'd scared her with their destruction.

When he'd assured himself the house was safe, he dialed 911 and walked out to bring Brianna inside.

She sent him a dubious look when she spotted the phone at his ear.

"Who is that?" she mouthed.

Police, he mouthed back.

Her eyes widened, and panic filled her face. She shook her head, whispering loudly, "No! Chris said no police!"

Hunter scowled at her, even as the emergency operator confirmed that a patrol unit was on the way. He muffled the phone against his chest before he answered her. "Don't you think he meant the police shouldn't be told about *him?* This can be handled as an average break-in."

"Except we both know it's not an average break-in. The people who did this want Chris. They—" she shivered "—want Ben."

The idea of someone coming after Brianna's baby sent ice to his marrow, followed quickly by the heat of fury toward anyone who dared to hurt Ben or Brianna. "I just don't see how it's a bad thing to alert the police to a potential threat against you."

"I can't explain it, but you heard Chris. He was very clear. He knows the situation better than we do. He's got to have good reasons for being so adamant."

Her sky-blue eyes pleaded with him, and the fact that she trusted Chris's judgment over his chafed. He didn't want to argue with her. Still, he was the one here, defending her, taking care of her postdelivery, putting his ass on the line to keep her safe. His Royal *Hideness* left her to fend for herself...with his newborn baby. Prince Chris was the one who'd *put* Brianna in danger.

Hunter took a deep breath and gritted his back teeth. *Jealous much?*

"Since the cops are already on the way, let's let them have a look around, take a report. It may turn out this was a simple break-in, nothing more sinister."

Brianna bit her lip, looking unconvinced, but the arrival of a squad car preempted further discussion. Hunter recognized the officer as someone he'd gone to high school with, and while Brianna watched, a frown denting her forehead, Hunter chatted up old times as he led the officer through the house.

"Anything missing?" the officer asked as he walked from the living room into Brianna's bedroom. "I see the flat-screen TV and jewelry are still here. Those are usually taken in a robbery."

"Um…" Hunter glanced to the living-room couch, where Brianna had settled with Ben. Thanks to her amnesia, she wasn't likely to remember what she'd owned or know if anything was gone. "I don't think she's had a chance to make a list of what's missing yet. Can we get back to you and add that as a P.S. to your report?"

The officer stuck his pen in his shirt pocket and nodded. "Just give the case number to the officer who takes your list. They can add it to the file I'll start."

"In light of the break-in, could you ask for patrol cars to keep a watch on her house for the next several days? I'm concerned about her safety."

"Will do. Often when there's a break-in like this, several more in the neighborhood will follow. We generally will watch the area for the perp to return."

Hunter didn't contest the officer's theory that this was a run-of-the mill break-in. He was satisfied simply knowing the police were willing to patrol the neighborhood and watch Brianna's house.

While the officer finished his search, Hunter joined Brianna on the couch, where she cradled her sleeping son in her arms. The policeman checked for signs of forced entry and footprints outside windows, then called for a forensics team to dust for prints on the doorknobs and surfaces of cabinets that had obviously been rifled through. Hunter didn't expect them to find much, if anything. He had a hunch the people who'd ransacked Brianna's place were professionals. What was more, he feared the thing they'd come to take was Brianna's life.

Chapter 7

That evening after the police had left and Hunter and Brianna had cleaned up the majority of the damage, Hunter ordered a pizza for their dinner. Brianna had protested when he told her his plans to hang around, believing the added police patrols would be sufficient protection. But he'd refused to leave, convinced that the people who'd rifled her house would be back. As long as she insisted on staying in her house, he was going to be her roommate and guardian, sleeping in her guest room indefinitely.

They were just sitting down to eat when someone rang Brianna's doorbell.

"Expecting company?" he asked.

Her response was a wry look that said, *What do you think?*

Wishing he had the handgun he kept at his apartment, he went to the front door and peered through her peephole. An attractive woman about his mom's age stood on the front porch, holding a bunch of blue balloons and a casserole dish. Relaxing the coil of apprehension in his gut, he opened the door and greeted Brianna's visitor.

"Oh, hi," the brunette said, a curious dent at the top of her nose. "I'm Robyn Rosenberg, Brianna's aunt. Are you the new daddy?"

"Uh, no. Just a friend. I'm Hunter." He took the balloons from her and ushered her inside. "Come on in. Brianna's in here."

Brianna's aunt swept in, setting the casserole pan on an end table and rushing to Brianna as soon as she spotted her on the couch. "Brianna, darling! Where's that new baby?" Her aunt bussed her cheek, then pulled back with a frown. "Oh, look at that nasty gash on your head! Have you regained your memory yet?" She waved a hand toward the dish she'd brought and chattered on without giving Brianna a chance to answer. "I brought you a chicken casserole, but…oh, I see you have dinner already. Well, never you mind. I'll just put it in the fridge for tomorrow. How are you feeling?"

Brianna blinked and hesitated, as if not quite sure she was supposed to answer or if she needed to wait on further verbiage from her aunt. "I'm feeling better every day."

Robyn straightened from greeting Brianna and planted a hand on her hip. She cocked her head to the side and twisted her mouth. "You don't remember me, do you?"

Brianna bit her bottom lip. "I'm sorry, but…no."

Aunt Robyn flapped a hand at her. "Don't worry. I'll help you fill in those blanks. I brought pictures and souvenirs to jog your memory, and I can answer all your questions. Hunter, be a dear and put that casserole in the refrigerator, then point me toward my great-nephew. I'm just dying for a peek at him!"

"He's—"

But Aunt Robyn spotted the bassinet across the room and cooed, "Oh, my! There he is!"

Hunter picked up the pan of food and sent Brianna a glance as her boisterous aunt scuttled across the room to swoon over Ben. Brianna's amused expression matched his own thoughts. In a word, *wow.*

Two hours and many family stories later, Aunt Robyn held Ben as he slept and paused from regaling them with an account of Brianna's high-school graduation to ask, "Am I helping at all or just confusing you more?"

"Um, you're helping. I just…" Brianna, whose brain had long ago reached information overload, rubbed her gritty eyes and tried to focus. She knew there were questions she needed to ask, critical pieces of her past she needed her aunt Robyn to fill in for her, but her head was swimming in a soup of teenage proms, family trips to Graceland and the details of the car accident that killed her parents when she was fourteen. According to her aunt, Brianna loved water sports of all kinds, worked as a biomedical researcher at Bancroft Industries and attended the local United Methodist church, where she served on a variety of committees.

Brianna closed her eyes and focused her thoughts on the tidbits her aunt offered. Water sports? While she couldn't remember specifics about ever swimming, surfing or skiing, she felt a kick of excitement when she pictured herself in the water. That had to be a good sign, right? And biomedical research? An image of a laboratory, of petri dishes, of test tubes in a centrifuge flashed in her mind. She could even see the photo of a bifido-bacteria microbe on the back of the laboratory door. *Bifidobacteria?* That wasn't a term she figured the average citizen knew. Maybe memories of her research *were* lurking at the edges of her recollections.

While this was all good information to have, she didn't feel any resolution to some of the bigger issues facing her.

"Maybe you could help her with some more recent history?" Hunter suggested, as if reading her mind. "What can you tell us about her relationship with Ben's father?"

Brianna sent him a sharp look. Chris had warned her about letting anyone know about him, and she wanted to keep Ben's royal heritage a secret until she figured out how she would address that issue.

"She would have been involved with him last winter," Hunter continued, not catching her warning glance. "From what you said earlier, I take it you didn't meet him, but do you remember Brianna mentioning a relationship last year? How they met?"

Aunt Robyn dabbed at a bubble of spit Ben blew as he slept. "Let's see. You weren't dating anyone steadily last winter locally that I recall. Not that you tell me much about your love life, mind you." Aunt Robyn smiled at her and patted Ben's diapered bottom. "As I recall, you went to the house at the Cape after Christmas for a while. You'd just wrapped up a huge project at work and decided to take some accumulated time for R and R."

Brianna thought about the key chain she'd had with her when her car flipped. I ♥ Cape Cod. "The Cape? Do you mean Cape Cod?"

Her aunt nodded. "Why, yes. The vacation home your

parents bought back in the eighties. You inherited it when they died. When you moved in with me, we sold your parents' house and paid off the mortgage on the vacation home. We both use it as a getaway when it's not rented to tourists. You get a tidy little income from the rental fees."

Hunter sat forward on the couch. "So that's probably where you met Ben's father. The timing is right."

"Do you have any other information about who or where this man is? He deserves to know he's a daddy." Aunt Robyn divided a look between Hunter and Brianna.

"Not much. He knows about Ben, just not that he's been born." Brianna rubbed her temple, just below the cut from the accident.

Aunt Robyn tipped her head and knitted her manicured eyebrows. "Honey, have I worn you out? I can go if you need to rest."

Brianna jerked her head up. "Go? You're not staying? But…"

Aunt Robyn pressed a hand to her heart, and the V in her brow deepened. "I'm afraid I can't stay. If I led you to believe otherwise, I'm sorry. I'm giving the keynote address at a nursing conference in Minneapolis tomorrow night. I'm catching the red-eye from the Lagniappe airport later tonight." She checked her watch. "In fact, I should probably head on to the airport now." Aunt Robyn rose from the sofa, kissed Ben's head and carefully settled the baby in the bassinet set up beside the sofa.

Brianna flashed her an awkward smile, embarrassed that she'd assumed her aunt was here on baby duty. The brevity of her aunt's visit stung a bit, too. According to Robyn, she was Brianna's only family—other than some uncommunicative cousins on her father's side. When

Brianna pasted a smile on her face, determined not to show her hurt, an odd déjà vu settled over her. Somehow, being on her own, battling a sense of isolation and disappointment, was familiar. She had a flash of sitting alone in a well-appointed living room with a beagle sleeping on the couch beside her.

Robyn pulled her into a hug as they headed to the front door. "I'll be tied up next week with work, but I've marked off the week after, your original due date, to come back and help you out."

"Aunt Robyn, did I have a dog as a kid?" she blurted.

Her aunt blinked and tipped her head. "Not as a child. Your father was allergic. But I got you a dog when you came to live with me. To keep you company while I was at work. Barney."

"A beagle?"

Robyn's face brightened. "Yes. You remember?"

"Just a flash. An image."

"Still a good sign," Hunter said. "Maybe the swelling's going down."

Brianna rubbed her hands on her slacks and worked up an optimistic smile for the two anxious pairs of eyes studying her. "Maybe."

While Hunter walked Robyn out to her car, Brianna checked on Ben, who'd rejected his pacifier in favor of his own thumb. Thumb-sucking might be a habit she'd have to break later, but tonight, he looked too precious for her to dissuade him from the self-comfort. Brianna had bigger issues facing her and years ahead of her to deal with parenting issues—such as, if Ben was forced to claim his royal heritage, how did she protect her son from a life of societal expectation, media scrutiny and dangerous political militants? Should she allow Ben the life of royal privilege and comfort his father's lineage afforded him? Even as that question niggled, an image of Hunter grinning at Ben worked its way to the front of her thoughts.

Where did Hunter fit into all this? She'd tried to cut him loose, give him her permission to walk away. But he'd stayed. And that loyalty, that commitment, his steadfast friendship, filled her with a warmth and security she treasured more than all the gold in Chris's royal account.

After Aunt Robyn left, Brianna wasted no time giving Ben his dinner, changing his diaper, taking a warm shower and tumbling into bed. She'd moved Ben's bassinet into her bedroom so she'd hear him when he woke for his midnight meal, and Hunter headed off to the guest bedroom for the night.

As tired as she was, Brianna spent long minutes staring at the ceiling and picturing Hunter's tall, muscular body squeezing into the small antique bed in the guest room. She made a mental note to ask Aunt Robyn the history on the beautiful bed, tiny as it was, next time she saw her, then her brain returned to Hunter. She imagined his long legs hanging off the end of the mattress, his wide shoulders filling the width of the bed and his chiseled face nestled on the pillow. Did he snore? Did he sleep in the buff? What would it be like to curl against his strength and sleep wrapped in his arms? To kiss him good-night, feel his skin against hers, have his hands—

Brianna scrubbed both hands over her face and stopped the daydream in its erotic tracks. Her skin tingled from her scalp to her toes, and a pleasant heat had curled in her belly. *Dream all you want, but don't get any ideas about acting on the fantasy.* Hunter wasn't hers to claim. And the doctor had specifically said no sex. For six weeks.

At the hospital, with her body still aching from the delivery, she'd thought, *No kidding. Like I'll feel up for that anytime soon!* Then she'd cut a side glance to Hunter and seen the rosy flush of awkwardness in his cheeks... and the dark smolder of desire and speculation in his eyes. Longing. Anticipation. The lure of the forbidden. And she'd known she would have tossed the doctor's instructions aside in a heartbeat, no matter how her body felt, for a few stolen moments of what Hunter's eyes promised.

Now she groaned, forcing thoughts of Hunter from her mind, and covered her eyes with her arm in search of sleep. Her body needed rest, and her life didn't need the complication of a relationship while she figured out where she stood with Chris. Had she loved him before the head injury stole her memory? Wouldn't she remember loving him if she had? So much to think about...

Dear God, she started praying instinctively. And why not? Aunt Robyn had told her she was active in a local United Methodist church. Praying felt natural, felt good. Calmed her mind. *Help me figure this all out. Help me get my memory back and do the right thing for everyone involved.*

The next morning, Brianna dragged herself out of bed when she heard Ben's first whimpers. She'd discovered last night that if she didn't respond to his mewls of hunger or discomfort promptly, he tuned up for a good cry and was all the harder to calm.

She crawled back into her bed to feed him and soon

Sorsha had joined them, meowing loudly and asking for her breakfast, as well.

"Wait your turn, Sorsha. I'll be there in a minute."

With a twitch of her tail, Sorsha sat down on the end of the bed and glared impatiently at the interloper who'd displaced her as first fed in the morning. Brianna stroked Ben's cheek as he nursed, then closed her eyes wearily. She'd been up three times overnight to feed, burp and change Ben's diaper. She'd had maybe four hours of sleep, at best. When Ben drifted to sleep at her breast, she eased him gently back into the bassinet and tiptoed to the bathroom.

She prayed she didn't look as haggard as she felt, but one peek in the mirror shot that hope down. She snorted derisively. Had she really been fantasizing at bedtime last night about having sex with Hunter? She'd be lucky if he didn't take one look at her this morning and run for the hills screaming.

She ran a brush through her hair, washed her face and pinched a little color into her cheeks. *Pitiful,* she thought, studying her reflection. *You look like just what you are—a sleep-deprived mother.* Shaking her head at herself, she stumbled back into the bedroom, checked on Ben—still sleeping, thank heavens—then crept quietly to the kitchen.

She found Hunter with his head in the pantry, scooping out cat food for Sorsha, who wound around his legs in a dance of anticipation and gratitude.

"Thank you," she said. "I could have done that."

He glanced up and grinned. "You had your hands full, and Sorsha claimed she was starving."

Brianna stooped to stroke her cat's silky fur. "Silly, impatient girl."

"I thought maybe if you were up to it we could head over to Bancroft Industries today and visit your office. Maybe seeing the place where your aunt says you work will trigger something for you."

She nodded. "Good idea. What about your work? Are you going in today?"

"I'll stop by a couple of work sites for a minute and talk with the crew, make sure everything's on target. You up to riding with me? I don't feel right leaving you alone here. Not knowing someone trashed the place yesterday."

The reminder of the destruction in her house sent a chill to her bones. She didn't want to be alone, either, not while there was still a threat to Ben's life. She pressed a hand to her swirling stomach and nodded. "I'm game."

In the end, the trip to Bancroft Industries didn't jog loose new memories, but it did confirm the flash of a laboratory she'd had while talking to her aunt had been her workspace at Bancroft. Her coworkers cooed over Ben, promised to bring food later in the week and wished her well for her maternity leave.

After stopping at a few of Hunter's construction sites, they spent the rest of the day assembling Ben's crib, a project she'd obviously started at some point and abandoned, based on the parts scattered on the nursery floor.

For dinner, Brianna heated the casserole Aunt Robyn had brought and soon after found she couldn't keep her eyes open any longer.

"Don't think you need to stay up on my account," Hunter said, giving her shoulder a squeeze. His strong fingers felt heavenly massaging her muscles, which were still stiff and achy from the car accident.

"In that case," she said, stifling a yawn, "since I

know I'll be up again in a couple of hours with the little prince…"

Hunter's grin faltered, then quickly recovered, though without the same luster as before. What had she said that bothered him? Perhaps her reference to Ben as royalty reminded him of the danger she was in? She knew the thought of the bullet holes in the back of her car hadn't been far from her mind all day.

Before turning out her light, as she crawled into bed, she rewatched the video message from Chris. Calling the number the video had been sent from led her to a disconnected number. A dead end. More frustration. Tired as she was, her worries kept her tossing and turning until after Ben had awoken for his midnight meal. Finally, she drifted off around 1:00 a.m.

A few hours later, Brianna was roused from a deep sleep, when something sharp pricked her wrist. She rubbed her arm and rolled over, only to have small feet walk on her.

"Mrow!" Sorsha's loud plea preceded a determined head butt to her arm.

"What? Sorsha, please. I'm tired." She cracked her eyes open far enough to see the feline's dark outline as she pushed her cat off the bed. "Leave me alone."

But Sorsha hopped back up onto the bed and bit her wrist again. "Mrow."

"Sorsha!" Groaning, Brianna sat up in bed and tossed back the covers. "Stop." She hated to shut the cat out of the bedroom, but she needed her sleep.

Then she smelled it. Smoke. She sniffed again, certain her nose was playing tricks. But again an acrid scent of burning greeted her. And suddenly Sorsha's agitation made sense.

Her house was on fire.

Chapter 8

"Hunter!"

Hunter jerked awake and sent a disoriented glance around the room he was in. Where—

"Hunter! Fire!" Brianna's cry shot cobweb-clearing adrenaline through him. In the next instant, he recognized the chemical scent of burning carpet and diesel fuel.

As he jammed his feet into his jogging shoes, he snatched his cell phone from the bedside table. He shoved the phone in his back pocket and ran to the hall, which was already filling with rolling clouds of black smoke. He pulled his T-shirt up over his nose, a feeble attempt to filter the toxic smoke, as he sucked in a breath to hold.

The flicker of flames danced on the wall near the living room…and the utility room at the opposite end of the hall. Hell! The fire was creeping toward them from *two* directions. Heat roiled through the house, blistering the paint on the walls and slamming into Hunter as he darted across the corridor into Brianna's room.

She stood over Ben's bassinet, coughing.

"We have to go out the window." He closed the door against the encroaching flames and smoke and trotted to the window. "The hall is blocked in both directions by the fire." He ripped open the blinds and flipped the metal hasp that locked the sliding panes. He grasped the bottom edge of the windowpane and tugged. The window didn't budge. Gritting his teeth, Hunter tugged harder. Still nothing.

"Damn it! I think the window's been painted shut. It won't open." He tried again, straining his muscles until they quivered. He sucked in a breath, worn out from his efforts, and choked on the smoke filling the room. Brianna held Ben close, blowing near his nose, but even the baby was coughing, gagging, crying. "Keep a blanket over his face!"

Hunter raised his T-shirt over his nose again and hurried into her adjoining bathroom. No windows there. Double damn!

Grabbing washcloths from the shelf, he doused them both in water from the sink, quickly rung them out and pressed one over his nose and mouth as he rushed back out to the bedroom. "Breathe through this!"

Brianna caught the rag he tossed her with one hand while hugging Ben close, cradled in the crook of her other arm.

Hunter glanced around the dark room, which was growing murkier as smoke billowed in and blinded him. He found a hefty lamp and snatched it up. "Stand back!"

As soon as Brianna had moved away from the window, he swung the lamp hard and shattered the window-panes. With a second whack, he knocked more glass out of the way before pulling Brianna's bedspread from the bed and laying it over the jagged shards on the bottom rim of the opening. "Give me Ben…" He stopped to cough. Breathing was growing harder by the second. "You climb out!"

Brianna's eyes were wide with terror. She gave the room an encompassing glance. "Get Sorsha, too! Please. She—" cough "—was here a minute ago."

"I'll try." He took Ben from her arms and glanced at her feet. "You need shoes. There's glass out there now." Spotting a pair of slip-on loafers near her dresser, he kicked them to her. "Hurry!"

She donned the shoes in seconds, and grabbing her purse from the dresser, she swung it through the opening in the window to the grassy lawn. Hunter steadied her as she clambered out the window. "Watch the sharp edges on the sides."

He swaddled the baby more fully in his blanket to protect him from glass shards and smoke. Ben wiggled and whimpered, and the infant's vulnerability punched Hunter like a fist to the gut.

Once she'd climbed outside, Brianna reached back through the opening for Ben. He handed her his phone, as well. "Call 911. I'll get the cat."

Lifting an arm to shield himself from the blast of heat seeping through the thin bedroom door, Hunter squinted into the corners of the shadowy room for Sorsha. "Here, kitty. Sorsha, where are you?" He coughed, knowing he had little time to grab the cat and get out before smoke inhalation got the better of him. How did he find a black cat in a dark, smoke-filled room? Anxiety tingled on his scalp. He loved animals as much as the next guy, and he hated the idea of Brianna losing her beloved pet. But his lungs were burning, his skin stinging from the building heat. "Sorsha!"

He dropped to the floor, where the smoke was thinner, and looked under the bed. Black. Complete darkness and shadow. He couldn't see anything, but he remembered Sorsha hiding in the back corner after the intruders tossed the house. He shimmied as far under the bed as he could and stretched a hand out. Found fur. Grabbed a handful of scruff and dragged the cat out. Sorsha meowed her fright and hissed once. "I know. I know. Easy, girl."

While holding Sorsha captive with one hand, Hunter yanked the rumpled sheet off Brianna's bed with his other hand and made a hasty cat-burrito. Swaddled in the sheet, Sorsha was safe from the glass and easier to handle, and Hunter was protected from the claws of a frightened feline. Holding Sorsha under his arm like a football, Hunter rushed to the window and climbed out. As he squeezed through the opening, his shirt snagged on something. He twisted sideways and groped with one hand to free himself. As he got loose and found his footing on the grass below, his gaze landed on the metal protrusion that had caught his shirt. A nail head. In the window frame. One of several intentionally driven into the frame of the pane. The reason it wouldn't slide open. A chill slid through him. Brianna's window, her escape, had been sabotaged. He bit out an earthy curse.

Already he heard the distant wail of sirens as he gulped in the fresh autumn air. Coughing and dragging in deep, rasping breaths, he carried Sorsha to his truck and shut her inside for safekeeping. "Do me a favor," he said hoarsely as he released the cat from the restraint of the sheet. "Don't trash the leather seats."

He staggered to the edge of Brianna's yard where she knelt in the grass, staring at the blazing house. Ben had kicked his legs free of the blanket and waved his arms angrily as he whined.

Hunter nudged her shoulder. "We should move farther back. In fact, I'm going to move my truck out of the fire engine's way. I've got Sorsha in the backseat. She's safe."

She didn't move, her gaze transfixed on the fire, and he worried she was going into shock.

"Bri?" He chafed her arm. "Hey, are you all right?"

She raised haunted eyes and blinked slowly, dazed. "What did I do?" Her voice sounded raspy from the smoke. "How did this…?" She coughed. "Did I leave something turned on? I can't think of…anything…"

Hunter took another lung-clearing breath of the night air and gritted his back teeth. "We don't know how it started. Don't assume it was something you did. Sometimes house fires start because of faulty wiring or lightning…" He glanced up at the cloudless sky and knew they could rule that cause out. He heaved a ragged sigh, and as he turned to stare at the raging fire that was devouring her house, he remembered his first impressions upon waking to Brianna's shout.

Diesel. He'd smelled diesel fumes.

He studied the size of the fire and thought about how quickly it had spread. From two ends of the house at once. When added to the nails in her window frame, Hunter could find only one explanation for the tragedy. The fire was no accident. It was arson. Whoever had tossed Brianna's house had come back. And tried to kill her.

* * *

Brianna sat with a blanket around her shoulders and watched an EMT check Ben over. She was still shaking, knowing how close they'd all come to burning up in the fire, succumbing to smoke inhalation. Not just her and Ben, but Hunter, too. Hunter, who'd gotten far more than he ever bargained for when he helped her at her car accident. Hunter, whose quick response may have saved her life and her son's. And her cat's. Hunter was her hero in so many ways…as was Sorsha. If Sorsha hadn't sensed the danger and woken her…

A shudder raced through her, and she moved the oxygen mask from her nose and mouth to ask the EMT, "Is he okay? He won't stop crying."

The female EMT glanced up and smiled. "I think he's fine. His oxygen levels are good." She lifted Ben to her shoulder and patted his back, obviously familiar with babies. "I'd wager his crying has more to do with the noise out here, having his sleep disturbed and maybe wanting a snack. I know my son ate every two hours when we brought him home from the hospital. And he hasn't stopped since! Wait until this one is a teenager. Whew!"

"Thank you. I—" Brianna coughed and replaced the oxygen mask over her mouth for another deep inhalation.

"Just the same," the EMT added, settling Ben in a borrowed baby seat, "I'd advise all of you to ride with us to the hospital and let a doctor check you."

She glanced across the yard to Hunter, who was deep in conversation with a police officer. Something about the dark scowl on his face told her something more was wrong than just their narrow scrape getting out of her burning house. Hunter led the officer over to the window they'd climbed out of and pointed to something on the frame. She furrowed her brow, wondering what could have their attention, when one of the firemen stepped into her line of vision.

"Ma'am, are you the homeowner?"

She regarded the firefighter, decked in turnout gear and boots. He'd removed his helmet and held a warped piece of plastic in his gloved hand. His expression was grim.

Uneasy with the firefighter's grave look, Brianna swallowed hard and winced as her raw throat burned. She gave the fireman a jerky nod.

"Are you aware that your smoke detector had no battery in it?"

"I—" She gaped at the twisted plastic. "That's my smoke detector?" she asked, knowing it was a stupid question but shocked by the damage. "You're sure there was no battery?"

The notion that she could be so careless, that her oversight could have killed them, horrified her.

He nodded. "See this?" He pointed to an empty hole in the melted device. "That's where the battery should have been." His glare was unsympathetic and scolding. "You're very lucky to have gotten out. In homes without a working smoke detector, smoke inhalation typically claims lives before fire does."

Hunter appeared behind the firefighter and split a worried glance between Brianna and the fireman. "What's wrong?"

"He says there was no battery in the smoke detector. How could I have been so delinquent? It doesn't make sense."

"Hell." Hunter's expression hardened, fury flickering in his eyes and flaring his nostrils.

Brianna cringed inwardly, knowing she deserved his anger. She was so caught up in her guilt over her lapse that she almost missed Hunter's reply.

"I doubt it was your fault. I think the people who broke in earlier took it out. I found nails in the window frame, and based on the condition of the nails and wood, the lack of weathering, I'd say they were put there recently. To keep you from escaping this fire."

Brianna gasped, and the firefighter pivoted to face Hunter.

"You suspect foul play?"

Hunter swiped a hand down his face. "Very foul."

The fireman glanced at the smoldering house. "Do the cops agree?"

"They agree the nails are suspicious. They're waiting for the fire marshal's report about the cause of the fire. But I smelled diesel fuel when I woke up. The fire was burning at both ends of the house when I reached the hall. My money is on arson." He gave Brianna a dark, concerned look. "I believe this was attempted murder."

After a thorough exam at the hospital for each of them, including Sorsha, whom Hunter's parents took to the emergency veterinary clinic, Brianna and Ben accepted the senior Mansfields' invitation to spend the rest of the night at their home. They'd all been treated for symptoms of smoke inhalation—mild for Ben and Sorsha to moderate for Brianna and Hunter. They'd all been given more oxygen at the hospital/vet's office, and the humans were sent home by early morning. Sorsha was to be picked up the next day after a night of observation.

Brianna's eyes were red and stung, and her throat was a tad scratchy, but she was alive and grateful that Ben had escaped the worst of the smoke thanks to the heavy swaddling over his face.

Julia and Stan Mansfield proved to be every bit as kind and helpful as their youngest son, and Brianna felt an instant affinity for them. She didn't miss the sparkle of speculation and intrigue in their eyes as they sized her up, however, and could imagine the assumptions they were making about her relationship with Hunter. He had, after all, been sleeping at her house when the fire broke out. Without a sane-sounding explanation to counter their presumptions, she had little to counter the private smiles and knowing glances.

Telling them her baby was of royal lineage and the target of assassins trying to overthrow the monarchy in Meridan sounded…well, crazy, even to her. And Chris had implored her not to talk about Ben's bloodline. Brianna, too, wanted to keep her son's parentage secret—at least until she knew what to do about his future. Could she burden him with the responsibility of the Meridanian throne? Did she have a choice?

Her suspicions about Julia Mansfield's assumptions were confirmed when Hunter's mother showed Brianna back to the guest room and helped her settle Ben. Julia cast Brianna a side glance as she changed the sheets in the crib where, as infants, her granddaughters slept when visiting. "I guess a couple of nights in a bed with pink bumper pads won't be too emasculating for little Ben. Perhaps we can get more masculine bedding for future visits."

"Future visits?" Brianna repeated, so tired her head throbbed and felt as if it were made of lead.

"Well, sure." Julia smoothed out the crib sheet she'd spread in the small bed, then shrugged. "I mean I'm assuming you'll be back to visit if you and Hunter stay together."

"Together?" She knew she sounded a bit like a parrot, and she rubbed her gritty eyes and rasped from her smoke-damaged throat, "We're not together. Not really. He's just helping me out. As a friend."

Julia's expression was a combination of crestfallen, skeptical and confused. "I see." She twisted her mouth in a thoughtful moue, then cocked her head. "Well, perhaps it's for the best that you see your relationship that way."

Brianna frowned. "Why is that?"

"Well…I don't want to see you get hurt. He wouldn't mean to hurt you, of course. My Hunter is far too sweet to intentionally break a girl's heart, but…"

When she hesitated, Brianna leaned forward, her heart thumping anxiously. "But what?"

Julia drew a measured breath, clearly choosing her words carefully. "Hunter's never showed any interest in marriage. He's never really had a serious relationship. I think he enjoys being a bachelor and playing the field. Not that he sleeps around, mind you," she hastened to add. "He just enjoys his freedom too much to settle down."

"Oh." A stab of disappointment jabbed her, though she couldn't say why. She had no designs on Hunter, had no right to presume anything beyond his friendship.

"I hate to be a Debbie Downer. I'd love nothing more than to see Hunter happily married. And you seem like a lovely girl." Julia's expression softened. "I just thought it fair to warn you. Hunter isn't the marrying kind."

Brianna forced a smile to her face. "Thank you for your concern, but really, we're just friends."

Julia nodded and cupped Brianna's cheek in a motherly gesture that burrowed straight to her heart. "If you need anything else, just ask."

Brianna had only a moment to digest what Julia had said about her youngest son before Hunter appeared at the bedroom door. "Everything okay in here?"

She looked up from where she was settling Ben in the crib, propping him on his side with a rolled blanket behind his back. "Yeah. He's already asleep, poor lamb. The last few days haven't been the most restful for him, either. Moved from one place to another, poked by doctors, noise and confusion."

"And you? Did you survive the grilling from my mother?" He flashed her a lopsided grin.

"She didn't grill me."

His eyebrows shot up. "Really? Because I saw the speculative look in her eyes when she brought you back here. I know she had questions for you."

"Oh, she was curious. But I assured her we were just friends."

"Sorry if she put you on the spot. Mom's a romantic, and I think she's worried I'll never give her grandchildren." He raised one eyebrow and gave her a curious glance. "Did she say anything else?"

Brianna hedged. She didn't want to put Hunter's feelings or intentions on trial. Especially when she was in no position to pursue a relationship, either. For all she knew, Meridanian law might require her to marry Chris or compel her to allow Ben to be raised in his father's homeland. But when she considered what it might be like to actually *have* a relationship with someone as thoughtful, handsome and protective as Hunter, her heart squeezed with longing.

She hesitated a moment too long, and Hunter clearly

took her reticence as reluctance to betray his mother. "Never mind. I'll set her straight."

"Oh. No, Hunter, I—"

"Hey, we're *not* a couple, so there's no reason *not* to clear that up with my mom." He stepped to the door of the nursery and sent her a forced smile. He seemed... disappointed? "Sleep well."

Her shoulders sagged, and she rubbed her chest where a raw ache gnawed under her ribs—a feeling that had nothing to do with smoke inhalation and everything to do with letting Hunter down. The sooner she regained her memory, the sooner she could put together the pieces of mystery surrounding her relationship with Chris. The sooner she could determine where her future, Ben's future, lay in respect to Chris's royal family line, the sooner she would know if a relationship with Hunter was even possible. Or was his mother right? If Hunter wasn't the "marrying kind," she was better off knowing that now. She had no use for another broken heart.

Another broken heart? Now, where had *that* notion come from?

Chapter 9

As much as Hunter appreciated his parents' hospitality the night of the fire, he knew it wasn't a long-term solution. Brianna's situation called for discretion. The threat to her from unknown members of the militant rebel faction meant an inherent danger he accepted for himself, but wouldn't impose on his parents. So the next day, after they'd all slept late and had been treated to one of his mother's mouthwatering, artery-clogging, happy-belly Southern breakfasts, he moved Brianna into his own apartment. His place was small, only one bedroom, but he'd splurged on comfy living-room furniture and wasn't opposed to sleeping on the couch.

They made a stop for baby supplies and inexpensive clothing on the way to his apartment and stocked up on some essentials Brianna had lost in the fire. A bassinet, diapers, baby clothes, slacks and shirts for her, undergarments…

Hunter's pulse accelerated when she tossed lacy bras, camisoles and panties in the cart, too easily imagining her in the sexy lingerie. She caught his look and hesitated, glanced back in the cart.

"You're right. Pretty bras can wait until I'm not nursing."

"I didn't say—"

"And cotton will be more comfortable until my body recovers from the pregnancy."

She replaced the lacy silk items, but even the cotton panties she tossed in the basket had sexy trim and feminine colors. He was still turned-on, damn it. Because it wasn't the underclothes that got him hot and bothered. It was the woman. Her curves. Her smile. The way her eyes lingered on him a few seconds longer than necessary. The spark that lit her eyes when she held his gaze. Hunter exhaled deeply and shook his head to clear it as he pushed the shopping cart down the store aisle, following her.

"I've been thinking about that video Chris sent me," she said over her shoulder, the mention of his competition effectively dousing him with cold water.

His competition? Since when was this a contest with Brianna as the prize?

"What about His Hideness?" he asked, hearing the surliness in his tone.

Her step faltering, she glanced at him with a curious look, and he realized he'd never told her his name for her ex. Assuming they were *ex*. It chafed to think there could still be feelings between them, a serious relationship. In the video message, the prince had talked about their plans for the future as a family.

Brianna continued down the aisle, scanning the shelves.

"Well, in light of the arson at my house, I'm rethinking the idea of going to meet him in New Orleans. Not only is he the best person, the *only* person really, who can answer all my questions about our relationship and Ben's future, I'm also thinking he has the right idea about going into hiding. He has professional guards to protect him, and—" Hunter's sigh stopped her. "Not that you haven't been a wonderful protector. You saved us last night and—"

He waved a hand. "You don't have to explain or prop me up. I'm one man, and he's got a whole royal security team at his disposal. I'm sure he can protect you better than I can." That truth irritated him, but he set it aside. "But strategically, is being with him the best plan in the bigger picture? I mean, he's the primary target of these rebels. Wouldn't it be better to keep Ben, his heir, in a separate secure location…in case the prince is found? As in you don't bury all your treasure in one spot. You put some under the mattress and some in the bank and some in stocks."

Brianna nibbled her bottom lip, her expression thoughtful. "I see your point. I'm just so eager to have some answers. I mean, Aunt Robyn definitely helped, but we're in danger because of Chris. My son's future is all up in the air. Does he *have* to assume the throne? Can he abdicate? Can I abdicate on his behalf? Should I keep his lineage a secret from the world? From Ben himself? I…"

She raked the hair back from her face and winced when her fingers hit the bandage on her temple.

"Look, I'm not saying *not* to meet up with him. Just… don't rush off until you think it through some more." Hunter squeezed the handle of the cart, feeling a pressing need to dissuade her. But were his reasons completely unselfish? "I still haven't figured out why the video bothers me, but there's something off with it. And you heard the doctor last night. You need to rest. Your body's been banged up and wrung out several times over the past few days. You're in no shape to travel." He glanced at Ben, his head lolling to one side in the baby seat, and he felt a catch in his chest. "And Ben's so small and vulnerable and—"

He glanced up and met Brianna's lopsided grin. "Okay. I won't rush off," she rasped. She wet her lips and rubbed the front of her throat as she swallowed. "But I want to watch the video again when we get to your place. Maybe we can figure out why it bothers you."

He nodded. "Deal."

An uneasy look crossed her face again, her eyebrows drawing into a frown. Hunter anticipated and intercepted her next question. "Yes, I'm sure I don't mind, and you're not an imposition."

She shot him a skeptical moue.

"I do need to arrange for someone to cover for me at a new building site for a couple of days and move a meeting with a contractor I have scheduled tomorrow," he said, thinking aloud. When her expression grew worried again, he raised a hand. "Easy. A flexible schedule is one of the perks of being your own boss. My family owns the construction company, and I worked enough hours this summer to take some personal time without guilt."

She took a pack of socks off a hook and tossed them in the basket. "I need to call Aunt Robyn and let her know what happened and where I am. If she were to stop by unannounced again and see the burned house, she'd freak."

Ben scrunched his nose as he woke from his nap and gave a mewl of discontent.

"Hmm, time's up. That's your warning to get this guy home, fed and changed before he sets up a major squall." Hunter pushed the cart faster. "Do we have the essentials? I'll head to the checkout."

Brianna nodded, and after paying for and loading their purchases in the back of his truck, Brianna changed Ben's diaper on the backseat and buckled him into his new car seat. They stopped by the emergency vet's office next and claimed Sorsha, who seemed glad to be sprung from the vet's cage, and headed to Hunter's apartment with all the booty.

Hunter took charge of unloading the truck and settling Sorsha in with a food bowl and litter box in the bathroom while Brianna draped a blanket over her shoulder to discreetly feed Ben his dinner on Hunter's couch.

When he finished with the last load, he collapsed in his recliner. Sorsha strolled through the living room, sniffing all of his furniture and scoping out her new digs. Brianna patted her leg and made a kissing sound that called Sorsha to her for a quick cheek scratch and head rub. Temporarily pacified, Sorsha pranced off, her fluffy tail twitching, to explore a different room.

Shaking cat hair off her fingers, Brianna nodded toward her purse. "If you want to get my phone out, we can watch Chris's video again. Maybe figure out why it bothers you?"

He rubbed his scratchy eyes, then retrieved her phone and moved to sit beside her. She smelled of baby powder and flowers, and the sweet scents prodded his protective instincts. He brought up the saved video, and His Hideness filled the screen. They watched the video through twice, and the same itchy feeling prickled his back. What was off?

"What do you think? It all seems pretty straightforward to me. Is it something in Chris's expression? His tone of voice? Something he said?"

Hunter dragged a hand across his jaw and hit Play again. "Or maybe it's not Chris at all. Maybe…" He shifted his attention to the background. Concentrated on extraneous noises. Studied the cityscape visible through the window behind Chris. And hesitated. Enlarged the image. "Is that a wrinkle? In the window?"

Brianna leaned closer to look, and he worked to keep his focus on the video and not the sweet scent of her skin or the tickle of her hair as it brushed his arm. He fisted his free hand to squelch the urge to run his fingers through her thick blond tresses.

"I see what you mean. Is that a defect in the video?"

"I'd say it means that's not a window at all but a photography backdrop."

Brianna angled a look at him. "Like a canvas or curtain?"

"Exactly." In fact, now that he really studied the image… "That's not New Orleans. Those buildings are too new. Too modern. The French Quarter, if that is in fact where he claims he made this, is mostly old brick and filigree ironwork, not glass skyscrapers."

"And look." She pointed to a spot behind Chris. "That's his shadow. Right?"

"I'd say so."

"So the strongest light is coming from the front. If that were a window with as much sunlight as pictured, he should have a shadow here." She pointed to the area beside Chris opposite the fake window.

"So the setup is a fake. This could have been taped anywhere." He tightened his jaw and shook his head.

"Why the deception? Why make you think he's in a city building where he's not? Why not film in the hotel room or safe house or wherever he is?"

Brianna shifted back on the couch with a puzzled look. "We don't know his intention was to deceive us. Maybe this setup just provided a better-quality video. Maybe—"

"Bri."

She stopped but sent him a defensive look. "I can't believe he would do something mean and deceitful. I mean, I knew him once, well enough to have a baby with him." She waved a hand as she defended the prince. "That tells me I cared about this man and trusted him. Maybe this wasn't filmed in New Orleans, maybe the video was staged in front of a photographer's screen, but I refuse to believe he sent the video as part of some grand plot or deception."

Hunter gritted his teeth, squashing the swell of bitter jealousy that rose in him as she argued the prince's virtue.

"If he says he's waiting for me in New Orleans, I believe him." She huffed a sigh and tightened her mouth. "At least, until we can prove otherwise, I choose to trust that Chris wants me safe and is working to reunite us and provide me the protection of his guards."

If he cared about you the way I do, he'd be here protecting you and his son, not hiding like a scared cat. Hunter swallowed the words and countered instead with, "Let's deal in facts. We know the video was staged. We don't know why. But knowing it was staged, I think we should proceed with an extra measure of caution until we're certain joining him is safe for you."

Under the blanket she'd draped over her shoulder for

modesty's sake, Ben peeped like a baby bird. Brianna peeked under the cover to check on her son. "All done, sweetie?"

She brought Ben out from under the blanket and held him awkwardly while maneuvering one-handed to rearrange her bra and shirt.

"Here. Let me have him." Hunter reached for the baby, and his elbow bumped her breast as he scooped Ben into his arms.

Brianna sucked in a light, quick gasp and raised a startled glance. Her eyes were wide and swirling with a heat unrelated to the smoke exposure. She trembled and released Ben to him as she licked her dry lips. "Thank you," she whispered, the rasp in her voice giving the soft tone a husky quality that shot fire to his core.

Damn it. How could she defend Chris one minute, pledging her faith in Ben's father, then look at him the next minute as if he was a chocolate sundae she was ready to lap up? He felt the crackle of attraction from her, but he wanted to be more than a fling on her way to bigger and better things with her prince.

A flippin', honest-to-Pete *prince.* Frustrated, he exhaled harshly, and his lungs gave a slight protesting wheeze to remind him of last night's danger. He drew Ben close to his chest; then, putting him and a burp cloth over his shoulder, Hunter rose to pace.

Sorsha trotted out of the bedroom and rubbed against Hunter's calves. Seeing her cat and the potential for tripping, Brianna patted the sofa cushion. "Come here, Sorsha girl. Good kitty."

The cat hopped up onto the sofa with a soft mewl, eager for the attention Brianna bestowed on her.

Hunter resumed his pacing as he patted the baby's

back with firm thumps. "What do you want to do, Bri? If you believe joining Chris is your best move, I won't stand in your way. I have no right to tell you what to do with your life."

"But you don't think it's safe, do you? Do you think this video is a trick to lure me into a trap? Is that what you're saying?"

Was that what he thought? Or was he just bothered by the idea of saying goodbye to Brianna and her son and sending her off to start a life with His Hideness?

"I'm saying it's your life, your baby, your choice. What I think shouldn't matter."

She finished her under-blanket maneuvers and set the cover aside. "But it does matter. I value your opinion and know you want what's best for us."

Ben gave a loud belch, and Hunter couldn't help grinning. "Good one, dude."

Splaying a hand behind Ben's head, he leaned the baby forward so he could wipe his milky mouth. When he'd resettled Ben and faced Brianna, she wore an odd expression. "What?"

"Every time you do something for Ben, help care for him, I have to remind myself you helped with your nieces, you have experience with babies."

He arched an eyebrow. "Yeah. And?"

"And…I love that you feel comfortable holding him and know what to do for him. I bet most bachelors would run the other way rather than voluntarily burp a baby."

"Well, not much scares me. As a kid I was always the one picking up snakes and frogs and other creepy-crawlies in our yard. Though the niece experience helps."

She cocked her head and chuckled. "Are you comparing my son to a frog?"

Hunter laughed. "No...although he is a prince. Aren't some princes frogs in disguise?"

"I think you have it backward. Some frogs are princes in disguise."

He angled his head to look down at Ben, whose eyelids were drooping. "Well, this little tadpole is ready for a nap. Want me to put him down?"

"Tadpole," she said under her breath and grinned. "Cute. No, I'll get him." She struggled off the couch and crossed the room to him. Before she took her son, she stood and beamed at Ben's tiny face as he slept against Hunter's shoulder. She gently stroked the baby's head and kissed his temple. She released a breathy sigh. "God, I love him so much already. So much it makes my chest hurt."

"You sure that's not the smoke inhalation?" he teased, quirking his mouth.

She sent him a wry look. "I'm sure." She moved to a better position to lift the baby from his arms and hesitated as she raised her arms. Her eyes met his in the same moment he realized the careful transfer of the sleeping infant would involve another intimate moment of their bodies touching. Anticipation zinged through his blood, and heat coiled low and heavy in his groin.

As she stilled, Brianna's pupils dilated, and a delicate pink blush rose on her cheeks. Her gaze dipped to Hunter's mouth, and her tongue darted out to nervously moisten her lips, leaving them dewy and tempting as hell.

Calling himself an idiot, Hunter groaned and plowed his free hand into Brianna's silky hair. Cupping the back of her head, he drew her close and caught her startled gasp with his kiss. Brianna's body was tense with surprise, but as he coaxed her lips with his, her muscles relaxed, and she melted against him. She flattened her hands against his chest, and a mewl of pleasure purred from her throat. The sexy sound only fired his desire, raising the temperature of his blood another dozen degrees.

With Ben safely nestled on his shoulder, he stroked his free hand from her hair down her spine, pulling her flush with his body. The press of her soft curves along the hard lines of his chest and hips sent intoxicating sensation spiraling through him. He could easily lose himself in this woman, her sweet mouth, her warm skin, her lush body.

When he opened his lips, deepening the kiss and teasing her with his tongue, her arms circled his waist, and she canted into him. Her lips tasted like seduction, and kissing Brianna felt like a homecoming. His body was humming, crackling, alive, and he sank deeper into the spell she cast. He'd parted her lips with his tongue, eager to tangle it with hers, when Ben squawked. And Brianna jerked away. She covered her mouth with her hand, angling her body from his and squeezing her eyes shut.

"I can't," she whispered in her smoke-rasped voice.

Disappointment tinged with rejection crashed over Hunter in a cold, breath-stealing wave. He clenched his back teeth and battled down the suffocating emotions before he spoke. "My bad. I shouldn't have pushed. I…"

Ben wiggled and complained, arching his back in discomfort.

Avoiding his gaze, she turned back to take her son. "Let me have him."

He passed Ben to her quickly, trying not to think about the soft glide of her skin against his when their arms brushed. "I think he needs to burp again. See how he's bowing his back? That usually means his belly hurts. He's got gas."

Grunting quietly, she shifted Ben into a more secure position and rubbed his back. "You know more about taking care of him than I do, and I'm his mother. I should know this stuff."

"I'm sure you did—" He stepped back. "B.C." When she furrowed her brow, he added, "Before Concussion. I saw a lot of parenting and baby-related books in your living room next to your romance novels and biochem texts. I bet you were well educated on how to handle Ben."

She nodded and laid her cheek on Ben's head as she started swaying, rocking her son with the gentle motion of her body. "So I knew what to do...*once.* One more thing I have to try to remember or relearn."

Fatigue filled her tone. Considering all that had happened in the past few days, he couldn't blame her for feeling overwhelmed. Still, he was compelled to buoy her spirits.

"You'll catch on. Women have been raising babies without instruction books for thousands of years." He took another step back, swiping a hand over his mouth, where he could still taste her kiss. Watching her soothe Ben, he tried to blot out the sensation of how well she'd fit against him and how right she'd felt in his arms.

I can't. But what couldn't she do? Have sex with him? He knew that. He remembered the doctor's chiding. Or did she mean she couldn't fall for him, didn't share his blossoming feelings? He knew all the reasons why involvement with Brianna was a bad idea, but his heart had shouted down his head. He'd always been impulsive, willing to take risks. But he had to think with something besides his libido when it came to Brianna. Her life was a complicated tangle of politics and danger and vulnerability and a baby…and another man.

No matter how strong the pull of their orbits, he had to give her time and space to figure out where she stood, where she was going. And whom she would share her future with.

Ben quieted as Brianna cooed to him, gently bouncing him and patting his diaper-padded bottom.

Hunter jammed his fingers into his pockets as he mentally shifted gears. He needed to focus on how to help Brianna, how to protect her. "According to my sister-in-law, you should nap whenever the baby is napping," he said. "That's about the only way you'll catch up on sleep."

"I don't—" A jaw-cracking yawn cut off her protest, and Hunter chuckled.

She blushed and sent him a wry grin. "Okay, maybe I do need a nap. You don't mind?"

"Of course not. In fact, I insist. You're going to need your rest in the coming days, handling both a baby and whatever this danger is that's out there for you and Ben."

A troubled frown dented her forehead. "Right. That."

He hated the black cloud of danger hanging over her. He hated that political unrest in another country could reach across the ocean and ruin what should be a magical, blissful time for Brianna with her new baby. He hated that His Hideness, Prince Shirks-Off, had put her in this position, royal duty be damned. And he hated that she seemed to feel a loyalty to the prince despite his abandonment.

But why wouldn't she feel devotion to the man? Chris was her baby's father. She'd had an intimate relationship with him. Deep down, a tug of admiration replaced the jealous twinge. Brianna's faith and confidence in Chris were heartening, qualities he respected. Qualities he wanted in the woman he eventually gave his heart to.

She headed for the sofa to lie down, and he caught her arm. "Use my bed while you're here. It's quieter back there, and I promise the sheets are clean. I already set up Ben's bassinet in there, so you're right beside him."

Brianna hesitated. "But...where will you sleep?"

"I'll be fine on the couch. It won't be the first time I've slept out here, and I'm sure it won't be the last. Go on. While you're napping, I'll start dinner."

Brianna gave him an uncertain look before finally nodding and heading back to his bedroom.

Rubbing his hands together, Hunter went into the kitchen and opened the freezer. His heart sank and his stomach growled when he encountered the frozen tundra of his icebox. He hadn't been to the grocery store in a couple of weeks, so his options were a small pizza—past its use-by date—margarita mix and a package of freezer-burned hamburger patties. Why hadn't he thought about groceries while Brianna was shopping for supplies?

Too distracted by the lacy bras to be thinking straight. He shook his head to clear it. He had to keep his head in the game if he wanted to keep Brianna safe.

As he stared into his empty freezer deciding what to do about dinner, he thought about the prince's video message. His Hideness had mentioned a romantic dinner where the prince had wined and dined Brianna with a shrimp dinner. Her favorite food, the message had said. He could do that. He was in Louisiana, after all, where fresh shrimp was abundant.

He'd have to make that overdue trip to the grocery

store and the local seafood market, but he was determined to make a better meal for Brianna than old pizza and questionable hamburgers. In fact, he wanted to surprise her with a sumptuous dinner that would put a smile on her face and a fond memory in her heart that rivaled the prince's dinner.

As he gathered his car keys and wallet, he paused. How could he leave her here asleep and alone with the baby while the Meridanian militants were gunning for her and Ben? He couldn't. But he had a neighbor who was a Lagniappe firefighter whom he trusted implicitly. And Riley Sinclair and his wife owed him a favor after Hunter spent ten days feeding and giving insulin shots to the couple's diabetic cat while they were on vacation.

Hunter knocked on his neighbors' door, and a tall blond man answered. "Hunter! How's it going, man?"

"Hi, Riley. I was wondering if you could do me a favor. I have a friend staying with me and, uh…her ex-husband is not a nice guy." Hunter felt bad about lying to Riley, but an explanation of the truth would take too long, and Brianna insisted they keep her situation a secret.

A dark scowl dented Riley's forehead. "One of *those,* eh? The bastard. I'm afraid I've had experience with abusive jerks through Ginny's work at the Women's Clinic."

"Um, yeah. So she's kinda hiding out at my place, but I have to run out and do an errand. Could you keep an eye on my place and make sure nobody bothers Brianna?"

"Sure thing. Let me tell Ginny where I'm going, and I'll watch the game at your place. How about that?"

Even with Riley on guard duty, Hunter felt compelled to hurry at the store. He grabbed a bottle of wine, a bunch of flowers, two steaks, shrimp, baking potatoes and fresh asparagus. When he got home, he thanked Riley for his help and fired up the hibachi on his back porch. In minutes he had seasoned skewers of shrimp, T-bones and the asparagus grilling, and potatoes in the oven. He set the table with an anxious flutter in his gut. About the time he set the vase of flowers on the table, he stopped and scowled at the table.

What are you doing, man?

He was prepping the table for a date. For a romantic evening. For a seduction. The memory of her soft mouth, of the sweet pull of her lips on his, sent a crackling energy through him. Hell, just the thought of her kiss set him on fire. But Brianna was not his date.

I can't...

She had a baby with another man...a *prince,* for cripes' sake! How could he compete with that?

He had no business romancing a woman who was a new mother—especially one in a vulnerable position the way Brianna was. With a disgruntled groan, he took the vase of flowers off the table and moved them to the kitchen. He replaced the wine with two bottles of cold beer in koozies. He was just taking the potatoes out of the oven when he heard the shuffle of bare feet behind him.

"Wow, something smells good." Brianna gave him a groggy smile, and Hunter's breath snagged in his lungs.

With her blond hair rumbled from sleep and her face free of makeup, Brianna should have looked a wreck. Instead, Hunter thought she looked provocative, as if she'd just been well loved during hot sex. Kicking himself mentally, he pinched the bridge of his nose to erase that image.

"What are you making?" she asked.

"I ran out while you were asleep and picked up some steaks and shrimp for us. They're right about to come off the grill." He held up his brewski before taking a sip. "I have cold beer if you want that."

"No, thank you, I think I better stick to milk while I'm nursing."

Hunter gritted his teeth, fighting the impulse to glance at her swollen breasts, and another wave of guilt washed through him for the sensual track of his thoughts. *Sure, she's curvy and gorgeous, but she's off-limits. She just had a baby. She needs you to protect her, not ravish her.*

She sidled next to him and peeked over his shoulder as he sliced open the foil-wrapped potatoes. "What can I do to help?"

"Just have a seat." He nodded to the table he'd set. "I've got it all done."

"Handsome, kind and you cook. How is it that you're not married yet? A guy like you should have been scooped up and dragged down the aisle a long time ago."

He flashed her a crooked smile. "Well, I guess the right girl just hasn't come along." *Until now.* His stomach swooped when the unbidden addendum whispered in his brain. Clearing his throat, he pulled her chair out for her, then retrieved the shrimp, asparagus and steaks from the hibachi.

Sorsha appeared at his feet, meowing hungrily and sniffing the air. He blew on one of the shrimp to cool it and slipped it into Sorsha's bowl. "Just one. And don't tell Brianna, okay?"

After he served the potatoes and grilled asparagus and poured her a glass of milk, Hunter joined her at the table. He lifted his beer and tapped it against her glass. "Here's to baby Ben and his mom."

"And to our rescuer and host, Hunter," she added. "I don't know what I would have done without you these past few days. You've gone above and beyond the call of duty. I think you qualify for sainthood."

Hunter almost choked on beer. "I know a lot of people who would disagree with that."

"Well, you've been a saint to me. Helping me at the accident, staying with me when I was alone and scared, taking me in after my house burned. That's way more than just being a Good Samaritan." Brianna took a sip of milk, then stabbed a shrimp and poked it into her mouth.

He was uncomfortable with her adulation. While he'd have helped anyone in trouble, would he have gone to such extremes, been so dedicated to protecting her, if he didn't feel this inappropriate attraction to her? Frowning at that thought, he cut his steak and watched her tuck into her dinner. "How is it?"

"It's…um, good," she said, though her face didn't reflect the same enthusiasm. "Hunter, about what happened earlier…" She bit her bottom lip and wrinkled her brow. "The kiss…"

His pulse kicked. "I'm sorry about that. I shouldn't have—"

"No, it's not—"

They stopped and stared at each other, a suppressed longing hovering between them. Like the dense southern humidity, the sensual pull stole his breath and made him feel feverish.

She wet her lips, and he muffled a groan.

"If I weren't—"

"I understand. Wrong time. Wrong circumstances." He held up a hand and forced a smile. "It won't happen again."

Brianna nodded, but her eyes reflected disappointment. Or maybe that was just wishful thinking on his part.

Fisting his free hand in his lap, he shoved down his own regrets and stabbed a bite of steak with more force than needed. They ate in strained silence for a moment before he noticed Brianna picking at her food.

"Is something wrong?" he asked. "I made shrimp because Prince Cristoff said it was your favorite in the video."

She gave him a small smile. "That was thoughtful." She stabbed another bite and stared at it with a furrow in her brow. "I wish I could say I remember shrimp being my favorite meal, but…" She ate the shrimp on her fork with a dubious expression on her face. "Somehow it doesn't seem right. While this tastes pretty good, I just can't work up a real excitement for it. If it's my favorite, why can't I work up any interest in it?"

She tried a bite of potato next, then a spear of asparagus. "Now, *this* is good. Delicious," she said, waving a buttery bite of potato at him.

Hunter shoved his own food around on his plate. "So is the little prince still asleep?"

She sent him a frown. "Don't call him that."

"Why not?"

"Because…" she began, then coughed and paused to take a sip of milk. "Regardless of his bloodline, I'm not sure I want him growing up as a royal, under the pressure of the crown. I want him to have a normal childhood."

She coughed again and took another sip of her drink. "I mean, can you imagine a childhood where you knew you had to lead a country when you were older? The pressure that'd put on him?"

He shrugged. "There'd be perks, too. For both of you. A posh castle to live in, a staff to serve you…"

She grunted. "Yeah, but look at the turmoil in the country right now. What would it be like to grow up with a bodyguard shadowing you all the time?"

"Are you saying you're not going to accept Ben's right to the throne? Can you abdicate on his behalf?"

"I don't know. I haven't figured any of that out yet. That's one of the reasons I need to find Chris, talk to him. I never bargained for any of this." She coughed again and covered her mouth with her napkin, her eyebrows dipping in a scowl. "Excuse me."

"Too much pepper?" he asked.

"No. It all tastes fine. I just have a tickle in my throat, and—" She coughed again, harder this time, then sipped her milk. As if to prove she was fine, Brianna forked another shrimp into her mouth and gave Hunter a bright smile. "Chris doesn't even know Ben's been born yet," she continued. "I need to tell him, and we need to reach an understanding about how and where Ben will be raised."

When she coughed again, pressing a hand against her chest, Hunter set his fork down. He noticed her face and hands we're beginning to swell, and red blotches were appearing on her neck. He narrowed his gaze on her, his concern rising. "Are you sure you're all right?"

She waved him off with a forced smile and a nod. "I'm just a little…short of breath…is all. Probably… because of…the smoke—"

Alarm prickled his scalp as she coughed harder and began to wheeze. "Brianna?"

Brianna pushed her chair back and clutched her chest. She wheezed louder, her face growing puffy, then raised wide, frightened eyes to him. He was out of his chair and at her side in a heartbeat.

"I…can't breathe," she rasped.

"Food allergy," he groaned. "You're in anaphylactic shock."

Chapter 10

Brianna reached for him, clearly panicked, and her fingers dug into his arm.

Adrenaline raced through him, spiking his pulse and pitching in his gut. *Adrenaline...* Hunter tensed, and a memory tickled his brain.

Last summer, while he'd been visiting Grant, his brother's little girl had been stung by a bee and had a similar reaction. Grant had since bought every member of his family an epinephrine injection kit to keep on hand for emergencies with his daughter. Hunter scrambled mentally to remember where he'd stored the EpiPen.

Brianna's face was turning red, and her cheeks were swelling with unnatural distortion. He had to hurry.

"I'll be right back." He gave her wrist a quick, reassuring squeeze and disengaged from her fearful grip. As he hurried to his bathroom, he dialed 911 on his cell phone.

"I need an ambulance!" he barked when the operator picked up. He answered the operator's questions while he ransacked drawers, cabinet shelves and storage bins overflowing with miscellaneous junk. Nothing. The emergency operator told him to stay on the line while she talked to the EMT dispatch. Pausing from his frantic search, Hunter dragged a hand over his mouth, forcing his brain to slow down. *Think.* What did the EpiPen package look like? Where had he put it?

He heard the scrape of Brianna's chair in the breakfast room, and a fresh wave of worry swamped him. He darted back to the dinner table to check on her.

Brianna's face was turning blue, and before he could reach her, she slumped in her seat and slid to the floor. "Brianna!"

He dropped to his knees and patted her face. "Brianna? Can you hear me? Help's coming, sweetheart."

Her eyelids fluttered, and she wheezed noisily.

Damn it! *Where* was that EpiPen? Tossing his cell aside, he ran to his kitchen cabinets and threw them open. He jerked open a drawer where he kept random items such as batteries, aspirin and postage stamps. He rifled through the odds and ends, nausea building inside him as Brianna's gasps grew fainter. *Dammit!* He was losing her!

Finally, he found the clear plastic tube with an orange tip.

"Thank God!" He snatched it out and rushed back to Brianna. "Hang on, Bri. I found an EpiPen."

Hunter scanned the instructions, then shoved her skirt up to her hip, exposing her slim thigh. As directed, he uncapped the outer tube, removed the autoinjector and pulled the safety cap off with his teeth. Spitting the cap out, he met her fading gaze. "Needle stick…"

With no further preamble, he jabbed the autoinjector against her outer thigh. Brianna's back bowed off the floor as he held the pen against her leg and counted out ten seconds. Removing the needle from her thigh, Hunter set the injector aside. "Okay, Brianna, you should start feeling better now."

He massaged the injection site, trying not to think about how smooth her skin was, how beautiful her legs were…

Huffing irritation with himself, he refocused and watched her carefully, anxious to see some sign she was responding to the epinephrine. What would he do if the EpiPen didn't work? What if he'd taken too long getting the antidote in her?

Sorsha, too, was sniffing and pacing around her mistress, acting agitated by the emergency. He'd heard cats had a sixth sense for trouble. Sorsha clearly knew something was wrong.

Brianna blinked rapidly, and her strangled gasps loosened as the swelling in her throat eased. Only when she dragged in a ragged lungful of air and her normal color returned to her cheeks did Hunter release the breath he'd been holding. Grasping her hand, he helped her sit up, then pulled her into his arms. Her body shook, both from the dose of epinephrine and fear, he was sure. He stroked her back as he tried to calm his own anxious jitters. "I got ya, Bri. You're gonna be fine. Crisis averted," he crooned, as much to reassure himself as her. That had been close. Too close.

He found his phone and reported in to the emergency

operator while Brianna patted Sorsha. Both Sorsha and Brianna seemed calmed by the pet/owner connection.

"Sounds like a food allergy," the operator said. "An ambulance is on the way, but I'll stay on the line until they arrive."

When he realized something he'd fed her had caused the allergic reaction, guilt kicked him hard. "So what do you think caused the reaction?" he asked Brianna. "Clearly you were allergic to something you ate."

She pulled back, meeting his gaze with teary eyes. "I have no…idea." Her voice still sounded hoarse and winded.

"The shrimp would be the obvious choice. Shell food is a pretty common allergen. But if it's your favorite, that implies you've eaten it before with no ill effects."

Brianna frowned. "Is it…my favorite?"

Hunter cocked his head. "That's what Chris said in the video."

"I know, but…" She drew another labored breath and struggled to her feet. Hunter rose as well and supported her when she wobbled as she returned to her chair. "It doesn't feel right. Especially since…I had this reaction."

Setting the phone aside, the line still open to the operator, Hunter pulled a chair close to Brianna and caught her hand in his. "Do you think Chris lied?"

She hesitated, still struggling to take deep, even breaths. "*Lied* is…a strong word. I just think…he was wrong."

Hunter twisted his mouth as he thought. "Maybe. But why—"

A pounding at his door interrupted and sent Sorsha scurrying for cover. "Emergency medical team. Anyone there?"

"Coming!" Hunter hurried to the door and let the EMTs in. "She's in the breakfast room." He explained what had happened and how he'd given her the injection as he ushered the emergency team inside. Over the next several minutes, the EMTs gave her an antihistamine, then checked and doublechecked Brianna's blood pressure, pulse and blood oxygen levels. While the readings weren't yet back to normal, she showed signs of marked improvement with each measurement. The medics tried to convince her to ride in the ambulance to the hospital, just to be sure she was all right, but she declined. "I've had my allotment of ambulance rides for this month, thanks."

"I thought you looked familiar," one of the medics said with a wry look. "Didn't we take you in a few days ago after a car accident? You were in labor?"

She gave him a sheepish grin. "That was me. And I went in last night after my house burned. For smoke inhalation."

The EMT's eyebrows shot up. "Seriously? Are you jinxed or is someone trying to kill you?"

The medic's partner chuckled, but the EMT's comment sent a ripple of suspicion through Hunter. Could Chris have *meant* for her to eat shrimp and have an anaphylactic reaction? Why would he have mentioned the shrimp so specifically unless there was some message behind it?

The little color that had been in Brianna's face leeched out, as well, telling him her thoughts had traveled a similar path.

"Just an unlucky streak, I think," she mumbled.

"Well, if bad luck comes in threes like they say, hopefully you're done now," the first EMT said. He rocked back on his heels and tipped his head. "You sure you want to pass on the hospital?"

She glanced at Hunter, then nodded.

He brushed a wisp of hair back from her eyes and tucked it behind her ear. "I'll keep an eye on her, take her in if needed."

When the medics had packed up and left his apartment, Hunter cleared the rest of their dinner from the table and joined Brianna, who was brooding in his living room.

After a moment of heavy silence, she voiced the question on both of their minds. "Why would Chris say shrimp was my favorite if I'm allergic to it?"

Hunter leaned his head back on the plump sofa cushion and closed his eyes. "Beats me. Is it possible that he wanted to hurt you?"

Tension rippled through Brianna. The possibility that Chris, someone she'd created a baby with, would try to hurt her shook her to the core. "Wh-why would he do that?"

Hunter blew out a frustrated breath and scrubbed his face with both hands. "Maybe he sees you or your knowledge of his whereabouts as a threat. Maybe he sees Ben as a threat to his claim on the throne or his power in his homeland. Maybe—"

"No. I can't believe that." Fatigue and stress drubbed her, pounding inside her. Denials screamed in her head. "I had an intimate relationship with him. I can't believe he'd try to hurt me."

Hunter sighed. "Bri, you can't rule out the possibility that Chris is behind the attempts on your life. The fire, the people who shot at your car and trashed your house. Maybe something happened between you before you split up that made him think you would betray him."

"I'd never—"

He caught her hand in his. "I know you wouldn't. But if he thinks you're a liability somehow…"

She shook her head. How did she explain the certainty that weighted her chest that Chris cared for her, even if they had ended their relationship? A memory lurked at the edges of her thoughts, just beyond her grasp. Gritting her teeth and battling the throbbing in her skull, she tried to call a clearer image to mind, but the message Chris had sent her replayed instead. "On the video, he said to think about that night." She paused to drag a breath into her aching lungs. "He said we'd made plans to be together…and be a family. If that were true—" another wheezy breath "—why weren't we together? If we were together and planning a future, why wouldn't Aunt Robyn have known?"

"Good question."

She turned on the couch to face him. The debate over Chris's loyalty added bite to the nausea swirling in her gut. She still trembled from the adrenaline and shock of nearly suffocating. She could tell her cheeks were still slightly swollen, and her voice was weak and raspy. "Hunter, Chris doesn't know I have amnesia. He mentioned the shrimp and scallops…thinking I knew about my allergy."

Hunter sat straighter, considering this angle. "You're right. So assuming he knew about your allergy, and that *you'd* know about your allergy…"

"What if it was a warning?" Her heart thumped as she warmed to the theory. "I'd know he was lying about the foods and…maybe he was trying to tell me to look at the rest of his message in the same light."

"Go on."

"I don't think we were planning a future together… even though I was having his baby."

"And if you weren't, then that makes two lies in the video."

She scowled at his terminology again. "I don't know what his intentions were for Ben, but—" She pressed a hand to her stomach as her nausea grew. A further reaction to the shrimp? To the EpiPen? Or just old-fashioned stress? She swallowed hard and finished her thought. "What if he was telling me *not* to believe him about a meeting in New Orleans? Maybe the lies about the shrimp and our future plans were to tip me off something was wrong…to warn me away."

Hunter nodded, clearly turning the notion over in his mind. "Could be. We've already decided the video was filmed in front of a fake cityscape backdrop. The whole message could have been given under duress."

Duress. The word sent shivers through her and made her sour stomach churn harder. "What if he's being held by the militants? What if the video was their attempt to lure me into a trap? An attempt to get Ben?"

Hunter drew and released a measured breath. "I'd say that's a safe assumption."

Brianna stilled. "But if Chris is being held by the militants, he could be—"

Bile surged into her throat before she could finish her sentence. She bolted off the couch and barely made it to the sink before what little supper she'd eaten came back up.

Hunter was behind her in an instant, fixing her a cool, damp cloth and hosing the sick down the drain.

Brianna rinsed her mouth out and wiped her face with the cool cloth. "Thank you."

He squeezed her shoulder. "This conversation can wait until you're feeling better. I think we're in agreement that going to New Orleans is out. We need to figure more out on this end, get you well, work on your memory, before we bring Chris into the equation."

"But he's Ben's father! We have to do something. If the militants have him, they'll kill him!" She grabbed Hunter's arms as another wave of nausea swelled in her. "We have to call the police or…or something!"

He speared her hair with his fingers, his frown wary. "Didn't Chris say not to involve the police because of the sensitive nature of the—"

Brianna spun away, back to the sink, and dry heaved.

Hunter stroked a hand down her back and helped hold her hair back from her face. In any other circumstance, she'd have been humiliated getting sick like this in his kitchen sink. But the situation was too dire to worry about her reaction to the EpiPen, bad news and a food allergy.

She wiped her face again and turned back to Hunter. He studied her with concern etched in deep creases around his eyes. He braced a hand under her elbow, which she welcomed, since she was trembling from shock and the extra adrenaline in her veins.

He led her back to the couch, and she dropped heavily onto the cushions. After three straight days of abuse of all forms, her body ached all over, and she was so weak she could barely move. She was in no condition to take care of Ben alone, much less chase after leads to where

Chris might be being held. If he was being held captive as they presumed. If he weren't already dead. A groan rose in her throat.

"Bri?" Hunter put a hand under her arm again. "You need to go back to the sink?"

She rocked her head from side to side. "I feel so helpless. Chris needs us. I know he does. But I can't even stand by myself without my knees buckling."

Hunter brushed his knuckles along her cheek. "I'm not going anywhere, Bri. I'm going to look out for you. As long as you need me."

She angled her face toward him and simply stared into his dark blue eyes for long moments. A sense of peace and security pushed aside the quiver of fear that had clutched her most of the past three days. "Why?"

Hunter blinked. "Why what?"

"Why are you with me? Why are you doing this for me?"

His cheek tugged up in a confused, lopsided grin. "I need a reason? Maybe I just want to help you." His wry grin faded, and his eyes softened, sending curls of warmth through her. "Because I care about you, Brianna. You and Ben. Maybe I was just being nice the day we met, but…now there's more to it." He swallowed hard, and she watched his Adam's apple work in his throat. "I'd have thought that was obvious."

She reached for his cheek, ran her fingers over the rough texture of his stubble and savored the feeling of his skin against hers. As much as she loved being near Hunter, treasured the way he made her feel, valued the help he provided, she couldn't grow dependent upon him. He wouldn't be around forever. *Hunter's not the marrying kind,* his mother had said.

An oddly familiar feeling whispered inside her, taking shape and growing more resolute. She'd had to learn independence the hard way. Because of her parents' untimely deaths? Despite Aunt Robyn taking custody of her, she sensed her teen years had been filled with lonely days, harsh lessons of learning to take care of herself. A nagging inclination that disappointment and abandonment had been frequent and familiar to her weighted her chest. An image flashed in her mind's eye. Quickly, and then it was gone. Chris. On a beach. Walking away from her.

The sharp, sudden sting in her heart stole her breath. Chris had abandoned her. Broken her heart. The certainty of it shook her to the core. Had he known about her pregnancy when he'd walked away that day on the beach? Had she known who he was, *what* he was that day?

When she looked to her future, she saw herself raising her son alone, dealing with whatever decrees were passed down from Meridan concerning her son's right, his obligations, to the throne. Unless she could keep Ben's paternity secret.

When the immediate danger to Ben had passed, when she regained her memory and located Chris, she felt sure Hunter would leave, as well. He cared about her, sure. But he'd been pretty clear that he was sticking around only to protect her. He felt an obligation to her because of her vulnerability and current needs, and Brianna refused to be anyone's burden or obligation. As soon as she could, before she grew too attached, too dependent on Hunter, she had to let him go.

Early next morning, Hunter and Brianna were just getting to sleep after a long night with a fussy baby, when Hunter's cell phone rang.

"Hey, man," Grant said, "are you going to be at the Henderson site today?"

"Wasn't planning on it. I'm taking a few personal days to help Brianna and her baby." He glanced at his watch. Six-thirty a.m. He'd had maybe five cumulative hours of sleep in the past two days. "You heard about the fire at her house, right?"

"Yeah, Dad mentioned it. Are you all right?"

"A little smoke inhalation. Sleep deprivation thanks to a cranky baby last night. Nothing major."

Grant chuckled. "You have my sympathy on the sleep deprivation. You remember the zombie I was last year when Kaylee was born?"

Hunter grunted. "Yeah." Sitting up on the couch, he muffled a yawn and scrubbed a hand over his face. "So... what's going on at the Henderson site?"

"What's *not* going on? We got the wrong shipment of faucets, and the owners changed their minds about the wallpaper for the front bathroom. The cabinet guy is behind schedule and can't install the kitchen cabinets until next week, which means the floors have to be delayed."

Hunter grumbled a curse under his breath. "I've been out for three days, and everything has gone to hell. What happened to Miller? He was supposed to pinch-hit for me."

"I haven't seen Miller in days." Grant hummed in thought. "I'd handle the Henderson mess myself, but I have a meeting with the state inspector over at the Brinkman building all morning. Can't you get away for a few hours? I need you to soothe ruffled feathers before this gets out of hand."

Hunter winced and shoved off the couch. He stumbled to the kitchen. Coffee. He needed coffee in the worst way. "Grant, I can't. It's not safe for me to leave Brianna and the baby alone."

"Not safe?"

"Long story." He put the carafe in the sink to fill with water, then reached down to pet Sorsha, who rubbed at his ankles, requesting her breakfast. "If there were a way—"

"Take them out to my place. Nancy, the nanny I hired to help with my girls, has training in first aid, child care and security issues. Nancy will make sure nothing happens to them."

"I don't know." Hunter rubbed his eyes and weighed Grant's offer. His brother's house was secluded out on the fringes of town. That isolation was good in terms of hiding Ben and Brianna, but not so good for emergency response time in case something happened. But the more he thought about the remoteness of his brother's country home, the more he liked the idea. Not just for today, while Hunter checked on problems at the Henderson site, but for the long-term. His house was bigger than Hunter's apartment, better suited for taking care of a baby—especially with Nancy around to assist.

He poured water in the coffeepot, measured out the grounds and started a pot of strong java brewing.

The downside of going to Grant's was if the people hunting Brianna did track her to Grant's house, Grant's family would be in the line of fire. Hunter's gut swooped at the thought of anything happening to his brother or his nieces because of danger he'd brought to them.

"Thanks, but…I can't risk it. I don't want to put you and the girls at risk." Hunter sighed and padded back to the living room, now worried whether they'd left any kind of bread-crumb trail to his place.

"Is the situation that bad?" Grant asked, concern heavy in his tone. Their family had endured a similar threat earlier in the year when a crime family targeted their brother Connor and his wife, Darby. Grant's wife, Tracy, had been a casualty of that danger, an innocent bystander caught in the cross fire.

"Afraid so. There've already been a couple of attempts on Brianna's life."

"Why? Who is she? What's going on?"

"I can't tell you. It's…complicated."

Sorsha meowed loudly, reminding him she still needed to be fed. Over the phone, he heard Grant huff his frustration, but Hunter's thoughts shifted to more pressing issues. Could the Meridianian rebels trace Brianna here? He'd been so preoccupied by the fire, Brianna's memory loss, taking care of Ben…

He grumbled a curse, and his head gave a throb of fatigue. *Think!*

"Hunter, what's wrong? You can trust me. Let me help!"

"I'm just trying to backtrack and decide if we've done anything that could lead the rebels here, to my apartment."

"Rebels?" Grant's tone was stunned. "What kind of rebels?"

Hunter groaned. "Forget I said that." He returned to the kitchen to pour food in Sorsha's bowl. How had they paid for the baby things yesterday? Brianna had used her credit card. Not good, but no link to him.

"Do the police know what's going on?" Grant asked. "Can they assign someone to watch your place?"

"Sort of." He returned the cat food to the counter

and checked the coffee's progress. "Not the whole story. Like I said, it's—"

"Complicated. Yeah, I got that. But if someone's trying to kill her…"

Rumpled and weary-looking, Brianna walked into the kitchen, pulling his attention away from what Grant was saying. Brianna flashed him a groggy smile, then gave the coffeepot a longing glance. As haggard as she looked, she still sent his libido haywire. He fought the impulse to pull her close for a good-morning kiss, to comb his fingers through the tangle of her bed-head hair and jolt her awake with a naughty tweak on her bottom as she bent to greet Sorsha.

"Hunter, you there?" Grant's voice drew him back to his phone call.

"Look, I'll find a way to get to the Henderson site today, but—" Hunter stopped short as a disturbing thought smacked him from the blue. Numbly, he lowered his phone from his ear and stared at it as he followed the thought through. Cell phone. Tracking. Chris's video.

He raised a horrified, disgusted look to Brianna. "Ah, hell."

"What?" Brianna paled in alarm, her body bristling.

"Hunter, what is it?" Grant asked.

"We've been using her cell phone. At the hospital and—" Another equally upsetting realization hit him. "Crap! I told the hospital I was her husband. They can link me to her! It's only a matter of time before they show up at my door."

Brianna gasped and pressed a hand to her mouth. Her knees buckled, and he hurried to wrap her in a supportive embrace.

"So I repeat…bring her to my place." Grant's voice

took on a commanding tone, a decisiveness and authority Hunter knew well from their childhood. Grant had always shown his younger brother a calm leadership and wise counsel. "Take the battery out of her phone and yours so they can't trace them. Buy a disposable phone."

Hunter squeezed Brianna tighter when she shivered and cussed himself for not thinking about the cell phone GPS sooner, about the implications of having given his name at the hospital. "What about your girls? We can't stay here, but we can't bring the danger out to Peyton and Kaylee, either. We'll…go to a hotel or something."

He leaned back to meet Brianna's eyes, and she nodded her agreement.

"No," Grant said. "If one Mansfield brother is good protection, then two Mansfield brothers are better protection. Mom and Dad have been talking about taking the girls to Disney World. I think now is the perfect time. You come stay here, and I'll help guard Brianna while you're at work."

"Grant, I can't ask you to—"

"You'd do the same for me, wouldn't you?"

Hunter grunted, knowing Grant couldn't be denied. "You know I would."

"Then it's settled. Just make sure you've cut any threads that you may have left before you come."

He didn't hear any condemnation or accusation in his brother's tone, but self-censure sawed in his belly just the same. "Right."

"And, Hunter…" Grant paused. Sighed. "Check your truck before you go anywhere. You know, for…tracking devices or…" His brother sounded embarrassed, stressed, awkward.

A car bomb, Hunter finished mentally, knowing where

his brother's thoughts had gone. Tracy had been killed by an undetected car bomb. Hunter would never call his brother paranoid, given his history, but clearly Grant was self-conscious over his hypervigilance.

"I will. I promise," he said, reassuring his big brother with an understanding tone.

His brother's wife had been murdered, and Connor and his family were in hiding. Violence and dangerous men had already taken a toll on his family in recent months, and Hunter vowed not to let any more tragedy hurt the people he loved…whatever it took.

Chapter 11

"Uncle Hunter!"

As Brianna and Hunter unloaded Ben, his diaper bag and their suitcases, a blond-haired girl charged across the shady grass lawn of the old clapboard-and-brick house where Hunter's brother lived.

Hunter's brow beetled for a moment in consternation before brightening as he greeted his niece. He scooped the girl into a bear hug, lifting her off the ground as she kissed his cheek. "Hey, squirt. How ya doin'?"

"Grandma and Papa are taking us to Disney World!" the girl said, positively vibrating with enthusiasm.

"So I hear. That's cool! You're gonna have so much fun." He kissed her head and set her back on the ground. "Peyton, this is my new friend, Brianna, and her son, Ben."

"Hi, Peyton," Brianna said and smiled.

The blonde girl peeked at her and gave a shy grin. "Hi."

The slam of a screened door drew Brianna's attention to the front porch, where a tall man with chocolate-brown hair strolled out, a baby in his arms.

"I thought you were sending Peyton to Mom and Dad's." Hunter's tone reproached his brother.

"They're on their way. A Disney trip doesn't happen in an instant." As Grant neared the car, Brianna saw the striking resemblance between Hunter and his older brother. Both men were breathtakingly handsome, though Grant had a few threads of gray at his temples and a few lines in his face that bore witness to the toll the months since his wife's death had taken on him. "Mom's making reservations and packing, and Dad is gonna pick the girls up after he settles some things at the office." Grant shifted his attention to her. "You must be Brianna. Welcome. *Mi casa es su casa.*"

"Thank you. I appreciate your help more than I can say." Brianna focused on the baby, who blinked at her with wide brown eyes. "Who is this doll?"

"My youngest, Kaylee. She's ten months." Grant wiped drool from the baby's mouth with the corner of the girl's bib, then kissed his daughter's dark hair.

Brianna cut a worried look to Hunter, then back to Grant. "Your parents are taking a ten-month-old to Disney World?"

Grant smiled. "I know. I'd never attempt it by myself, but my mom is Superwoman. She's looking forward to it." He jerked his head toward the house. "Shall we? I've got the upstairs guest room ready for you."

"Sure. Let me get Sorsha." Hunter opened the back door of the extended cab and took out the cardboard pet carrier. Sorsha meowed unhappily, and the scrape of pawing sounded from the box.

Grant turned around, startled. "You have a cat?"

"We did mention it. Didn't we?" Hunter asked.

"A cat?" Peyton hopped up and down with youthful exuberance. "Yeah!"

"It's not for us, Squirt. It's Miss Brianna's cat."

Brianna bit her bottom lip. "If it's too much trouble—"

"I don't mind. We'll have to see what Cinderella and Sebastian say about it."

Brianna sent Hunter a curious look, which he answered with an enigmatic grin.

As the group bustled inside Grant's country house, Brianna caught a flash of brown fur scurrying from the staircase to the living room.

"That was Cinderella," Hunter said, setting Sorsha's carrier down and opening the top flaps. "She's shy at first, but she'll warm up to you in time."

Sorsha poked her head up and sniffed the air. With a wary look around the foyer, she hopped out of the box and crept behind Grant's umbrella stand to survey her new environment.

Ben whined tiredly, and Brianna patted his back. "Is there someplace I can go nurse?"

"Wherever you're most comfortable." Grant started up the steps. "I'll show you your room, and you can decide what suits you best."

She followed her host upstairs and was admiring the cozy room and handmade quilt on the queen-size bed when a loud yowl reached them from downstairs.

"Uh-oh." Hunter led the charge back down to the foyer, where they found Sorsha bristled and glaring across the room at an orange-and-white tabby. The tabby, presumably Sebastian, flattened his ears and swished his tail. Peyton stood to the side, wide-eyed and watching the tense cats with trepidation.

Sorsha growled and hissed at the tabby.

"Sorsha, no!" Brianna fussed.

"It's to be expected. Cats are notoriously territorial," Grant said, his smile understanding.

Brianna nodded. "Sorry. I'll take Sorsha upstairs. She can stay up there, away from your cats."

"Let me. You have your arms full." Before she could reach her cat, Hunter scooped the unhappy long-haired cat into his arms and started back to the guest room. Sorsha hissed again and thrashed her tail as Hunter toted her upstairs.

An hour later, the cats were all settled in separate parts of the house, Ben had been fed, and Hunter had unpacked much of what they'd brought into the closets and dresser of the guest room.

After putting Ben down to nap, Brianna followed the sound of voices to Grant's kitchen, where Hunter, Grant, the senior Mansfields and a dark-haired young woman Brianna didn't recognize were gathered around an oak table.

"Ah, there she is," Hunter said when Brianna entered. "Bri, you've met my parents, but this—" he motioned to the young woman "—is Nancy Sawyer, Grant's über-nanny."

Nancy rolled her eyes at Hunter, then stood to lean across the table to shake Brianna's hand. "Nice to meet you."

"You, too. So what makes you *über?*"

"Hunter's imagination," she said drily.

Hunter raised his hands in defense. "I'm sorry, but anyone trained in martial arts and weapons for the purpose of protecting the families of high-ranking U.S. officials in dangerous parts of the world gets the *über* qualifier in my book."

Brianna's eyes widened. "Wow. With all that training, what are you doing in Lagniappe?"

"Why is she working for a nobody like me, you mean?" Grant said with a grin.

"I didn't say that!" Brianna waved a finger at Grant.

Nancy laughed. "I was in Colombia until about six months ago. I followed my husband back to the States when he got a job with Bancroft Industries as their head of security."

"Oh! Maybe you know him?" Julia Mansfield said, brightening. "You did say you are in the R and D department there, right, Brianna?"

"I did, but I don't…um," Brianna said awkwardly. "I—"

"Mom," Hunter said under his breath.

Julia gasped and winced. "I'm sorry. I forgot…your amnesia."

Stan grunted and pushed back his chair. "Come on, Julia. Time to get on the road. Mickey Mouse awaits." He glanced into the adjoining family room and called, "Hey! Anyone in there want to go to Disney World with me?"

Peyton gave a loud, happy squeal as she bounced into the kitchen and jumped into her grandfather's arms. "Me! Me!"

Julia took Kaylee from Grant, and Grant saw his daughters off with the grands, leaving Hunter and Brianna in the kitchen with Nancy.

"After his wife was killed, Grant was understandably

anxious about his girls' safety," Nancy explained. "Does he need a babysitter with a license to kill out here in the boonies? No. But if it makes him feel better about leaving his kids when he's at work, where's the harm? And I love his girls. They're precious."

"Even though Squirt and her sister are headed to Mouseville, Nancy has agreed to stay here with you and Ben while Grant and I handle a few problems at work." Hunter pushed his chair back and rose. "You okay with that?"

"I... Sure." Brianna gave Nancy an awkward grin.

"I won't be gone long." Hunter bent to kiss the top of her head and headed for the door.

A shiver of apprehension chased through Brianna. "Hunter?"

He stopped and turned, hand on the doorknob.

She swallowed, not sure why she'd called out to him, other than a gut-level impulse, the tickle of dread over being separated from him, even for a few hours.

Great, Brianna. You know you have to cut him loose in a few days, and you're squeamish over him leaving for a few hours?

"Yeah?" he prompted when she only stared at him for several taut seconds.

"Uh...good luck with the Henderson site."

He lifted a corner of his mouth. "Thanks."

She turned to Nancy after the door closed and flashed her another awkward smile. "So..."

Nancy lifted a hand. "You don't have to entertain me if there's something you need to do."

"I—" Brianna sat back in her chair and released a deep breath. She did have a list of things she'd been meaning to handle since the accident, but one disaster after another had made mere survival a priority. She needed to contact her insurance company about the car accident. And the fire. She cringed, knowing she'd get a fight from the insurance company in light of the clear evidence the fire had been arson. She prayed the police report would clear her of culpability. But her most pressing need was to research Meridan and the laws concerning succession to the throne. After that, she needed to make some tough choices about her next steps in putting her life back in order.

"Hello? Anybody home?" Hunter called as he entered Grant's house that evening. It had taken most of the day to get the problems at the Henderson work site straightened out, and he'd worried about Brianna the whole time. Now, as he returned to his brother's home, the kitchen and living room, typically buzzing with the activity of two young girls and their caregiver, were eerily silent. "Brianna?"

He heard the shuffle of feet, and Nancy appeared at the door to the hall. "Oh, hi. I didn't hear you drive up."

"Where's Brianna?"

"Upstairs, I think. She's been up there working on her laptop, taking care of Ben or napping most of the day. I just stayed out of her hair. Is Grant with you?" Nancy looked past him toward the door.

"No. But he said he'd be home in an hour or so." Hunter's gaze shifted to the stairs. He was eager to see Brianna and find out how she was doing. "Any trouble today? Anything suspicious?"

Nancy shook her head. "Nope."

"Phone calls?"

"Just your mom calling to say their flight had arrived

safely in Orlando." Nancy hitched her head toward the staircase. "Go see for yourself. They're safe and sound. I'll start dinner. Fried chicken sound okay?"

Hunter's stomach growled at the suggestion. "Sounds fantastic. I'm starved!"

"Alrighty, then."

With that, he headed upstairs and knocked softly on the guest-room door.

Brianna answered, "Come in."

"Hey," he said, his smile already in place as he stepped into the room. "It's me."

Brianna had pillows propped behind her back, sitting on the bed with Ben nursing greedily. She greeted him with a smile that was pure sunshine and warmed him to his toes. "Hey, you. Did you get the problems with the Henderson project worked out?"

He could get used to coming home to that smile, her beautiful face. "Yeah. For now. Little crises seem to pop up every few days in my line of work. Nothing I can't handle, but..." He dropped his gaze to her chest where Ben suckled, realizing she hadn't covered herself. Not that she was especially exposed, given her modest nursing blouse and that Ben's head hid her breast.

She followed the path of his gaze, and her cheeks pinkened. "Oops. Want to hand me the blanket over there?"

She pointed to the bassinet, but he ignored her request, moving instead to the edge of the bed. "Don't cover up on my account. I can leave if you're uncomfortable feeding him with me in here. I just wanted to check in."

She blinked, ducked her head to gaze at her son for a

moment, then raised a smile to him. "No, stay." She patted the bed beside her. "Tell me about your day."

He moved to lean against the headboard next to her, careful that he didn't kick Sorsha, who was settled at the foot of the bed sleeping. As Hunter settled in, he reached over to stroke Ben's tiny head. "Not much to tell. I made phone calls, talked to contractors, soothed irate customers. Yada yada. I want to hear about your day. Did Ben say his first word? Get accepted to Yale? Score a touchdown for his team?"

Brianna chuckled. "Oh, right. All of those things. And he has a lead on cold fusion for his science-fair project."

Hunter grinned. "Attaboy!"

"He did get a good nap today, though. So I had a chance to do some research of my own." Her attention remained fixed on her son, the loving pride in her eyes burrowing deep to his core.

"Yeah? What'd ya learn?"

"A little more about Meridan. The history, the culture, the economy."

Intrigued, he angled his gaze toward her. "And?"

"Seems like it would be a nice place to live, the current political unrest aside."

"Huh." A squiggle of disquiet wormed through him at the thought of Brianna moving overseas. Without him. He gritted his back teeth and fought the swell of disappointment. *Deal with it, man. That's probably how this will end.*

She cut a quick side glance to him before returning her focus to Ben and dabbing with Ben's bib at the milk on his chin. "I found a little about their laws regarding royal succession. Ben is the legal heir to the throne whether Chris and I marry or not."

Hunter's gut tightened. He hated the possibility that Brianna would be forced to marry Chris, regardless of her feelings for His Hideness. A prick of jealousy stung him, along with a twist of regret. Clenching his back teeth tighter, he reminded himself this scenario was nothing new, no matter how he'd fooled himself into believing he and Brianna might have a future together. Political imperatives meant he had better come to grips with reality, or he'd get burned.

"An heir can abdicate the throne, but only after turning twenty-one, only given certain circumstances," she continued, "and only if another suitable heir is available to take the throne."

"What were the allowed circumstances?" he asked.

"Treason was the first cause, and in those cases, the Royal Senate imposes the abdication and the traitorous royal is put to death."

Hunter grunted. "Next."

"Marriage to a person deemed unworthy of the crown."

"Unworthy? By whose judgment?"

"The Royal Senate's."

"And who is in this Royal Senate?"

"Nine men who inherit their positions just like the royal family inherits their position." When he shot her a look of disbelief, she sighed and nodded. "Members of the aristocracy. An antiquated tradition passed down from past centuries."

"And the citizens of Meridan are okay with this?" He arched an eyebrow. "Or is that what the rebellion is about? An attempt to install a democratic government?"

"Nothing so noble. There wasn't much on the internet about the coup attempt, but what I could find indicates the rebellion is more about control of natural resources and money. They've discovered a great deal of natural gas beneath the country, and the current law says the ruling family controls the natural resources and any wealth resulting from mining, drilling…or fracking. This was never a big deal before, because they didn't have much in terms of commercially valuable resources. But with hundreds of millions of dollars at stake now, a group of citizens has risen up, demanding a rewrite of the law to gain control over the income from the natural-gas reserve."

"And the monarchy has thwarted that movement," Hunter guessed.

"Actually, the recently assassinated king, Chris's father, was in favor of the change. Other powers in the government were fighting him on it."

"The Royal Senate?" Hunter asked.

She touched a finger to her nose. "Bingo. They want to preserve the old ways and keep the wealth for the wealthy."

"What a mess."

"Aren't most civil wars?"

"True." He furrowed his brow. "But you said the ruling family would inherit the profits from the natural gas. So how does killing the king help change that? Now Chris inherits the throne…and the millions from the natural-gas reserves." A chill skittered through him. "Who inherits the throne if Chris's family is murdered?"

"I haven't gotten that far. I couldn't find anything this afternoon." She scrunched her nose and rubbed her eyes. "Ugh. Can we change the subject? I've been thinking about Meridan and the country's problems all afternoon, and it's given me a headache. All I want to do is hold my son and savor these moments with him. What with the house fire and all the cloak-and-dagger of trying to hide Ben, I haven't had nearly enough time to just sit still and enjoy this beautiful little boy."

Brianna curled her lip in and caught it with her teeth as her eyes filled with happy tears. The love that lit her face made his heart perform a tuck and roll. What would he give to have her look at him with that much joy and affection?

"Would you mind holding him while I switch sides?" she asked.

Hunter blinked and flashed her an embarrassed grin, having been caught staring. He hoped his expression hadn't given away the direction his thoughts had traveled. "Oh…sure."

She angled her body away as she moved Ben from her breast and twisted at the waist to hand him back to Hunter.

He took Ben and shifted the baby to his shoulder. "Here ya go, buddy. How about a midmeal burp, huh?"

Brianna held out the burp cloth she'd had draped on her arm. "Don't you want a—"

With a little hiccup, Ben spit up milk all over Hunter's shirt.

"Whoops," Brianna said, clearly struggling not to laugh.

Hunter groaned and frowned at Ben. "Seriously, dude? You couldn't have waited five seconds until I got the cloth from your mom? It's right there. Three feet away."

The chuckle Brianna had been suppressing now filled the room, her laughter a musical sound that moved something deep in Hunter's soul. Making Brianna laugh was well worth baby barf on his shirt any day of the week.

His chest tightened at realizing he was falling hard and fast for both Brianna and her cherubic son. He was already halfway to heartache. *Damn it.* If he didn't rein in his feelings, he was sure to get his heart crushed when the inevitable scenario with the prince played out.

The next morning, Brianna woke to the bright beams of golden light streaming through the window. The cheery sunshine lifted her mood and put a smile on her face. She stretched lazily, realizing she actually felt rested for the first time in days. She'd fed Ben at 3:00 a.m. and hadn't heard a peep from him since. Rolling to check the bedside clock, she squinted at the numbers. *Eight twenty-five?* That had to be wrong. Ben woke up and ate every three hours.

Tossing back the covers, she stumbled over to Ben's bassinet. Sorsha was curled up in the baby bed, snoozing comfortably. But Ben was gone.

"Ben?" Panic gripped her heart, and she spun around, her gaze sweeping the room for some clue where her son could be. She raced to the door, unmindful of her dishabille, and ran down the steps toward the kitchen. "Hunter? Hunter!"

"In here."

She followed the sound of his voice to the family room, where Hunter sat kicked back in a recliner with Ben asleep on his chest. His bare chest, she realized after her concern for her son abated. She heaved a huge sigh of relief, and her pulse should have calmed to a normal cadence. But the sight of her son resting peacefully against Hunter's taut chest and tanned skin was so sexy and sweet at the same time her breath stilled. She gaped at Hunter's muscle-sculpted shoulders and arms, his flat, hair-dusted abs... Brianna's pulse stutter-stepped. Who needed coffee in the morning with that sight to get your blood pumping?

"Morning," he said with a lopsided grin that melted her heart. Dear Lord, this man wore down her defenses. What would she give to be able to wake to this man's warm smile and sexy chest every morning?

Her fingers itched to feel all that warm skin, and she envied Ben, who snuggled against Hunter. She balled her hands at her sides, squelching the impulse to dig her fingers into his biceps and run her fingers over his chest. "Morning," she answered, her voice croaking. She cleared her throat and added, "I kinda freaked when he wasn't in his bed. I can't believe he's still asleep."

"He woke up at six-thirty, and I brought him down here before he could wake you. I figured you needed your sleep."

She blinked and moved to the side of the recliner to gently stroke her sleeping son's back. "Didn't he need a diaper change? To be fed?"

"I changed him and gave him a bottle, and he went back to sleep."

Brianna tipped her head. "A bottle of what? How did you feed him?"

Hunter flashed her a cocky grin. "Grant still had some of Kaylee's powdered baby formula." He aimed his thumb at the bottle on the lamp table next to him. "He sucked it right down."

"Formula? But..." Brianna raked a tangle of hair back from her face and sat on the edge of the couch. "I read that switching between bottles and breast milk can lead to nipple confusion. And because some formulas are sweeter than mother's milk, babies will learn to prefer the formula over the breast milk."

"Yeah, seems Darby said something about that when Savannah was born. But I didn't think one bottle would hurt him. And sleeping in was definitely in your best interests." Hunter paused, then gave her an odd look. "Wait…you say you read that? When?"

She shrugged. "I…"

When *had* she read it? She could visualize the book, the diagrams, the illustrations and charts. "Before he was born." She raised a wide-eyed look to Hunter. "*Before* he was born!"

Hunter's smile brightened. "Your memory is coming back."

She flopped back onto the sofa and conjured the image of the baby-care book again. "It is. I remember reading books and blogs about newborn care, about feeding regimens and first aid and…" She pressed a hand to her mouth as relief swamped her and tears pricked her eyes. "Oh, thank God."

"Rest. Time. Healing. The doctor said that's what you needed." Hunter's eyebrows drew together in a wary frown. "Do you remember anything else? Anything… about Chris?"

Grant's brown tabby, Cinderella, hopped up onto the couch next to Brianna and sniffed her. She reached for the cat, letting Cinderella smell Sorsha's scent on her hands before scratching the feline's cheek and chin. Patting the cat helped her relax as she searched her memory for details about her relationship with Chris. She tried to bring images to mind of quiet times with him, laughter, making love to him. Surely something as intimate and important as sex would have made a significant impression in her brain. But when she closed her eyes and tried to pull that memory from the void, she saw herself with Hunter instead. Holding Hunter, kissing Hunter, wrapping her limbs around Hunter's naked body.

Feeling her nipples tighten and her blood heat, she shook her head and rubbed her thumbs against her eyes to erase the image. She was in trouble if instead of memories her mind could conjure only desires and fantasies of what could be, what she wanted to be real.

"What? Did you remember something else?" he asked.

She raised a wary gaze, praying he couldn't see the truth in her eyes. "Not a memory of Chris."

"What, then?" Hunter's gaze held hers for a moment, then, as if he read something in her expression, his eyes grew smoky.

Her mouth dried, and she forced enough moisture into her mouth to swallow. "I… Nothing." A restless energy prickled her skin, and she shifted on the cushion, pulling an afghan from the back of the sofa around her shoulders. Lifting her gaze to Ben, she cleared her throat. "Do you want me to take him?"

She reached for Ben, and he waved her off. "Nah. Why bother him? I'm okay. There's coffee in the kitchen if you want it. Decaf, since I know you're watching your caffeine consumption."

Coffee sounded wonderful to her, and she pushed off the couch, taking the afghan with her, in pursuit of a large mugful. She padded into the kitchen and, after taking a mug with *Mansfield Construction* in gold lettering from the cabinet, Brianna pulled the carafe from the coffeemaker. Her hand trembled as she poured the hot brew, and it sloshed onto the counter.

She groaned as she replaced the carafe and found a rag to wipe up her spill.

Hunter naked. Making love to her. Where had that image come from, and why couldn't she get past this… this infatuation with him? He and his family had been generous and hospitable to the extreme. He'd already given more than she had any right to expect from him. Thinking he might want to stick around and be a father figure to Ben, be her companion, her *lover,* was crazy. "It's selfish."

Hearing a squeaky sort of meow, she glanced down at her calf, where Cinderella rubbed against her and then blinked up at her with big green eyes. She set her coffee down and scooped the brown tabby into her arms. "So you agree it's selfish, Cinderella?" A loud purr rumbled from the feline as Brianna scratched the kitty's head. "Hmm. I'll take that as a yes." She laid her cheek against the feline's soft fur. "How can I think of dragging Hunter into a situation so full of complexities and unknowns? I haven't even talked to Chris about Ben yet. I don't know what my future holds, what Ben's life will be like. I can't make plans with Hunter and then call it off because my son has to take the throne in Meridan," she reasoned aloud to the cat. *Even if Hunter is where my heart lies.*

The thought caused a pang in her chest and a stab of guilt. She needed to put her son's welfare before her own. She needed to stop feeling sorry for herself and what she couldn't have with Hunter and concentrate on rec-onciling her past relationship with Chris to the current situation. She didn't know if Chris was dead or alive, where he was or what he might be suffering. An entire country was in upheaval, its monarchy threatened, and she was bemoaning her slim chances of having a relationship with Hunter?

Cinderella gave another squeaky meow before hopping out of her arms. Brianna dusted cat hair off her nightgown and lifted her mug for a giant sip. She missed caffeine. Maybe if she had a hit of caffeine to start her morning, she could think straight, sort out the knot of emotions and fill in the blanks in her memory.

As she drank her decaf, she stared out the window of the back door, which led from the kitchen to a small deck. The wood was newer than the rest of the house, and she guessed that Grant had had it built in recent years. Beyond the deck was a large yard with a jungle gym, a giant live oak with a tire swing, a covered sandbox and a pink playhouse. The entire yard was framed by dense woods of pine trees and hardwoods. The perfect playground for Grant's daughters. The autumn sun shone through the fall foliage and dappled the lawn with a buttery light. She hoped when Ben got older, he'd have a magical place like this where he could run, climb, make believe and explore to his heart's content.

As if on cue, a plaintive whine drifted in from the next room, shattering her daydream and calling her back to the present. A present in which she had no home, thanks to an arsonist. Tearing herself from the view of Grant's idyllic backyard, she headed into the living room to relieve Hunter of babysitting duty.

Finding a new, safe home for herself and Ben needed to be a priority. As she left the kitchen, the word *home* resonated inside her. But it wasn't an image of the house she'd gone to after the hospital that flashed in her mind's eye, but a clapboard beach house with gray shutters and window boxes with red geraniums.

On the heels of the image, a swell of longing and nostalgia swept through her, and her knees buckled. Her mug of coffee sloshed onto her hand, and she set it on the nearest surface, a bookshelf, so that she could grab the doorframe.

"Bri? Are you all right?" Hunter surged out of his chair with Ben tucked in his arms and hurried to her. "Your face paled as you came in here. You look ready to pass out."

"I just had a memory. A house at the beach. A house I loved and considered home."

"Your parents' place in Cape Cod maybe? The one your aunt Robyn told us about?"

She nodded. "Probably. That makes sense." She glanced at the dripping mug and frowned. "Oh, no, I'm getting coffee on your brother's floor."

"He has kids. No doubt worse has been spilled. I know for a fact I dumped red juice on the dining-room floor when I was seven, back when the house belonged to our grandparents."

Pushing away from the wall, she caught a few drips with her free hand before Hunter offered her the burp cloth he'd been using with Ben. "Speaking of your brother, where is he?"

"Already gone into the office. He's an early riser, thanks to Kaylee."

"Oh." She wet her lips and glanced around the quiet family room before returning her gaze to his. "What about you? Do you need to go into work today?"

He shrugged. "Nah. Not really." A devastating grin

spread across his face. "What do you want to do today? I'm all yours."

All hers? Her pulse ramped up at the thought. If only that were true...

Over the next several days, Brianna savored the quiet beauty of Grant's rural home. Borrowing from her host a backpack-style carrier for Ben, she took walks with Hunter through the woods surrounding Grant's house. The fresh air and chirping birds refreshed her soul. Hunter held her hand on their strolls and regaled her with stories of his adventures in those same woods when he and his brothers were boys. The portrait he painted with his tales of a loving family and idyllic childhood tugged at her heart. She wanted that life, not just for herself but for her son. She pictured Ben romping in those woods, and the longing swelled to an ache.

In addition to the nature walks, she had plenty of time to nap, and the rest worked wonders healing her body. She had a follow-up appointment with the neurologist, who took new scans of her concussion and seemed pleased with her progress. The doctor reiterated his opinion that time for the swelling to recede and rest for her stressed body were her best medicines. As predicted, her memories took their time returning, though she did regain spotty moments of her past. The returning events and people were a collage with no particular rhyme or reason, like a jigsaw puzzle being built one painstaking piece at a time.

She remembered a doll she got from her father at Christmas one year, and the thrill of winning a swim meet as a preteen. She recalled bonfires with hot dogs, fireworks and marshmallows, but the friends around the fire remained faceless. Details of her research at Bancroft Industries returned, and Hunter drove her back to her laboratory to retrieve files and articles to study while she was on maternity leave.

Though her past was slowly coming together, her recent history, including her relationship with Chris, remained frustratingly dark and elusive.

Grant proved a gracious, if somewhat reticent, host. Though he was kind and thoughtful, like Hunter, he seemed distant at times, and his eyes held a sadness that broke Brianna's heart for the widower. Nancy stayed with her a few afternoons, giving Hunter time to check in at the construction sites and keep his building projects on track. In the evenings, though, Hunter was as attentive to her and Ben as a new father would be. He took turns holding Ben while they watched TV with Grant, and he listened patiently to her stories of almost-smiles and nap schedules as if she were recounting an intriguing travelogue instead of her newborn's day. By pumping her milk, Brianna was able to share feeding duties with Hunter. He volunteered for one late-night feeding each night, letting her get a few uninterrupted hours of sleep.

But her healing body and quality time with her son aside, the most significant change during the past week at Grant's house was the deepening bond she felt for Hunter. Despite the warnings she gave herself about falling for someone she couldn't commit to, his charm and magnetism drew her closer every day. The need to settle the unresolved questions concerning Chris, Ben and her future became more and more urgent to her, because only with closure in her relationship with Chris could she even entertain the notion of the life she had started dreaming of with Hunter.

As much as she hated leaving the safety and comfort of Grant's home, the resolution she needed lay in reconstructing the days she'd spent with Chris at her parents' beach house on the Atlantic coast. Decision made, she announced her plan at dinner the night before the older Mansfields were scheduled to return home from Disney World with Grant's daughters.

"I want to go to Cape Cod," she said without preamble over the breakfast of bacon and eggs she'd prepared for the men. "I want to find the vacation house my parents left me, the one where I must have been staying when I met Chris. Maybe there are answers there, people who remember seeing us together, people who could tell us what happened last winter."

Hunter exchanged a startled look with his brother before sending her a skeptical frown. "Don't you think if the Meridianian militants could track you to your house, they've got eyes on the house at the Cape?"

She sighed. "Do you have a better idea?"

He flattened a hand on the table. "You mean other than staying here where you're safe?"

She turned both palms up, exasperated. "For how long? When will this be over? What if Chris is killed and I never get to question him? I need to know all I can about my son's father, for medical reasons if nothing else. I need to know what's expected of Ben, what his future holds, what my options are, where my relationship with Chris stood when we separated."

"Give it more time. Other memories have come back. Surely your time with Chris will return in a few more days."

"We don't know that. The doctor couldn't guarantee how much I'd eventually remember. Visual prompts have helped trigger my memories before. I think seeing the house, being in Cape Cod, will help fill in the holes."

Hunter glanced at his brother. "Grant, help me out here?"

Grant raised an eyebrow and faced Brianna. "Nancy and I can watch Ben for a week or so if you're worried about taking him with you on this fact-finding mission. I'll guard him with my life."

Brianna's pulse stuttered. "I know you will."

"That's not what I mean!" Hunter exploded. "Grant, what are you thinking?"

"I'm thinking a life on hold is no life at all." Grant picked up a mug of coffee and sipped. "Brianna needs to do what her heart's telling her to do. She needs closure, answers, before she can move on."

"Thank you," Brianna said with a nod to Grant.

Hunter shook his head. "I still don't like it. But if you insist on going, I'm going with you."

Chapter 12

Leaving Ben in Grant's and Nancy's capable hands, Brianna and Hunter flew out two days later, having gotten directions from her aunt Robyn to the vacation home on the beach at Cape Cod. They rented a car in Boston and drove the remaining miles, an anxious anticipation humming through her.

The sights and sounds of Cape Cod did little to jog her memory as they made their way through town, and disappointment grew in her chest. But as they neared the address she'd jotted down for her parents' vacation home, something familiar stirred in her brain.

"This is it," Hunter said as he parked the rental car on the crushed-shell driveway, and Brianna looked up at the weathered clapboard house. According to Aunt Robyn, she'd spent many summers here with her parents. This unassuming beach house with gray shutters and a screened porch jutting out toward the ocean had been a second home to her as a child.

She felt Hunter's gaze on her, knew he was watching her reaction to the house, sensed his eagerness for the past to spill its secrets. She stared hard at the front door, the empty flower boxes under the windows, willing her brain to work.

Relax. Don't force it. Let the memories find you. Remembering the doctor's advice, she closed her eyes and took a deep breath. She rolled the tension out of her shoulders before opening her eyes again and sending Hunter a lopsided grin. "Ready?"

As she climbed out of the car and walked toward the wood-plank boardwalk leading to the front door, she inhaled the salty scent of the sea air, spiced with a hint of fish and the smoke of a nearby chimney. The smells were familiar, and she clutched the railing of the boardwalk as memories rushed over her, pulling at her like a riptide. She could hear her mother's voice warning her not to go too deep into the waves. She could see her father in his lucky fishing hat and hear his hoot of victory as he reeled in a prize catch from the ocean. She felt the prick of sunburn and the sting of jellyfish from summer days gone by.

"Bri?" Hunter stroked a hand down her back, yanking her from the onslaught of memories.

She tipped her head up to meet his worried gaze, and he thumbed away a tear from her cheek. She'd been so lost in sweet recollection that she hadn't realized she was crying.

"Are you all right?"

She nodded and chuckled through her tears. "I know this place. I belong here. I remember my parents, summers here, laughter. Good memories. So many happy memories—they're all coming back."

He cupped the back of her head and drew her close to kiss her temple. "That's great, Bri. Thank God. Any-thing…else?"

Something dark and uneasy shaded his eyes, and lines of strain framed his mouth when he smiled. Though he didn't say it, she knew he was worried what she might remember about Chris, what it might do to their budding relationship. Because they could deny it all they wanted, but something special had grown between them. They had a bond, an affection, a physical chemistry that went beyond friendship.

The ocean breeze mussed Hunter's hair, leaving it sexily rumpled. She couldn't help but comb her fingers through it, savoring the silky strands as she rearranged them, only to have the wind whip his hair into disarray again with the next damp gust. Her heart clenched as she studied Hunter's rugged face in the bright autumn sun. Little girls dreamed of being rescued by a hand-some prince, being swept away to a life of luxury and romance. How ironic that she'd had a real-life prince enter her life, yet Hunter's was the face that filled her dreams. He was the one who'd saved her life, been her champion…and won her heart.

If she were honest with herself, she'd have to admit to being more than a little scared herself of what she might learn in the next few days about Ben's father, the romance they'd shared, the promises they'd made. If her memories of last winter returned, if old feelings for Chris resurfaced, how could she say goodbye to Hunter, knowing it would hurt him? How could she walk away from a man who meant so much to her?

Swallowing the knot of grief that thought brought, she scanned the beach and spotted a few chairs planted along the water's edge. A handful of people meandered along the sand or ventured knee-deep into the cold Atlantic waves. "Maybe we should talk to the neighbors, see if anyone knows me and remembers Chris."

Hunter firmed his mouth and jerked a nod. "Lead the way."

Brianna took a breath for courage and held her hand out to Hunter. He laced his fingers with hers and squeezed her hand as they followed the wood-plank boardwalk through the sea grass and down to the beach. Brianna slipped off her shoes and socks and carried them in her free hand, enjoying the feel of the cool sand between her toes. They walked down to the water's edge, his pace quickly matching hers stride for stride, their bodies in sync. Brianna canted toward Hunter as they walked, thinking of the many ways they fit. After so short a time together, he could finish her sentences, and she could read his moods from subtle changes in his eyes. Their easy rapport came as naturally as the change in seasons. His companionship, his steadfastness, comforted her, buoyed her in a way she sensed no one else had in many years. Surely if Chris had been this in tune with her, she'd remember more about him.

When a wave rolled in and soaked her feet, Brianna yipped at the shock of the cold water.

"Mmm-hmm. That's why I left my shoes on," Hunter said with a chuckle. "This Southern boy prefers his beach balmy and his salt water warm." He wrapped an arm around her as they strolled down the beach toward a family building a castle in the sand.

"Excuse me," Brianna said to the parents. "I know

this will sound odd but…do you know me? Are you regular residents here on the Cape?"

The husband, a balding man with wire-rimmed glasses, squinted up at her and shook his head. "Sorry, no. We're borrowing a house from my law partner for a little R and R. Is there a problem we can help you with?"

"No." She flashed him a smile, hiding her disappointment. "Thanks anyway. Enjoy the day."

Farther down the beach, they encountered an older couple digging for clams. When Hunter called to them, over the sound of the waves and squawking seagulls, the gray-haired woman glanced up. Holding her floppy hat in place with one hand when the sea breeze buffeted her, the woman sized them up as they approached. Gasping, she cried, "Glory be! Brianna Coleman, is that you? Harry, look! It's Brianna. How in the world are you, darling?"

Brianna exchanged a look with Hunter. Mission accomplished.

"Good morning, ma'am. How are you?" Brianna dropped Hunter's hand to shake the woman's in greeting.

"I'm fine, honey," the woman said with a scoff as she folded Brianna into a hug. "But what is this *ma'am* business? What happened to Aunt Mimi?"

Brianna blinked. "You're my aunt?"

The woman canted back, holding Brianna's shoulders, and frowned. "Honey, don't you recognize me?" She glanced at Hunter and furrowed her brow. "You're not Chris."

Brianna's heart tripped. "You remember Chris?"

"Of course I do. It's only been, what? Ten months or so. I'm not senile yet!" The woman laughed, but her puzzled look remained. The elderly man shuffled up, stretching his back and setting his bucket of clams aside.

Hunter extended his hand to the gentleman and introduced himself. "We're actually hoping you could fill in some blanks for us. Brianna was in a car accident recently and lost her memory."

The woman—Aunt Mimi, she called herself—gasped. "Oh, Brianna!"

"It's coming back as I heal," she hastened to add, "but we're looking for answers about my relationship with Chris last winter."

"What sort of answers?" the man asked.

"I...I'm sorry. Who are you? You seem familiar, but like we said, my memory—"

"You poor child! How awful for you." The woman pressed a hand to her chest. "I'm Miriam Hartley, and this is my husband, Harry." She motioned to the man, who nodded to them. "We've been your neighbors here for twenty-five years. That's our house, the blue one." She pointed to the large, brightly painted home near Brianna's. "You played with our daughter, Helen, every summer from the time you were two until your parents died. After that, you still came for a week here and there, when your aunt could get away or when you could come stay with us."

"Helen." Brianna closed her eyes and saw a giggling, freckle-faced redhead buried in sand so that only her head and neck showed. "We ate Popsicles on your back porch. Grape was her favorite. Cherry was mine."

Miriam brightened. "Yes! You do remember!"

"Bits and pieces. Coming up here, seeing the house and beach in person, is helping bring back scattershot memories."

"Well, why don't we go inside, get some hot tea and see if we can't help you remember more about those days? And you say you need answers about Chris?" Miriam lifted a hand to her mouth. "Gracious. I'm surprised you don't remember him. More surprised he's not still with you. I felt sure you two would be married by now."

Beside her, Hunter tensed, and Brianna's stomach swooped. "We were close, then? In love?"

"Oh, boy." Harry hoisted his bucket and, taking his wife by the arm, hitched his head toward their house. "Sounds like we have our work cut out for us. Let's get lunch, and we'll help you out as best we can."

Hunter placed a possessive hand at the small of her back as they followed the Hartleys across the beach and up the warped wooden steps to their back porch. Shedding their shoes, the couple stopped at a hose and rinsed the sand from their feet before heading inside. Brianna followed suit, and Hunter toed his shoes off by the back door, entering the house in his sock feet.

"Harry," Miriam said, waving a finger toward a cabinet in the corner of the family room, "while I fix us tea and sandwiches, show Brianna and Hunter the photo albums."

"Oh, good idea." Harry pulled out a couple of fat books and patted a spot next to him on the overstuffed couch. "Sit with me, Breezy."

Brianna cocked her head as she settled next to Harry and Hunter next to her. "Breezy?"

"Yeah," the older man said with a grin. "That was your parents' nickname for you. We adopted it because it fit so well. You were always a happy child, without a care in the world. Friendly, outgoing…breezy."

She glanced at Hunter, and he arched an eyebrow and smirked. "I like that."

Brianna felt her cheeks flush, and she turned back

to Harry. "That's the sort of thing I want to know. The details that made us a family."

He cracked open the dusty photo album, and she smiled at the old snapshots encased in plastic sleeves. Right away she spotted the redhead she remembered, flashing a toothy grin and showing off a handful of shells. "That's Helen, isn't it?"

"Our pride and joy."

"Where is she now? What is she doing?" Brianna asked.

"Teaching school in London. She's married and has two boys. Ryan, who's five, and Billy, who's seven."

"He's eight!" Miriam called from the kitchen. "You were at his birthday party last month. Remember?"

Harry chuckled and swiped a hand over his mouth. "So I was. Wow, the rascals are growing up fast."

"Helen's in London?" she asked. "Why there?"

"That's where her husband is from. It was tough on all of us when she moved overseas. She's our only child, and she was your best friend. You were in graduate school at the time and took it hard. You moped around here for days after her wedding like she'd died instead of moving to England."

Brianna stared into near space, a hollow, lonely feeling engulfing her. A new memory sifted from the corners of her mind. "She gave me my 'I Heart Cape Cod' key chain before she left. She said a piece of her heart would always be with me in Cape Cod."

"That sounds like our Helen. She's sentimental that way."

Brianna looked to Hunter as the memories of her best friend's wedding and subsequent departure played out in her mind's eye. She had been devastated when Helen left. She'd felt the loss as deeply as when her parents had died.

Hunter put his arm around Brianna. He leaned close to see the pictures as they flipped pages and Harry told her stories of days past. She shoved down the melancholy of Helen's departure and focused on the fond memories Harry recounted. When Miriam brought in hot spice tea and ham-and-cheese sandwiches, they shared the meal and laughed over the Hartleys' tales of shenanigans Brianna and Helen got into as children.

"I don't know who told her honey and lemon would remove freckles," Miriam said, wiping tears of mirth from her eyes, "but by the time I found you girls, Helen was covered in the sticky mess and your experiment was drawing the attention of flies, bees and ants."

"You were very scientific about it, though. You had one clean patch saved on her arm as the 'before' spot for comparison."

"A control," Brianna said, the term popping freely to mind.

"Early evidence of the research scientist you'd become." Harry raised his tea to her before he sipped.

"I figured you had a mischievous side." Hunter grinned at Brianna and massaged her nape with his fingers, his arm still draped possessively behind her on the couch. A tingle raced from her scalp to her toes, and she shifted slightly on the couch so that her leg touched his from knee to hip. She tried to refocus on the anecdote Miriam told next, but her body hummed, hyperaware of Hunter winding a wisp of her hair on his finger and the feel of his firm muscles pressed along her thigh.

"But enough about your antics with Helen." Harry

clapped his hands on his legs. "You asked about Chris. Your relationship with him."

Beside her Hunter stiffened, and Brianna's pulse stumbled, yanked from her sensual sidetrack at the mention of Chris's name. Guilt shot through her, as cold and sobering as the Atlantic waves on her feet. *Chris.* The father of her son. Likely a political prisoner.

Miriam tipped her head and set her teacup on a lamp table. "What specifically did you want to know?"

Hunter removed his arm from the couch behind her and cleared his throat as he folded his arms over his chest. Brianna mourned his withdrawal, feeling a draft-like chill sweep over her.

She rubbed her palms on her slacks and met Miriam's gaze. "Everything. How did we meet? How serious were we? Did we talk of marriage? Of a future together? Obviously we had an intimate relationship. Ben is proof of that, but—" Brianna stopped when she saw the woman's reaction to the mention of Ben. "Oh. You don't know. I had a baby. A little boy. Two weeks ago. Chris's son."

Miriam and Harry looked at each other, then smiled.

"Congratulations, Breezy." Harry sent an awkward, pointed glance to Hunter.

Hunter said nothing, but he inhaled a deep, silent breath and rubbed a hand on his chin.

"No wonder you're so interested in Chris," Miriam said. She sat forward in her chair and furrowed her brow in thought. "Well, as I recall, you said you met him in town. At a coffee shop. Something about sharing the last cinnamon roll in the pastry case, which led to a lunch invitation and…well, several more dates. Several weeks spent together. We had the two of you over several times.

For the Super Bowl, for Harry's birthday dinner, for lunch after the Sunday church service once."

"What was our relationship like? Did we seem… close?" The question felt ridiculous. Uncomfortable. Obviously she'd been close enough to Chris to make love to him, make a baby with him. But sex didn't *have* to mean they'd shared an emotional bond…although the notion that she'd sleep with someone she didn't love didn't feel right to her. It didn't fit her instincts about herself. Maybe she was hoping she hadn't loved Chris so she'd feel less compunction for the feelings that were blossoming in her for Hunter.

"Well, you never said so, per se," Miriam said carefully, "but based on my observations of the two of you when you were together, I'd say you were very close. In love, even."

Brianna held her breath, a fist of something—regret? guilt? disappointment?—gripping her lungs. Even with all the evidence pointing toward that truth, she'd been reluctant to accept that at one time she'd been in love with Chris. She found some comfort in knowing Ben had been conceived in love. But if they'd been in love… what happened?

The same image that had brought a painful ache to her a few days ago, a flash of Chris walking down the beach, away from her, drifted through her mind like a mist.

"He made you so happy, and we were happy for you, considering all the heartache you'd suffered throughout your life." Miriam shook her head slowly. "I don't know why you would have split up."

Harry cleared his throat and cast her a guilty side glance. "I might. I never mentioned it, but I pulled him aside once and asked him about his intentions. You're like a daughter to me and with your own father gone…" He huffed a sigh and scratched his cheek. "Well, he said he wanted a future with you but that he had—what was the word he used?—*complications* he had to straighten out before he could propose."

"Complications?" Hunter echoed. "Did he explain what he meant by that?"

Harry shook his head. "But he loved you. I was sure of that."

Brianna swallowed hard and held Harry's gaze. "Sure…how?"

The older man's cheek twitched in a grin. "It was in his eyes, the way he looked at you. The way you looked at each other." He paused and arched one graying eyebrow as he tipped his head toward Hunter. "The way this young man looks at you, and you him."

Brianna's heart stilled, and her breath caught. Was Hunter *in love* with her?

She hazarded a glance his direction, and her gaze collided with his. His expression reflected the same shock that skittered through her. But as their eyes held, the surprise faded, and a wistful longing and poignant warmth shone in his gaze.

Did she love Hunter? Could Miriam and Harry see something she'd refused to see, hadn't admitted to herself, because a relationship with Hunter seemed… unlikely? Ill-advised? Fraught with complications?

Complications. The word Chris had used to describe what stood in the way of his future with her. His obligations to the throne. Politics. Royal tradition. The same issues still complicated her life and stood in the way of being with someone she loved. Because she couldn't plan a life with Hunter until she settled the past with Chris, until she knew Ben's fate, until the unrest in Meridan had been put down and the danger to her son's life eliminated.

Although she couldn't deny her feelings for Hunter, Harry had also said that she and Chris had loved each other.

After lunch, Brianna promised to visit the Hartleys again before they left town, then hugged the older couple before she and Hunter headed back to unpack and rest.

When they reached her parents' beach house, they unloaded their bags from the rental car and crunched over the broken shells to the porch.

"I want to call Grant and see how Ben is doing," she said as Hunter keyed open the door. "Then I need time to…" *Pump my breast milk.* She stopped before she said it and chuckled that she'd almost said the words aloud, almost overshared. A private detail like that might be a natural thing for a husband and wife to discuss, but did she really need to tell Hunter every intimate piece of her life?

"You need to what?"

She grinned and waved him off. "Never mind. I almost overshared."

"Ah." He tweaked her cheek. "The dreaded overshare. Remind me to tell you about the night Darby and I celebrated the end of exams in college." He pulled his face into a comical grimace, and she flashed him a smile.

"I look forward to that story."

That it felt natural enough for the share to have almost tumbled from her tongue didn't escape her. She'd reached a point with Hunter that she was comfortable sharing every part of her life, from her fears to her foibles. She'd relaxed her inhibitions enough that nothing seemed too personal.

Hunter stood aside and let her enter the beach house first. Another wave of nostalgia rolled over her as she scanned the nautical decor. A yellow glow spilled through open window blinds, filling the living room with a warm, homey aura. Though the house smelled musty and stale from being closed up for the past several months, the overall impression of the pale blue walls, ivory-toned furniture and open floor plan was airy and bright. Cheerful.

"I'll take these upstairs. Is there a room you prefer I stay in?" Hunter asked.

She shook her head. "Any of them. Wherever you'll be most comfortable."

With a nod, he disappeared up the steps with her weekender tote and his duffel bag.

Taking her burner cell phone from her purse, she called Grant and talked long enough to learn that all was well in Lagniappe. She thanked Hunter's brother again for his help and disconnected the call, turning her attention to the house she'd shared with her parents.

She brushed her fingers along the back of the couch as she strolled deeper into the room, glancing at the family pictures on the mantel over a stone fireplace. Brianna thought of the stories the Hartleys had told them, the smiles she'd worn in the pictures in the photo albums Harry had brought out. She'd been happy here. She'd had a loving, blessed childhood before her parents were killed in the car accident.

A sharp ache, a flash of memory, sliced through her. A state trooper at her door. Aunt Robyn consoling her. A weighty sense of loneliness and abandonment.

Sucking in a deep breath, she shoved the painful

memory aside to focus on happier thoughts. She wanted
to remember the good parts of her younger years. She
wanted to recall the crabbing, the picnics, the sailing
and swimming and laughter she'd known at this house.

And she needed to remember the details of her time
here with Chris.

She moved into the kitchen, opening cabinets and
picking up whimsical odds and ends—a pair of seagull
salt and pepper shakers, a lighthouse magnet on the
fridge, a smiley-face mug full of pens and markers by
the phone.

Her pulse tripped when she noticed the light on the
answering machine was blinking. She had messages.
Heart hammering, she stepped over to the machine and
pushed the play button.

"Hi, Brianna. It's Miriam. I'd hoped to catch you before you left for the airport to say goodbye and safe trav-
els. I'll try your cell. Take care, honey. We love you!"
The time stamp played, indicating that message was
from February. Brianna deleted it.

The next message was a hang-up from February,
which she also deleted.

"Hi, Brianna. It's me." A male voice. Chris? A tickle
of familiarity skittered down her spine. "Are you there?
Please pick up." She bit her bottom lip, her chest tight-
ening. She started to reach for the phone, as if the caller
were there now, as if she could talk to him and ask him
questions and hear what he had to say about the tragic
turn of events between them.

"I…I wanted to apologize for the way I left town.
There are things…things I haven't told you about me.
About my life and…" The man muttered harshly, a word
she didn't recognize. A foreign word?

She held her breath, knowing this had to be Chris, knowing he'd tried to reach her after she'd left the beach house. But why?

"Bri, love, I want to be honest with you. I want you to know why I had to leave."

The thump of footsteps on the stairs signaled Hunter's return.

"I loved you. Still love you, darling," Chris was saying, and Hunter stopped at the foot of the stairs, jerking his head up.

"What's that?" he asked, brow dented as he pointed toward the answering machine.

Brianna waved a hand, shushing him.

"But I have responsibilities to my country. I have to decide how—" The message cut off with a beep, and the time stamp announced the message had arrived in early March.

Brianna groaned. "No! You have to decide what?" She slapped the counter with one hand and raked her hair back with her other. "Call back. Call back! Please tell me he called back!"

"That was Chris," Hunter said, striding across the living room to her, an odd, worried look in his eyes.

"Yes."

"And?"

The next message started. Brianna held up a finger, asking Hunter to wait, then leaned closer to listen.

"It's Cristoff…" A grunt. A sigh. "*Chris* again. Look, just call me on the number I gave you. It's my private line. We need to talk, love." A pause. "Please. I miss you." Another sigh. "Okay, goodbye." The date stamp announced that call had come in just after the last one that got cut off.

Brianna raised a palm. "What number? He left me a number to call?"

"Maybe it's written down around here somewhere."

"For all the good it will do now if Chris is being held somewhere. I doubt his captors left him with his phone."

Another message, a wrong number, came in at the end of April.

The last message was Chris again, but his tone, his manner, was far different. "Brianna, it's Chris. Damn it, if you're there, *pick up*. It's important! You're in danger. Please, pick up. We have to talk. Brianna? Please. Are you there?" A ragged sigh. "Damn it, where are you? It's vital that I talk to you!" He grumbled what was likely a curse, then, "Brianna, call me *immediately* when you get this message. Your life is in danger. I'm sorry. It's my fault. I wish— Hell, just *call me!*"

Chapter 13

Hunter met her gaze, and even knowing all she did now, the panic and anxiety in Chris's tone caused a flutter of alarm in her gut.

The date stamp placed the call just days before Ben had been born. Chris had been looking for her just before the car accident, just before someone had shot at her car.

Brianna wiped her slick palms on her jeans and stumbled over to the couch. She dropped heavily onto the plush cushions and shook her head in disbelief, trying to absorb this new information.

"So…" Hunter joined her on the couch, swiping a hand down his face, then casting a hesitant side glance. "He was looking for you, trying to reach you."

"Yeah." A memory tugged at her, and she stared across the room at a painting of a sandpiper, trying to pull the lurking image to the forefront.

"So why not call your cell phone?" Hunter asked. "The video message he sent you tells us he had that number. Or at least he acquired that number at some point more recently. Had you changed cell providers since last winter?"

Brianna cut a quick look toward Hunter. "I...I don't know. I—" The ghostlike scene flickered again, distracting her. She closed her eyes, hoping to better capture the wispy vision.

"I suppose you can check your records, past bills to see if—" Hunter turned his body toward her. "Bri? What is it?"

"My legal name is Cristoff, not Chris. Cristoff Hamill. I'm the crown prince of Meridan and next in line to assume the Meridanian throne after my father, King Mikhail Hamill. If the baby you're carrying is my son, then he is of royal blood and is heir to the throne after me."

"If the baby is yours? You think I'm lying?"

"You wouldn't be the first woman to try to pass your baby off as a royal's child—"

"I'm not trying to pass my baby off as— Damn it, Chris! You know me better than that! At least I thought you did."

"Brianna, I only meant—"

"My baby is yours. There's been no one else. I didn't know you were a...a prince, for crying out loud. I don't even know how to begin processing that! I don't care about... I don't want..."

"Brianna, calm down. This is exactly why I didn't tell you. I wanted a normal relationship for once."

"Normal?"

"But the fact remains, I am a prince, and if your baby is mine—"

"Stop saying 'if'!"

"The fact that you are pregnant with my child complicates things. You're in more danger than ever. You have to hide. You have to protect our baby."

A shiver rolled through Brianna as the conversation came back to her. She could picture Chris standing in her living room, could recall the shock that had gripped her. She remembered the men who had burst into her home carrying weapons.

Her chest clenched, and acid roiled in her gut. "I remember…"

More images flickered. Past terror resurfaced, as real as the first time. They'd grabbed Chris, and he'd yelled for her to run. She'd fallen. Pain had gripped her belly. Loud staccato blasts of gunfire…

"Bri?" Hunter's fingers wrapped around her arm, and she startled. "You're white as a sheet. What's wrong?"

"I know what happened. I remember the day of my car wreck, before the wreck." She swallowed hard, choking down the taste of bile. "I remember the men shooting at me, Chris yelling for me to run."

Another full-body shudder raced through her, and she stopped to draw an unsteady breath.

"Hey…" Hunter guided her onto his lap and stroked her back. "You're safe now. I'm not going to let anyone hurt you. Not while I have breath in my body."

She rested her head on his shoulder and allowed his soothing caress to calm her ragged nerves. But his promise sent a different kind of quiver through her, because she knew he meant what he said. Hunter would defend her to the death. And she feared the dangerous men who'd invaded her home that day two weeks ago, who'd burned her house down around her, who were likely hunting her still, might kill Hunter to get to her.

"I don't want that," she whispered.

"Don't want what?"

"I don't want you to die protecting me."

He gave a short, wry laugh. "I don't want that, either, but I'll do what I have to for you."

She shook her head. "No. I mean I can't stand the thought of losing someone else I—" She caught herself before she said too much. Someone else she *loved*.

Her parents. Helen. Even Chris. The Hartleys said she'd loved Chris, and that matched her memory of being desolate and heartbroken, watching him walk away from her on the beach. She had to have cared deeply for him to be that hurt by his desertion.

But it wasn't only Chris's departure that haunted her. The past few days had given her a much better picture of her past, and an understanding of the lonely, hollow feeling that filled her when she contemplated recent years. She'd lost so many people she loved, had felt alone in the world many times.

"I'm not going anywhere, Bri," Hunter said, as if reading her mind. "Not until this danger's past."

His qualifier dropped her heart to her toes. "And then?"

"I don't know. I guess that will depend on what you choose."

"Me?"

He took a moment to answer, his dark eyebrows knitting, his expression troubled. "I'm not blind to the fact you have feelings left for Chris. And he's Ben's father. Then there's the whole heir-to-the-throne angle, the possibility you'll have to raise Ben in Meridan." He paused and sighed heavily. "I won't mess that up. I can't stand in the way of your chance, Ben's chance, for a better life than what I could give you."

Brianna blinked, stunned by what he was saying. The last thing she wanted was to repay Hunter's kindness and sacrifice by hurting him. "Hunter, I…"

She stopped when her voice cracked, and before she could catch her breath, he'd cupped the back of her head and caught her mouth in a deep, searing kiss. Brianna looped her arms around his neck and clung to him, returning his kiss with a fervor she hoped spoke for her heart.

His kiss was gentle but urgent, coaxing her lips to part as his tongue swept in to tangle with hers. A sweet lethargy flowed through her, and she sank into him, savoring his warmth, the strength in his arms as he held her close. She buried a hand in his thick hair and curled her fingers against his scalp. Her other hand flattened against his chest, feeling the powerful thump of his heart, and she sensed her own pulse synchronizing with his, a spiritual connection strengthening between them.

She'd tried to keep her feelings for Hunter in check, because of the uncertainties in her future. But alone with him, touching him, kissing him like this, she couldn't contain the tender emotions spilling from her heart. He was dear to her, essential to her, woven into the fabric of the person she'd become since the car accident. Her past and future were still riddled with holes, empty unknowns, but in this moment, right now, she felt whole. Because of Hunter.

She angled her head and deepened their kiss, a mewl of contentment forming in her throat. He drew on his lips with seductive persuasion, molding her mouth and sending ribbons of pleasure to her core.

Heat building inside her, she dipped her hand under his shirt and smoothed a hand over the taut skin of his back. She wanted more, wanted his hands on her, wanted to wrap her body around his and show him the depth of her feelings for him.

With a deep-pitched groan, he laid her back on the sofa cushions. Brianna held her breath until he shifted and stretched out beside her, half of his body pressing her deeper into the couch. He stroked a hand along her arm, then briefly cupped her breast before moving his hand across her belly and hip. "I hope you know how much you mean to me, Bri."

She framed his face with her hands and tugged him closer for another kiss. "I do. And I care deeply for you, too. Really, I do. I just can't make promises about—"

He cut her off, slanting his mouth over hers and giving her nape a gentle squeeze. "I'm not asking for promises. I know where we stand. I only wanted you to know how I feel. In case there was any doubt."

"I've never doubted you, Hunter. I knew from that first day at the accident that I could trust you. I've wanted you beside me, a part of my life, from the very start. You make me feel safe and cherished. And happy." She flashed him a sad smile. "I wish I could give you more. You deserve better. You're a good man, Hunter. If things were different—"

"But they're not." His eyes darkened, and he pressed his mouth into a grim line. "So let's deal in realities. Take each day as it comes. Huh?" He blew out a sigh and levered his body off hers. Rising to his feet, he raked a hand through his hair and glanced toward the stairs. "I think I'm going to call it a night."

His disappointment was palpable, and her heart hurt for him. She opened her mouth to offer him comfort and reassurance, but caught herself. She knew he wouldn't welcome what he'd likely see as pointless platitudes. Instead, she nodded. "Good idea. I'm tired, too."

He held out a hand, helped pull her to her feet.

"Which room did you put my bag in?" she asked.

"The master bedroom. You are the lady of the house. It should, by rights, be yours."

She flashed him a small grin of acknowledgment. "Thanks. Don't wait on me. I'm going to lock up and set the coffeemaker to brew in the morning. I'll be up in a moment."

"You don't need any help?"

"Setting up the coffee?" She pulled her grin into a teasing smirk, hoping to lighten the bittersweet turn in the mood. "No, I think I can handle it."

"I meant…" He laughed softly. "Never mind. I'm going up."

Brianna shuffled into the kitchen and pulled the dust-cover off the coffeemaker. She opened the cabinet above the brewer and found a canister with coffee grounds. She blinked. How did she know that was where the coffee was kept? Logical, obvious storage spot? Lucky guess? Or were her memories of smaller details about her life coming back along with the big points?

She sniffed the grinds. A little stale but they'd suffice for one morning. She definitely would see about going to the local market for fresh beans tomorrow, though.

When she finished checking the locks on all the

doors, Brianna climbed the stairs and made her way to the master bedroom.

"Are you one of those people with a side-of-the-bed preference?"

She stopped short and snapped her gaze to the bed. Hunter sat on the edge of the mattress wearing his boxer briefs, no shirt and a come-hither smile.

"What...what are you doing?" she asked, her gaze locked on his broad chest and muscle-sculpted arms.

"You said for me to take whichever room I'd feel most comfortable in, and..." He waved a hand around the room. "I'll feel best staying close to you." His dark blue eyes twinkled. "The closer the better."

A warm flush swept through her. She'd like nothing better herself. She found Hunter oh-so-sexy. But...

"You're forgetting the doctor forbid me to have sex for six weeks. It's only been three."

"I'm forgetting nothing. I promise not to ravish you, tempting as you are." He cocked his head and narrowed one eye in speculation. "I'll go to a guest room if you want me to. I was looking forward to holding you, though."

She drew a tremulous breath. She'd like nothing more than to have Hunter's arms around her while she slept. He calmed her, centered her, made her feel as if there was hope she'd survive this tangled mess with Meridanian politics and have a normal life again. A happy, fulfilled life with her son...and maybe a man. This man. This gentle, protective, strong, good-to-the-marrow man.

She took a deep breath and nodded. She might not be able to give him the intimacy they both craved or certainty about the future she wanted to promise him, but she had this night. This moment. And she wouldn't waste it.

He flipped back a corner of the covers, and she slid between the crisp, cool sheets. After snapping off the bedside lamp, he snuggled close to her. His body heat quickly chased away the chill, both external and deep in her core. As she laid a hand on his chest and closed her eyes, her soul gave a satisfied sigh.

This man, an internal voice whispered to her.

"What did Grant say when you called earlier?" he asked.

She angled her head to see his face in the dim light seeping through the window. "All was well."

"No signs of trouble?"

"You mean from the men who burned my house?"

Hunter gave an affirmative hum.

"He didn't mention anything."

"And Ben?"

"Ben is napping for him, only crying a little, taking the bottles of breast milk I left." An awkward prickle skittered through her, and she remembered her almost overshare from earlier. She had no reason to be embarrassed about her breast feeding or anything related to it, but she didn't want Hunter's primary thoughts of her breasts to be in their motherly feeding capacity. She wanted him to see a desirable woman. A sexy figure.

She snorted. Not likely in the next few weeks, until she lost some of her postdelivery sag and roll. She loved being Ben's mother, but carrying him had stretched and reshaped her body in ways she'd never have imagined.

"What was that little grunt about?"

"Nothing. Just a private reality check."

He rolled onto his side to face her, his hand sliding

along her hip to her waist. Brianna tightened her taxed stomach muscles as best she could, self-conscious over the weight she still carried.

"Keeping secrets? Already?" he teased.

"I…" She ducked her head and chuckled. "No, I just… was wishing I had my pre-baby body back. I was realizing how far I have to go and the hours at the gym ahead of me."

"Cut yourself some slack. It's only been three weeks. And for what it's worth, I think you—"

She raised a hand to his mouth, silencing him. "Please. No empty compliments to make me feel better about my baby body."

He kissed her fingers, then took her wrist gently and tugged her hand away. "Not empty at all. In fact…"

His fingers sank into the tumble of her hair, and he cradled the back of her head as he lowered his lips to hers. The heat that had flowed through her earlier returned with a vengeance, swamping her senses and melting her bones. She sagged against him, wanting to meld with him, fill herself with the sweet sensations he stirred at her core. With a tingle, her nipples tightened, and she curled her fingers against his back.

"I think you're beautiful, Bri," he whispered as he trailed kisses along her chin and the curve of her throat. "Inside and out."

"Hunter…" His name was a sigh, a plea. She arched her neck, giving him access to the tender pulse points just above her collarbone and down the valley between her breasts. His dark hair brushed her hypersensitive skin, sending a current of heady sensation through her.

She stroked a bare foot along his calf, winding her leg around him, then sliding her thigh against his hip. He rolled her to her back, covering her with his body, and she felt the proof of his arousal nudge her belly.

"We can't…" she reminded him, her own regret a deep pang, even as she gripped his buttocks and clung to him.

"I know." His disappointment hung heavy in his tone. "But your doctor's orders are the only thing stopping me from making love to you right now." Capturing her lips again, he echoed his words by stroking his hands sensuously along her body, pausing to mold her breasts with his fingers, then squeezing her bottom and drawing her more firmly against his erection.

Brianna moved both hands to frame Hunter's face. "I want that, too. If things were different, if I could…"

She plowed her fingers into his hair and raised her mouth to his, finishing her sentence with a demonstration of her feelings for him. She poured everything she felt for him into her kiss, drawing hard on his lips. Hot, deep and full of promise.

This man, her soul whispered again, and a viselike pressure grabbed her heart.

Hunter pulled away and rested his forehead against hers. "You're worth the wait, Bri. I'll wait as long as it takes."

She lowered her gaze, feeling a blush heat her cheeks. "Thank you. I'm just…impatient. I feel like so many things in my life are on hold. Because of my memory loss, because I can't find Chris, because I have to wait for my concussion, my body to heal." She huffed in exasperation.

He caressed her cheek with his thumb. "I know you're frustrated. I wish I could tell you things would be different soon, but you are getting a little of your memory back every day. We'll figure things out as they come. As far as the rest of it…no rush. After Darby had Savannah, it took her almost a full year to get back to her pre-baby weight. Her theory was that it took nine months to gain the weight, so nine to twelve months to take it off wasn't a bad thing."

His mention of Darby caused a funny tickle in her gut. "She had a point." Brianna bit her bottom lip, weighing the wisdom of raising a sticky issue with him. "You, um…talk about Darby a lot." Was she being silly worrying, especially since she had no claim on Hunter herself?

"Do I?" He threaded a finger through the hair on her forehead.

"It seems that way to me."

He lifted a shoulder. "She's my sister-in-law. And she's been one of my best friends since college."

"I know. But you also proposed to her. I was just wondering if—"

He barked a laugh and nudged her chin up. "Are you jealous of her? Are you worried I'm in love with her?"

She flattened her hand against his chest, feeling a little ridiculous for having broached the topic. But she'd stuck her foot in it now, so she plowed forward. "I know you say you don't love her, but she's clearly on your mind a lot, which would indicate…" She let her voice trail off, not sure how she wanted to word her statement.

What *was* she suggesting? Why did she care so much? Darby was married to Hunter's brother and living in Witness Security. Hunter might never see his sister-in-law again. So why was she pushing the issue?

She peeked up at Hunter awkwardly, and he was smiling at her. He kissed her nose and said firmly, "I'm *not* in love with Darby."

Nodding, she took a cleansing breath, prepared to let the issue drop. She'd revealed too much as it was about her own feelings by even raising the question.

But as Hunter shifted off of her to lie on his back, he added, "There was a time I think I might have believed I was in love with her, before she started dating Connor."

Brianna tipped her head toward him, hearing an unspoken sadness or disappointment in his tone. "It must have hurt when she fell for your brother over you."

He folded one arm behind his head and drew her closer with the hand at her waist. "That's the thing. It didn't hurt in the way you might think. That's how I know it wasn't really love I felt for her. Not romantic love anyway. I loved her as a friend. Still do. But…"

When he hesitated several seconds, she propped herself up on an elbow to gaze down at him. "But what?"

"Oh, it's stupid. Petty really."

"Now who's keeping secrets?" She grinned and traced the line of his jaw with her knuckle, enjoying the scratchy rasp of his five-o'clock shadow.

His mouth twisted into a wry moue. "Okay. Here it is. Don't judge me. Being the youngest of the family, I've always felt on some level Grant and Connor got the best of everything and I got the leftovers. The hand-me-downs. Mostly that was a big deal when I was a kid, and it made me competitive with them in a lot of ways. Typical sibling-rivalry stuff. But when Darby and Connor became an item, I felt a little like…well, like he took her from me. She didn't have as much time for me anymore and, while I was happy that they were happy, I felt…dismissed. Rejected."

"I can see that. Especially if you had a little crush on her."

"Then when I proposed and she turned me down, my reaction was…complicated."

He slid his hand up her back to tease the hair at her nape, and Brianna felt a tingle race through her. When he shifted his body to angle a look at her, his bare leg brushed hers and the crinkly hairs on his thighs tickled her, making her hyperaware of how snugly he held her against him.

She took a slow breath through her nose, trying to squelch the erotic sensations tempting her and focus on what Hunter was telling her. "Complicated how?"

"Well, I really thought she'd accept, so I was surprised she said no to start with. And because I thought us getting married when she learned she was pregnant was what was best for her, I was a little…frustrated."

"She thought Connor had died at the time, right?" she asked, trying to keep facts straight.

"Yeah. It was a tough time. We thought Connor was dead, then Darby learned she was pregnant. I thought she needed me, thought marrying her would fill the void of Connor's absence." He flashed her a sheepish grin. "I think knowing she didn't need me stung my male pride a bit."

Again, an uneasiness squirmed low in Brianna's gut. Was Connor with *her* just because she made his male ego feel useful and fill a void? Was his loyalty to her based on a sense of her neediness?

"And while her reasons for turning me down made sense—she loved my brother, not me, and she wanted me to be able to marry someone I truly loved—I still had moments of…I don't know…call it 'little-brother syndrome.' I still felt like I had lost out to my brother. Stupid and small-minded, I know, but it bothered me. I'd kinda warmed to the idea of being her husband by the time I proposed. We made a good team, and I thought we could make it work. So her 'no' was disappointing. Like I said, complicated. It was a lot of things, feelings and circumstances I'd rather not repeat."

Brianna closed her eyes, her conscience screaming. Her life was nothing if not complicated. She had no right to entertain any ideas about getting involved with Hunter. She could give him only more confusion and disappointment. Regardless of what she *wanted,* the fact was she was tangled up with the royal family of Meridan and all the political intrigue and danger that went with that relationship. In order to avoid hurting Hunter, she needed to make her position clear now. Continuing this way, leading him to think there was any chance of a future for them, was doing him a disservice. The pain that assailed her heart in the wake of that decision took her breath away. She hadn't realized just how much she had been hoping to make a life with Hunter, a life that it seemed would never be.

Her heart aching and her thoughts in turmoil, she snuggled close to Hunter's warmth and eventually fell into a fitful sleep with dreams of state troopers, lost friends and empty years.

The next morning, Brianna woke to the smell of fresh coffee and the chill of an empty pillow next to her. "Hunter?"

She heard noises downstairs and tossed back the covers to swing her feet out of the bed. She turned to make the bed before she joined Hunter, and as she was tucking in the sheets, she felt something hard beneath the mattress. Curious, she wiggled her hand farther between the mattress and box springs and withdrew a small book. She cracked it open and read the handwritten words on the first page—"Dear thirty-year-old me…"

She chuckled as a wave of familiarity and remembrance flowed through her. Her childhood diary. She fanned the pages, written in all shades of neon ink, and caught glimpses of phrases such as "best night of my life," "swimming tourney tomorrow" and "sooooo awesome!"

Grinning, she headed downstairs with her find and found Hunter in the living room cradling a cup of coffee and studying a family portrait. "Morning."

"Morning, Breezy." He flashed her his trademark heart-stopping smile, and her pulse ramped up.

She grunted playfully at his use of her nickname and waved the diary at him. "Look what I found."

He arched an eyebrow in query. "A book?"

"My diary."

"Oh, yeah?" Setting his mug aside, he stepped closer and snatched the journal from her.

"Hey!" She swatted at him. "Give that back! A girl's diary is private."

"'Dear thirty-year-old me, I kissed Ronnie Nash at the bonfire tonight. Squeal! He is sooooo hot!'"

He chuckled, and she grabbed the diary back and mock-growled at him. "I was thirteen. Give me a break."

He tugged his mouth into a devilish grin. "Kissing boys at thirteen? You got an early start."

Lifting her nose with an indignant sniff, she tucked the book under her arm and strolled into the kitchen for coffee. "You're going to tell me you weren't kissing girls at thirteen?"

He shrugged. "Maybe I was, maybe not." He took a

seat at a stool behind the bar dividing the kitchen from the living room. "So why the 'Dear thirty-year-old me' bit instead of 'Dear diary'?"

She ruminated on his question as she sipped her coffee. She saw herself as a preteen, the covers over her head, flashlight in her teeth as she wrote in her journal at night. "I think I considered my diary an account of my life, my hopes and accomplishments for when I grew old. To me being thirty was old." She shook her head, grinning. "Now that I'm staring down thirty in the next couple of years, it doesn't seem so old."

Hunter shot her a teasing look. "Was kissing Ronnie Nash one of your accomplishments?"

"When I was thirteen, it was!"

He nodded to the book under her arm. "What else does it say?"

She carried her mug toward the living room. "None of your business."

Hunter chortled and dug the car keys from his pocket. "Fine. You read up on your teenage angst, and I'll go buy us something sweet and artery clogging from that place on the corner for breakfast."

He kissed her temple as he headed out the door, locking it behind him, and warmth and affection spread through her. Remembering the seductive pull of Hunter's lips on hers last night, she'd wager Ronnie Nash had nothing on the man in her life now.

Sitting cross-legged on the couch, her mug in her hands and the diary on her lap, Brianna lost herself in the pages of her youthful writing. She smiled at entries about her adventures with Helen, groaned at her preteen hyperbole and teared up over accounts of time spent with her parents. Page after page, the events came to life, and images of that happy time in her life paraded through her head in full color, alive with sounds and scents. At one point, the book slipped as she was turning a stiff page where she'd glued an old snapshot, and as she straightened the tome on her lap, it fell open to a page at the back. The handwriting here was more mature, and Brianna set her mug aside, a curious knit in her brow.

"Dear teenage me," the entry started, "I'm twenty-six now, and my life has taken so many turns since I started this journal. Mom and Dad are gone. Helen's married and living overseas. I've earned my master's degree in biology and have a great job doing research for Bancroft Industries. The only thing missing is someone to share my life with. Miriam says I just need to be patient. He's out there and when the time is right, I'll find him. Sometimes waiting for what you want is hard. Guess I'll just focus on my career for now."

Brianna pulled her bottom lip between her teeth. Her twenty-six-year-old self had sounded so lonely. The entry was evidence of the empty yearning she remembered when flashes of her late-teen years came back to her.

She turned the page and found similar entries, and then, "Dear teenage me, I met someone. His name is Chris Hamill, and he's wonderful and handsome and funny and intelligent and kind and romantic and has the sexiest accent! He's the one I've been waiting for. I know he is. I've only known him about six weeks, but I'm already in love. Yes, love. I love him, and he says he loves me, too. I can see myself spending my life with him and raising a family with him. He hasn't asked me to marry him…yet. :-) But I think he will."

Brianna's stomach clenched, and she closed her eyes to take a deep breath. Here was her confirmation of her relationship with Chris. She'd been head over heels for him. She'd suspected as much, but the proof was here in her own handwriting.

Swallowing hard, she turned the page and kept reading, her heart pounding against her ribs. She read about walks on the beach, making love in a lighthouse, dinners by candlelight, a day trip to Boston and the birthday dinner for Harry that Miriam had mentioned yesterday. And on every page, the colorful descriptions and intimate details of her love affair with Chris spoke for the deep emotion she'd felt. The *love* she'd felt.

Brianna paused from her reading and glanced out the window. She stared at the view of the beach—the ebb and flow of the waves, the flutter of seagulls and shimmer of sunlight on the golden sand—and remembered. Pieces slowly clicked into place, and she saw herself laughing with Chris, kissing him, making love to him, dreaming with him.

Her breath froze in her lungs, and her heart twisted painfully. Chris. Ben's father. The man she'd fallen in love with last winter.

Tears pricked her eyes as she lowered her gaze to the next entry.

"Chris asked if he could come by tonight. He said he has something important to talk to me about. I think this is the night! I think he's going to propose!"

Her heart did a slow roll as she turned to the last handwritten page. "Chris left. He told me he was sorry to hurt me, but he had to go home to someplace called Meridan. Some sort of crisis or family emergency. He said he had obligations, restrictions on his life, and couldn't marry me. He said he had a plane to catch, and he just walked away. Just like that. I'm such an idiot. I thought he wanted to marry me, but it was just a fling for him. It hurts to be here. Everything reminds me of him. I'm leaving in the morning if I can get a seat on the six-thirty plane to Lagniappe. Why does love hurt so much?"

Feeling the tickle of moisture on her face, she wiped her cheek and snapped the diary shut. Chris had broken her heart. He'd walked away from her on the beach just as she'd remembered. If she'd known about her pregnancy at the time, she hadn't mentioned it in her diary, and that seemed like a rather important fact to have forgotten. So Chris hadn't known he was a father when he left. Not that she'd ever use a pregnancy to lock him into a marriage he didn't want. Yet in his phone messages he'd said he loved her and—

The front door opened, and Hunter strolled in with a bakery box. "Apple fritters. Get 'em while they're hot!" He met her teary gaze, and his dark eyebrows snapped together in a frown. "Bri, what is it?"

"I loved him…Chris. I wrote in the back pages about him, and…I remember feeling…happy."

Hunter's jaw tightened while the rest of his body seemed to wilt. His shoulders sagged, and he set the fritters on an end table as he took a seat across from her. "Well, I guess we suspected that, huh? I mean, you did have a baby with him." The smile he sent her didn't reach his eyes. "What else does it say? What do you remember?"

"I wanted to marry him. Hoped he'd ask me." She read him the entries, told him the feelings and memories that had washed through her as she'd pored over the pages. With a stiff tone, she relayed the words of the last notation and her heartache. "I remember that night. I was devastated. I thought he didn't care. But his phone messages…"

Hunter dragged a hand over his mouth, his palm scraping over his shadow of a beard. "So what now?"

She turned her gaze to the window, the beach beyond. "I don't know. In a sense, nothing's changed."

"Hasn't it?"

Her gaze darted back to the wounded look in his eyes. "Hunter, I—"

He stood abruptly, his body vibrating with tension, emotion. "I, uh…think I'm gonna go for a walk." He strode briskly to the door that led to the deck and walkway to the beach.

"Hunter."

"I just…need some air. To clear my head." He disappeared outside and quickly jogged down to the water's edge.

Her heart ached for him. Despite her vow to herself not to hurt Hunter, their relationship had become more complicated, more confusing in the past few days. She wasn't sure what she'd say to him, but she couldn't ignore the wounded look in his eyes.

Darting upstairs, she dressed quickly and hurried out after him. Given his head start, she didn't catch up with him until they reached a small oceanside café.

"Shall we eat since we're here?" he asked her, aiming a thumb at the deck of the establishment.

"Will you talk to me?" she asked, touching his arm and denting her brow.

He flashed her a lopsided grin that was bracketed with lines of tension. "It'd be pretty rude of me not to talk to my table companion."

"About us. About what I found in that diary."

He smoothed the windblown hair back from her face. "No need. I'm fine. Really. You just…caught me by surprise. All I need now is a cup of coffee and a big omelet. I'm starved."

Though she didn't quite believe he was as fine about their situation as he pretended, it was clear he had no intention of discussing the new closeness they shared… and what it meant for the future.

Shoving her own confusion aside as best she could, Brianna ordered a blueberry muffin and tried to enjoy the time with Hunter. She had as many answers about Chris as she was likely to learn here, short of finding Chris himself, and she was eager to get home to Ben.

They walked home via the streets of town, window-shopping and enjoying the cool autumn weather. Brianna stopped at the Hartleys' long enough to tell them goodbye and promise them she'd email pictures of Ben soon.

"I'll call the airline and see if we can get on the next flight out," Hunter said as they reached her beach house, and he keyed open the front door. Then froze.

"What?" she asked.

"It wasn't locked. I thought I'd locked it behind me earlier."

"Not that I remember." She pushed the door open, heading inside. "You had the bakery box and—"

"Brianna, wait…" He reached for her arm, but—

"Brianna Coleman. At last."

She jerked her head up with a gasp.

Across the room, a man in a crisp suit sat in her father's recliner, flanked on each side by large, frowning thugs. In a heavily accented voice, he said, "We've been waiting for you."

Chapter 14

Adrenaline shot through Hunter.

Get Bri out of here. Seizing Brianna's arm, he turned and pulled her with him back out the front door.

But before he'd gone two steps, another man materialized from behind the bushes and blocked his path. "Inside," the man ordered.

Hunter's gaze dropped to the pistol aimed at his gut. His brain ticked, calculated. What was his play? If Brianna weren't a factor…

But she was. She was the most important part of the equation. Protecting her, defending her. At all costs.

"Let him go," she said, trying to move out from behind him. "He's not part of this. You don't need him! Please!"

When she moved into the line of fire, Hunter stretched an arm out and pushed her behind him again. "Stay back, Bri."

"No one's going anywhere until we talk."

Hunter spun ninety degrees so he could see Mr. Snazzy Suit, who now stood in the front door. He edged backward, keeping Brianna behind him and dividing his gaze between the two men who had him cornered.

"Please, come inside out of the chill," Snazzy Suit said with a European accent Hunter couldn't quite identify. He waved a hand toward the living room. "Olaf, please." He raised a quelling hand at the man with the gun. "Put that away. We don't want to frighten our guests."

"Guests?" Hunter scoffed. "This is Brianna's house. You're the trespassers."

Snazzy Suit tipped his head and furrowed his brow. "And you would be Mr. Mansfield. Hunter Mansfield. Correct?"

"Who are you?" Brianna sidestepped again, moving from behind his protective stance. "What do you want?"

"If you would?" The intruder swept an inviting hand toward the living room again. "I shall explain everything."

When they didn't move, Olaf stepped closer, glaring at them. "You heard him. Go!"

Hunter bristled, pulling his shoulders back as his temper rose. Sure, the other guy had a gun, but Hunter chafed at being ordered around. He didn't do submissive, and he'd be damned if he'd roll over for these men who'd lain in wait for Brianna.

When he stood firm, meeting Olaf's challenging glare with his own, Brianna placed a hand on his arm and whispered, "Don't, Hunter. Let's hear him out."

He sent her a skeptical glance. "Bri, I have a bad feeling…" he muttered under his breath.

"Ms. Coleman, please," Snazzy Suit urged, then said, "Prince Cristoff is with us, in a secure location."

Brianna's head snapped up, her eyes widening. "You have Chris? Where? Is he all right?"

The hope that lit Brianna's face, the fear in her voice for the prince's well-being, shouldn't have needled Hunter. But it did. Her worry sounded like a lot more to him than platonic concern.

"We will take you to him, but first, we talk." Again Snazzy Suit motioned for them to come inside, smiling amiably.

Brianna started into the house, and Hunter grabbed her arm. "Bri…"

"They have Chris, Hunter. I need to hear him out." She wrenched her arm free, and Hunter had no choice but to follow her inside. His body hummed with tension, his senses all on alert.

As they entered the house, one of Snazzy Suit's thugs took Brianna's purse from her and tossed it onto the floor in a corner.

"Hey!" she protested with a glare.

"You won't be needing it," the thug coolly replied.

Frowning her discontent, Brianna took a chair across from Snazzy Suit, who resumed his post in the recliner with his thugs flanking him, as if the large chair were his throne.

Perched on the edge of her seat and leaning expectantly toward the imperious man, Brianna clipped out, "Where is Chris? Who are you?"

"My name is Senator Renaule Viktor. I am a member of the Royal Senate in Meridan. Our country is in the midst of an attempted coup, an attempt to unseat the royal family and install a new government."

Hunter moved to Brianna's side, standing over her with a hawklike vigilance. "We're aware of the unrest, the rebels. They've sent assassins over here to kill Brianna and her—"

Brianna grabbed Hunter's hand and squeezed hard, stopping him. She glanced up at him, a silent signal for caution in her eyes.

"Before we go further—" Brianna's tone said she was striving for calm rationality, but Hunter heard the tremor that gave away her nerves "—I want proof that Prince Cristoff is safe. That he is really with you, really under your protection."

"Proof?" Viktor sighed and glanced away for a moment. "Will a picture satisfy you?"

"Why can't I talk to him?" Brianna asked, pushing the issue. "Call him? Surely there are phones—"

"Phones, yes. But reception, no." Viktor steepled his fingers. "I'll have a picture texted to you. How is that?"

Brianna nibbled her bottom lip. "I need to know it is a current picture."

"Have him hold up three fingers on one hand and a fist with his other hand," Hunter suggested.

Viktor cocked his head, his eyes wary. "Why? What is the significance of this?"

Hunter shrugged. "No significance. It's just a random gesture. That's the point. You relay that message, and if he complies, we know he's all right. That he's alive and in your custody."

Viktor jerked a nod and sent a look to Olaf. "Send those directions to His Highness. Tell me when Prince Cristoff responds."

Olaf pulled a phone from his breast pocket and began thumbing keys.

"Meanwhile, we talk." Viktor drummed his fingers on the arm of the recliner. "We know that you had a love affair with His Highness the Prince last winter, Ms. Coleman. We know because His Highness revealed this to us himself. He told us this when he returned from America and spoke of changing Meridanian laws so that he could marry you."

Brianna gasped. "Marry me?"

Hunter's heart plunged to his toes, his worst fear confirmed. Brianna and Chris had been in love, had wanted to marry. Even if it meant changing Meridanian laws. What chance did he have against a man with that much power and position?

Brianna felt Hunter stiffen beside her. She knew how this news must have hit him, especially in light of their recent discussion about her feelings toward Chris. But this news of Chris's intentions toward her didn't jibe with her memory of Chris breaking up with her, walking away from her, ending things with an unquestionable finality. His lack of communication for months. Her inability to reach him in order to tell him about her pregnancy.

Did she believe this man about Chris wanting to marry her? He claimed to be a member of the Royal Senate, but she had no way to verify that claim.

"D-did the law get changed?" she asked, her heart drumming.

"Not yet. His father, King Mikhail, was pushing for the law to be enacted. The king wanted to preserve the royal succession, and Prince Cristoff, an only child, was threatening to abdicate his claim to the throne if the new law, allowing the prince to marry a foreigner, was not passed. Before the vote could be taken, King Mikhail was assassinated, and Cristoff disappeared."

"So..." Brianna swallowed hard, fighting the swell of nausea in her gut. "If you've found Prince Cristoff, if he's safe in your custody, why do you need me?"

"You were the reason he threatened to abdicate. We need Prince Cristoff—now our king in light of his father's death—to fill the power vacuum and put down the rebellion once and for all. We need him to show strength and leadership, not vacillation, pining for an American he met while on a winter retreat."

"So you're reuniting us so we can marry?" Brianna shook her head, still confused. "So Chris can have both marriage and the throne?"

"That would be one solution. If the law were changed." Viktor lifted one eyebrow. "We'd also been told you were with child. That you were carrying Cristoff's baby."

Brianna worked hard not to visibly react. Until she knew for certain whether she could trust these men, she couldn't reveal anything about Ben. Beside her, Hunter remained tense, still, quiet.

A beep sounded in the taut silence, and Olaf said something to Viktor in a foreign language. Viktor waved his hand toward Brianna and Olaf stepped close, shoving his cell phone in front of her.

An image glowed on the screen. *Chris.* Grim-faced, but seemingly unharmed. He held up three fingers with one hand and a fist with his other, just as Hunter suggested. Proof that he was still alive and in Viktor's custody. An odd tangle of relief and dread knotted her stomach. Though she was glad Chris was safe, she didn't know where this situation was headed. Would she be forced to marry Chris? What would happen to Ben if she refused to be Chris's wife?

Hunter leaned close to study the picture with her, and his proximity gave her a measure of comfort. At least she wasn't facing all of this alone.

"Are you satisfied now that we have been truthful with you? Do we have your cooperation?" Viktor asked.

Brianna bit her bottom lip, quickly searching the picture for clues to Chris's whereabouts. Was there evidence, as in the video he'd sent, that all was not what it seemed? The background didn't yield much help. He was standing in front of a generic-looking blue wall, the corner of some sort of cabinet visible at the edge of the frame. Before she could give the image any further scrutiny, Olaf snatched his phone back and thumbed the screen, likely deleting the photo, before stashing his cell phone in his breast pocket again.

She raised her gaze to the Meridanian senator and drew a slow breath. "As you can see, I'm not with child. Who told you I was?"

"Prince Cristoff for one. Some of the palace guards who saw you with Cristoff a couple of weeks ago confirmed this."

A tingle ran down her spine. The palace guards… who'd shot at her.

Hunter straightened his back and pulled his shoulders back. "Your sources are partly right. She had a baby a few weeks ago, but Prince Cristoff is not the father. I am."

Chapter 15

Brianna jerked her chin up, her startled gaze snapping to his. Hunter knew his move was a gamble, but he'd do whatever it took to protect Ben.

Senator Snazzy Suit gave him a skeptical, one-eyed squint. "Yours?"

"Mine. Check his birth certificate if you don't believe me."

Viktor's eyes shifted to Brianna, who leveled a surprisingly steady gaze on the Meridanian senator. "The Royal Senate will require paternity tests for confirmation. With the royal succession at stake, you understand the need for verification?"

Hunter placed a hand on Brianna's shoulder in a gesture of support and felt the small shudder that rolled through her.

Lifting her chin, she said, "My son is an American

citizen, and he's protected by American laws. You won't touch him without my consent."

The senator stared silently at Brianna for several seconds before exhaling harshly and nodding toward Olaf. "Perhaps you will feel differently if we give you the opportunity to talk with Prince Cristoff."

Brianna shifted on her chair and divided a wary glance between Hunter and the senator. "You're going to bring him here?"

When Viktor stood, Hunter squared his feet, his senses on alert. He angled his body to keep both Viktor and Olaf in view.

"No," the senator said, signaling to his bodyguards. "I'm taking you to him. Olaf, please ask Gunther to escort the prince to the rendezvous point."

Brianna rose to her feet and placed a hand on Hunter's arm. Her expression said she was torn between hope and alarm. Clearly she wanted to see Chris, wanted to believe he was safe, but her refusal to tell the men anything about Ben told him she didn't trust the senator and his men any more than he did. Hunter wrapped an arm around Bri's shoulders and leaned in to kiss her head by her ear, whispering, "Stay alert."

She sent him a look that said she understood and agreed with his warning.

When they hesitated to follow the senator out the front door, Olaf seized Brianna's arms and hauled her toward the door.

Hunter saw red. Shoving between the henchman and Brianna, he grabbed Olaf's wrist with an iron grip and snarled, "Let go of her!"

Brianna gasped and flicked a worried glance from Olaf to Hunter.

Olaf held Hunter's steely glare for long seconds and flipped back the edge of his jacket to reveal the pistol he wore in a chest shoulder holster.

Hunter didn't back down from the thug's unspoken threat, and finally, the senator spoke from the door.

"Is there a problem?"

The henchman answered in a foreign language, but he released Brianna's arm and stepped back. He jerked his head toward the exit, and Brianna headed slowly toward the door. As she left the living room, she cast a longing look toward her purse, where her phone poked out of a front pocket, but when she slowed her steps, Olaf stopped beside her. He blocked her path to the purse, the cell phone, and with a shuddering sigh, she followed the senator out of the beach house.

Hunter patted his pockets, feeling for his phone, and groaned internally, remembering he'd left it in the rental car, plugged into the charger. They had no means to call the police if things went sideways.

Unless he could overpower Olaf and get the phone from his breast pocket. But there was still the matter of the pistol under Olaf's jacket and the weapons the senator's other thugs were no doubt carrying somewhere hidden from view. Hell, Senator Snazzy Suit could even be packing. Not good odds.

He caught up to Brianna in two long strides and laced his fingers with hers, giving her hand a squeeze of comfort and encouragement, as they walked outside.

A large white SUV pulled onto the crushed-shell driveway behind their rental car and stopped. Thug One and Thug Two flanked the senator as he approached the car, then Thug One, who sported a spider tattoo on his neck, slid into the front passenger seat while Thug Two opened the back door for Viktor.

Hunter and Brianna were steered into the middle row of seats next to the senator and Olaf, and Thug Two took the third row at the back of the SUV.

Hunter tried to plan, to run the logistics of various escape scenarios through his mind as they rode to their destination, but soon after they pulled away from Brianna's beach house, Viktor spoke up again.

"I'm surprised you would leave your son with him so young."

Brianna flinched, then sat straighter. "He's safe. And I only plan to be away from him a couple of days."

"In Meridan, mothers spend hours a day, *every* day, bonding with their newborns." The senator's tone held reproach, and Hunter bristled on Brianna's behalf. He saw the guilt that warred with irritation in her expression.

"Until this trip, I spent every hour since his birth with my son." Her voice cracked, evidence the emotion Snazzy Suit's comments had riled.

Hunter put a hand on her knee and said quietly in her ear, "He's trying to get in your head. Don't let him."

"What's that, Mr. Mansfield? Please share," the royal senator said, calling him out as if he were a child in school.

"I said you're a bastard, and she should ignore you," Hunter growled, his temper spiking.

Viktor leaned forward to glare across the seat at him. "Is that so?"

"Yeah." Hunter flashed him a sour grin.

"Hunter," Brianna warned, squeezing his hand.

Viktor met the gaze of Thug One in the visor mirror and gave a small nod. Turning to the backseat, Thug One leaned over and slammed his fist in Hunter's jaw.

Brianna yelped in shock and distress, and Hunter, having grown up with two older brothers, instantly reacted by surging toward his attacker and grabbing the scruff of Thug One's neck. No sooner had he grabbed his opponent than Thug Two snaked a beefy arm around Hunter's throat from behind and yanked him back onto the seat, strangling him.

"No!" Brianna cried, slapping and clawing at the man's arm. "Stop it! Let him go!"

Hunter wrestled with the choke hold, but the henchman had both a size advantage and better leverage.

"I will not be disrespected. I am a member of the Royal Senate of Meridan, and I will not be insulted again." Viktor sent Hunter a menacing scowl. "Do you understand?"

His lungs ached, and blood pounded at his temples as the senator's henchman squeezed his throat. The last thing he wanted to give the miserable pompous man was respect, but he couldn't protect Brianna if he let Olaf take him out now over a test of wills.

"Let him go!" Brianna continued tugging on the thug's arm, her tone desperate and frightened.

Finally, as the SUV drove into a more populated part of town, Viktor jerked a nod. "Enough, Axel."

The thug—Axel, Viktor had called him—released him, and Hunter gasped in deep gulps of oxygen.

Brianna whipped around on her seat, fury rolling off her. "Why are you doing this? I'm nothing to you. And Hunter has no part of any of it. Let him go!"

"I'm afraid that's not possible. If I release him now,

he'll go to the police, try to play the hero for you and Meridan's wayward prince."

A chill ran down Hunter's spine as he read between the lines of the senator's explanation. The possibility of them going to the police *after* the rendezvous with Chris should have been as big of a concern. But Viktor didn't mention it. Because Viktor didn't intend for there to be an *after*. After the meeting with the prince, if that was even where they were going, Hunter felt sure he and Brianna—and probably Chris, as well—would be dead.

Chapter 16

A frisson of ice slithered through Brianna as the SUV pulled to a stop at a small private harbor where a handful of boats from small sailing vessels to mammoth yachts were docked. She cast a harried glance about for anyone she could shout to, anyone who might see them as they left the car, but the harbor was suspiciously empty.

Her stomach roiled, and she mentally kicked herself for having trusted the senator. When he'd said he had Chris safely in his custody, she'd believed he was on their side, that he was trustworthy. Or perhaps she just *wanted* so much for him to be trustworthy, wanted to believe Chris was safe and this whole frightening chapter of her life could be resolved, that she'd fallen for his smile and easygoing manner. Hunter hadn't. Hunter had sensed trouble from the start, but she'd convinced him to go along with the senator, to hear him out. She should have listened to Hunter. Instead, he was now in danger. They were both in danger. Because it was quite clear to her now these men were not allies with Chris.

As the SUV stopped, the hulking men in the front seat got out and opened the back doors. The senator climbed smoothly from the vehicle and ran a hand down his suit coat. The driver glared into the SUV at her and waved for her to step out.

She clenched Hunter's hand tighter and exchanged a dubious look with him that silently asked, *What do we do?*

"Ms. Coleman, please," Viktor said with what she now considered an oily smile. A snake's simpering grin. "This way."

"No. Take me back to my house," she said, knowing in her heart of hearts the chances of that happening were less than zero.

The senator's brow furrowed in irritation. "We have an appointment with King Cristoff to keep."

"Bring him here. I'll wait in that bait shop over there." She pointed to a dilapidated building at the far end of the weed-infested parking lot.

"Get out of the car," Olaf groused behind her. He fisted his fingers in the shoulder of her sweater and tugged her toward the vehicle door.

Hunter clamped his hand on Olaf's arm, despite the other thug's rough treatment of him earlier, and grated out, "Let. Go. Of. Her."

Viktor stepped into the space between the open car door and the backseat, ducking his head to glare back inside. "Ms. Coleman, I'd advise you to cooperate. Do not forget that we have Cristoff in our custody." He twitched her a leering grin. "And we know that Mr. Mansfield's brother has your son at his house. If you care anything for the safety of either of these men or your child, you will come with us quietly and do exactly as we say."

Brianna felt her gorge rise, and she had to swallow several times to force the choking bitterness back down her throat. Trembling to her core, both with fury over the senator's intimidation tactics and fear that he'd make good on the threats, Brianna slid to the end of the seat and climbed out of the SUV.

The henchman with a spider tattoo on his throat grabbed her upper arms and hauled her close to drag her toward the pier. Though the man didn't draw his weapon, she could feel the bulge of the gun under his coat jabbing her side. She stumbled as the man yanked her along, leading her across the cracked parking lot. She twisted, glancing behind her for Hunter, praying at the same time that he could manage to escape and that they were bringing him with them. As selfish as it was, she didn't want to be alone in this ordeal, felt safer with him near her.

But that same selfishness and fear of being alone were what had dragged Hunter into this nightmare in the beginning. She'd pleaded with him that first day at the car accident to stay with her. And he had. Faithfully. For far longer than most men would have. For longer than she had any right to ask. And now he might die because of her, because he'd been kind enough, brave enough, loyal enough to stick by her through all kinds of hell.

He'd stood by her as no one else in her life ever had. That realization sent a bittersweet, heart-squeezing pang to her core.

Senator Viktor and his men marched them down the buckled wooden pier to a large speedboat, tethered in a slip at the far end of the dock. The thump of their feet on the wood-plank dock echoed hollowly, reverberating inside her like the slow, dread-filled beats of her heart. Were they really going to meet Chris or were they simply going to ferry them out into the ocean, where they could shoot her and Hunter and easily dispose of their bodies?

If she fought back, tried to run from them, did she have a prayer of escaping, or would she be guaranteeing she and Hunter would be killed in the attempt? Olaf stood directly behind him, and the angle of the henchman's arm told Brianna he held his gun at Hunter's back, out of view.

"Search them," Viktor said, waving a hand toward her.

Immediately, the man with the spider tattoo patted her down, touching her in intimate places and making her skin crawl. Hunter was given a similar frisking, and Olaf took Hunter's pocketknife and keys and slipped them in his shirt pocket before once again jabbing his gun in Hunter's back.

As the senator's thugs boarded the speedboat, she met Hunter's eyes. His creased brow and keen, assessing gaze told her he, too, was looking for an escape, weighing the risks.

What do we do? she asked with her eyes. She couldn't just let Viktor's men lead them to their slaughter like meek little lambs.

Hunter gave her a tiny, almost-imperceptible nod, saying he understood, he agreed—then reared his head back into Olaf's nose. While Olaf staggered and howled in pain, Hunter spun to face the henchman, grabbed Olaf's wrist and thrust his arm, and the gun in the man's hand, into the air.

Though startled by Hunter's move, Brianna took advantage of the other men's distraction and shoved hard on Mr. Spider Tattoo. He lost his balance at the edge of the pier and teetered into the water.

The SUV driver, who'd already climbed into the boat, scrambled back toward the dock. Hunter stopped him with a swift kick to the chin, knocking the man back on his butt.

"Run!" Hunter shouted.

She did. But the spike of adrenaline fueling her blood was not enough to counter the dragging effect of her postpartum body, her concussion-mending skull and short legs. She'd made it only to the parking-lot end of the dock when Axel caught up to her and tackled her from behind. They fell together, the broken pavement scraping her skin and the henchman's heft knocking the wind from her lungs. Though breathless and aching, she fought the man's grip, struggling to wiggle free of his grasp. He wrapped a muscled arm around her waist and hauled her to her feet. When she continued fighting, he lifted her like a sack of flour and tossed her over his shoulder. Still she flailed, hoping she'd get in a good lick or two to the thug's groin or kneecaps or spleen or—

The sound of a single gunshot sent ice through her veins and stilled her heart. "Hunter!"

She jerked her head up, twisting to search the pier for Hunter. *Please, God, let him be all right!*

She spotted him, still locked in hand-to-hand battle with Olaf. Spider dragged himself back onto the dock, glowering at her, then with a rough twist on Hunter's arm, helped restrain him. Grunting in pain, Hunter cast a side glance toward her and visibly sagged when he saw that she'd been recaptured. A trickle of blood leaked from his nose, and the area around his eye was starting to swell. Her heart hurt seeing his injuries, but she saw no evidence he'd been shot and gave thanks for that much.

Axel let Brianna down, setting her feet on the dock but keeping a grip on her arms.

Senator Viktor stepped forward, clearly displeased with their little show of rebellion. He stuck his nose in Hunter's face and growled, "You are dispensable. I recommend you not try that again."

Hunter scoffed, "Don't you plan on killing both of us anyway?"

Viktor shrugged. "Perhaps. But you have family in Louisiana. If you cause problems for us, we can settle the score in creative ways."

Nausea roiled in her gut. That was the second time he'd threatened Hunter's family. She hated the idea that the ripples of this horror could continue, more lives be destroyed. Because Hunter had been loyal to her had risked everything to help her, protect her. No matter what else happened, he was her hero. A chill that went beyond the cold wind burrowed deep into Brianna's bones, and she longed to cuddle close to Hunter's protective warmth. Her heart gave a bittersweet throb as the thug at her elbow shoved her toward the speedboat.

"Get in. We're taking a little trip," Axel groused.

With a worried glance to Hunter, she shuffled across the dock and boarded the watercraft. She knew compliance, stepping into that boat, was as good as stepping up to the gallows. But as long as she and Hunter were still alive, she held to a hope that they could escape. Hunter had never let her down, and she had faith that even now he was working out a plan to rescue them.

* * *

With a gun at his back and his nose bleeding, Hunter followed Brianna into the boat. His brain clicked through scenarios as fast as he could, kicking out the ideas that were too risky for Brianna and those that weren't logistically possible. Keeping his expression as neutral as possible, he continued sorting through their circumstances, their resources, their chances of survival. He didn't like the odds, but he refused to give up. His years in the army had trained him well, and he wasn't about to give up hope of getting Brianna safely home. She had a son to raise, and he intended to see that she got that opportunity.

He shuffled across the speedboat to sit close to her but was jerked back and shoved onto a seat on the opposite side. The motor roared to life as Olaf untied the ropes that tethered the boat in the slip. Soon they were skimming across the water, bouncing on the waves with the icy blast of sea air rushing past them.

They drove for several minutes, farther and farther from shore—and help. Soon their destination became obvious as a small yacht came into view on the horizon. The man who'd driven the SUV steered the speedboat up to the side of the yacht, and a man sporting a soul patch under his bottom lip tossed a rope ladder from the deck of the luxury craft.

The senator climbed up first, then Olaf. The tattooed henchman Brianna had shoved into the cold water by the dock aimed a gun at her. "Your turn. Go."

Her legs trembled visibly as she moved to the ladder. She cast Hunter a side glance that searched his, and he wished he had other options. But while they were outgunned and outmanned, he saw no alternative except to cooperate. As long as they were alive, he still had a chance to save them.

"Go!" Spider jabbed Brianna with the muzzle of his weapon, and Hunter tensed. He narrowed his eyes on their captors, working to suppress the hatred and anger that only served to muddle his thinking. He needed a clear head. Needed to stay alert. When his opportunity to act came, it might be available for only a split second. He had to watch, listen and be prepared to act.

Brianna began climbing the wobbly rope ladder, and Hunter stood without being told and took his position at the base of the ladder, ready to follow her up. He had to stay close to her in order to protect her.

When Brianna reached the deck of the yacht, Olaf seized her arm and dragged her forward, toward the interior cabin. Hunter hustled up the last rungs and vaulted onto the deck. He hurried to tail Brianna, to keep her in his sights.

Moving from sunlight to the dimness of the main cabin, he needed a moment for his eyes to adjust. Before he could see clearly who or what was in the room, he heard a harsh gasp, and a man rasped, "Brianna!"

She jerked her head up, squinting across the cabin in the direction the voice had come. A man Hunter recognized from the cell-phone video as Chris stood in a small kitchenette, his gaze fixed on Brianna.

Despite their grave circumstances, relief and joy flooded her face at the sight of Ben's father. She tugged free of Olaf's grasp and raced across the room. Throwing her arms around the prince's neck, she clung to him as happy tears filled her eyes. "Chris! Oh, thank God you're all right!"

Brianna's affection for Chris was unmistakable and

clearly ran deep. Had seeing Chris again, touching him, brought back memories of their relationship, memories of the love they'd shared?

Hunter's stomach swooped. He'd known Bri and Chris had made a baby together, which spoke to the strength and depth of Brianna's feelings toward him. But seeing them together, knowing that when all was said and done she might go back to Ben's father and pick up where they'd left off…hurt. Jealousy bit hard, and he gritted his back teeth to stanch the green monster.

Chris bent his head to Bri's, laying his cheek against her temple, then burying his face in her hair.

Hunter looked away, scanning the rest of the cabin as his eyes adjusted to the low light. A bald, beefy guard stood with arms crossed in a corner of the cabin, his shrewd eyes assessing the new arrivals. Adding the man who'd let down the ladder for them, Hunter now counted six henchmen with Senator Viktor to his, Brianna and Chris's three. *Olaf, Soul Patch, Baldy, the driver, Spider and Axel. Damn. Not good.* Especially since he'd wager every one of the hulking men had a weapon, even if he hadn't drawn it yet.

"Oh, Brianna, you shouldn't have come," Chris murmured softly, yet loud enough for Hunter to make out his words. "I'm so sorry I got you into this."

She tipped her head back, her face paling with fresh apprehension, and for the first time, Hunter realized Chris hadn't returned her embrace.

"Chris, what—" she started, stepping back and holding him at arm's length.

With the rattle of chains, he showed her that his arms were shackled behind him, and he was chained to a large hasp bolted to the wall.

"Oh, my God! Chris!" she cried.

The man guarding Chris grabbed her from behind and hauled her back.

Hunter seethed at the repeated manhandling of Brianna but swallowed his fury, seeing the value of biding his time and waiting for the right time to make his move.

Olaf stood at the door of the cabin, and Axel moved up behind Hunter to poke a gun in his back.

As Viktor brushed past Hunter and took a seat in the cabin, Brianna cut a sharp glare to her captor. "This is how you treat your king? You said he was unharmed!"

Viktor lifted a palm. Calm. Unconcerned.

"I assure you my cousin is not hurt. For now."

Brianna jerked her back straighter, and Hunter's skin prickled.

"Your *cousin?*" she repeated.

The senator's face was smug. "Oh, did I not mention that earlier? Yes, Prince Cristoff… No, I'm sorry, Your Majesty…" He gave a mocking bow toward Chris. "*King Cristoff* is my cousin. A distant cousin, yes, but I am his closest male relative in the Hamill bloodline." He paused, arching one menacing eyebrow. "Which means if he dies—and any of his heirs with him—I am next in line for the throne of Meridan."

She whipped her gaze back to Chris. "Is this true?"

Chris's face hardened, and he jerked a tight nod. "It is. I only learned this myself in the last few weeks, when I threatened to abdicate my claim on the throne. Just before my father was murdered, and I fled the country to find you, warn you."

"As the next in line to rule, I was more than happy to let you resign and be with your American lover. But of course your father had to be dealt with first."

"So you're behind the coup attempt," Chris said, his tone bitter, and his eyes narrowed in rage on the man who had betrayed him. "Are you the one who murdered my father?"

"Your father was trying to change too much, trying to please the people rather than keeping the monarchy strong."

Chris shook his head. "He was trying to help the people. He was trying to do what was right for the citizens!" His jaw tightened. "Don't pretend this is about anything but your own greed. You want the profits from the natural-gas reserves for yourself."

Victor strode closer to Chris and shoved his nose in his prisoner's face. "They belong to the monarchy. But your father was going to give away millions of dollars in valuable natural-resource rights. Millions of dollars that belong to the ruling family, to my family! He might not care about that money, but I do. The profits from mining the natural-gas reserves will be mine. The current laws will be preserved, and I will return Meridan to its former glory."

"The people want a voice. The citizens should share in the proceeds of resources mined from their land!" Chris returned, his face reddening with anger.

Viktor opened his mouth as if to argue, but closed it again, his expression modulating. Taking a deep breath, he stepped back from Chris and divided a glance between Brianna and Hunter. "Secure them."

The senator's minions rushed forward to do his bidding, and Hunter's pulse jumped. Each of his arms was seized, Soul Patch and Axel flanking him. He struggled against their imprisoning grasp, seeing his chances of escape diminishing quickly. At least if his hands were free, he had a shot at overtaking one of the thugs and fighting his way off the yacht with Brianna.

A shackle was snapped on his wrist, and he battled to keep his other hand free. He head-butted Soul Patch and threw his full body weight against Axel, knocking his opponent off balance.

Across the room, he heard Brianna cry, "No, don't! That's... Ow!"

He jerked his gaze toward her, found her twisting and fighting with Olaf as he yanked a plastic zip tie around her wrists so tightly it cut into her skin. "Brianna!"

He surged forward, trying to reach her, only to be jerked back by the chain already clamped on his left wrist. Undeterred, Hunter swung a leg up and caught Soul Patch in the kidney. The man doubled over but kept a tight grip on the chain clamped to Hunter's wrist. Shifting his weight, Hunter kicked out again. Soul Patch blocked the strike, but Hunter managed to graze the man's hip and send Soul Patch stumbling back a step. Seeing Axel assume a fighting stance, Hunter braced his feet, ready to take on the thug.

He never got the chance. Baldy snaked an arm around Hunter's neck from behind and jerked him back, adding his brute strength to subdue Hunter. The air in his lungs whooshed out as he was slammed to the floor. Baldy wrenched Hunter's arm to an awkward angle and pain shot through his shoulder. The math Hunter had calculated earlier proved insurmountable. He was outnumbered, outmuscled.

"Hunter!" Brianna cried as Baldy and Axel dragged Hunter toward the built-in cabinets that were part of the yacht's interior wall.

He continued to flail against his captors' grips, kicking out at their shins, their knees, anywhere he could strike, unwilling to simply give up. As he struggled, he felt something hard in Axel's jacket pocket poke his side. While he thrashed and fought the men who held his arms, he slipped his fingers into Axel's pocket and snagged the keys they'd taken from him on the dock earlier. He'd have preferred his pocketknife, but he'd take any tool he could get. The army had sharpened his fighting skills and taught him resourcefulness. He curled his hand around the keys and kept his fist low and out of sight.

He continued to kick, drawing the men's attention away from his hands.

"Bind his feet," Baldy ordered, and Soul Patch quickly secured a zip tie around his feet and a second plastic tie from his bound feet to the handle on a low cabinet drawer. With two men holding Hunter, Soul Patch snapped the other end of the short chain to Hunter's free wrist. He felt like a trussed pig waiting to be roasted. Frustration roiled in his gut along with a gnawing sense of having failed Brianna. He'd promised to keep her safe, but if he didn't think of something fast, they would both die. He squeezed his fist tighter and felt the bite of metal against his palm. A set of keys wasn't much, but at least he had a shred of hope.

The plastic strips binding Brianna's wrists were so tight she was losing feeling in her hands. But her hands were of secondary concern to the rough way the senator's henchmen had treated Hunter. She was sick to her stomach with guilt over getting him embroiled in this nightmare. He sat on the floor with his feet bound, his face bloodied and swelling, and his hands chained behind his back. But the expression on his face was pure defiance, and the fire in his eyes said he wasn't done fighting.

"Is this brutality really necessary?" Chris said darkly. "I don't even know this man." He jerked his head toward Hunter. "Release him and Brianna. Your fight is with me!"

Senator Viktor heaved a sigh, as if the circumstances pained him. "Yes, Your Highness. I would much prefer doing this a different way, but you left me no choice. You were supposed to abdicate the throne."

Chris's face hardened. "That was my plan…."

Brianna gasped. So it was true. Chris had hoped to marry her, even if it meant giving up his claim to the throne. Her head spun, and she raised a stunned gaze to Chris.

His eyes softened as he met her glance. "I love you, Brianna. I wanted to be with you. Even before I found out about—"

She gave her head a small, sharp shake and warned him with her eyes not to give anything about Ben away.

Thankfully, Chris realized his near slip and schooled his face. "Before I found out about my father's murder."

Her pulse pounded in her ears. How could he say he loved her when he'd left her without any explanation last winter? She didn't want to have this conversation in front of so many strangers, but the answers she craved taunted her.

"Did I know this? Had I said yes?"

Chris's eyebrows drew together in a frown. "What?"

She licked her lips and cut a quick glance to Senator Viktor, who followed the conversation with a smug grin.

"I was in an accident, and my memories of us are… gone. Most of them anyway."

Chris's face fell, and he shook his head. "But…you're here. You looked for me."

"And aren't I lucky she did?" Viktor gloated.

Chris tore his gaze from her and shot a glare at Viktor. "The point is moot because you murdered my father! *I'm* the king now. I will serve my country and lead them through this crisis." His eyes narrowed on the senator, and he growled, "I will not abandon my people, my duty, my heritage."

On a cursory level, Hunter followed the back-and-forth between Chris and his political rival, but his attention was fixed on the henchmen. He couldn't risk having one of the senator's thugs see what he was doing and sound an alarm. While attention was focused on the argument between Chris and Viktor, Hunter had shifted to a position that allowed him to saw on the plastic zip ties with his keys. He had to go slowly to keep the keys and his shackles from jingling, and the minute progress he was making frustrated him. But one millimeter at a time, he cut the plastic tie.…

Chapter 17

Brianna tensed when Viktor pushed out of his chair and strolled toward Chris. "So Prince Cristoff has gained a conscience, a loyalty to his country and his inherited duty to the throne. How noble. But as you say, the point is moot. Because you're going to die today."

Chris stiffened, his head held high and his glare full of spite. "You'll be hanged for treason, Viktor. Make no mistake."

"Oh, not I. I'll take the throne. Because the American authorities will call your death the result of a lovers' spat. This is why we brought Mr. Mansfield along rather than dispose of him earlier. You see, Mr. Mansfield has military experience, including explosives."

In her peripheral vision, Brianna noticed Hunter jerk his head up. She glanced at him, and the shock and dread on his face bore out the truth of what the senator was saying. Nausea swirled in her gut. What did Hunter suspect?

"The American police will find our new king and his girlfriend were victims of a jealous man with deadly skills," Viktor continued, but Brianna kept her focus on Hunter. He'd changed position, now kneeling with his back to the wall. When the senator turned to stalk toward Chris, Hunter's arms moved slightly behind his back. Brianna's pulse leaped. Had he found a way to get loose from his handcuffs?

The henchmen all watched Senator Viktor's grandstanding and Chris's reaction to Viktor's threats, but if any of the guards glanced in Hunter's direction, Hunter's slight movement stilled.

He *was* working on escape! She was sure of it. Her breath caught in her lungs. She had to keep the senator and his thugs distracted, buy Hunter time to act.

"What are you threatening? Hunter's not my boyfriend. He has no part of this!"

"Oh, but he does now. The three of you will die in a terrible boating tragedy. A revenge killing," Viktor said and waved a hand toward his head henchman. "Olaf, you may set the timer. Gale, Thom, prepare the boat." He hitched his head toward the door, and the man with the soul patch and the thug with the spider tattoo headed out.

Olaf walk to the small galley adjoining the main cabin and opened a cabinet. Inside, a small digital clock and a block that looked like grayish clay sat in the shadowed recesses, attached to an elaborate tangle of wires.

A chill curled through Brianna's blood as she remembered action movies where a similar gray block was referred to as C-4, a powerful explosive.

Mr. Mansfield has military experience, including ex-

plosives. Her heart sank, heavy and full of fear and regret. Not only did the senator plan to blow them up, he planned to frame Hunter for the crime. As if assassination wasn't enough, the hateful man intended to ruin Hunter's good name in the process. Indignation raged in her on Hunter's behalf.

Olaf flipped a switch, and the timer on the bomb started counting down from fifteen minutes. Enough time for Viktor and his men to get away. But was it enough time for her, Hunter and Chris to free themselves from the shackles and get off the boat?

Chris paled as he watched Olaf step back from the bomb, then lunged for Viktor, only to be brought up short by his chains. "You won't get away with this. I have allies back home who will see to that! The Hamill family line will not be removed from power!"

Brianna shot a discreet glance toward Hunter. Was his escape plan working? How much more time did he need?

Relief curled through Hunter when the zip tie around his feet finally broke. Gritting his back teeth, he began working the chain binding his wrists over his heels, down his soles. Inch by inch he worked his hands around his feet to his front....

"Ah, yes." Viktor faced Brianna, and she yanked her focus back to the senator. "We heard the rumors that your mysterious American lover was pregnant, that our new king could have a bastard heir. And our job of securing the throne for me became a bit more complicated. But once we found Ms. Coleman, we had no trouble guessing where she'd hidden your heir. When we finish here, my men will return to Louisiana and take care of your son, eliminating any threat that he'll try to steal the throne from me."

Horror punched Brianna's gut. "No! Leave my baby alone! No one but us knows that he is Cristoff's son. Let him live. Please, let him grow up. No one else needs to ever know who his father is or about his claim to the throne."

"I wish I could oblige, Miss Coleman. I'm not happy about killing a little baby. But when you and Cristoff disappear together, there will be questions. It will be investigated. Someone could test your baby's DNA, and I can't leave any loose ends."

"There's a special place in hell for people like you," Chris snarled.

Tears stung Brianna's eyes. She prayed that Grant would keep Ben safe. If only they could warn Grant about Viktor's men...

And when she thought of Ben losing both his parents, her heart wrenched. She knew the pain of losing both a mother and father. Biting her bottom lip, her pulse racing, she glanced at the bomb timer. The counter was down to 13:46.

Viktor followed the direction of her glance and pulled a crooked grin. "You're right. Time's wasting. Men..." He flicked a hand toward the door, and without a backward glance, Viktor headed for the deck...past Hunter.

Springing to his feet, Hunter threw his chained hands over Viktor's head and pulled the chain tight against the man's throat.

Olaf drew his weapon and aimed at Hunter, but with lightning-quick reflexes, Chris swung a leg up. He kicked the gun from Olaf's hand, and the weapon skittered across the floor, stopping a few feet from where

Brianna was chained. Seeing her opportunity, she lay down on the floor and stretched her bound hands as far as she could, but the pistol still lay inches from her fingers. She clenched her teeth, growling her frustration.

The bald thug retrieved Olaf's pistol, then hurried to lend his muscle to Axel, who fought to free Viktor from Hunter's choke hold. The bald man cracked his elbow against Hunter's head, and Brianna gasped in horror. But though Hunter's knees wobbled and his face contorted in pain, his grip kept the chain taut across Viktor's throat.

A grunt called her attention across the room as Olaf whirled toward Chris and swung his arm in an upward arc. Olaf's hand caught Chris under the jaw and sent him stumbling backward. When he recovered, Chris ducked his head and lunged at Olaf. Though hampered by his shackles, Chris managed to catch Olaf low in the gut and knocked his opponent back.

Across the room, Hunter released Viktor and the older man slumped to the floor. Unconscious? Dead? Axel dropped to his knees beside the senator to render his boss aid, while the bald man shoved Hunter back against the wall and held him pinned with a meaty hand around Hunter's neck.

Adrenaline flooded Brianna's blood as she divided her gaze between the two battles. She had to do something, had to help in some way. But what? Her hands were bound, her leg chained. But Hunter had gotten his legs free. Maybe she could…

She bent her head and started gnawing the plastic ties at her wrists. *Please, please,* she prayed. *Help us!*

The bomb timer continued counting down. 9:21, 9:20, 9:19…

While she chewed at the plastic strip with her teeth,

she cut a wary gaze to the scuffle between Olaf and Chris. Olaf had stepped back from the fight and glared at Chris, his chest heaving from exertion. Moving across the room with long strides, Olaf seized his pistol from the bald man and stalked back to Chris.

The fine hair on the back of her neck rose. No!

Chris was squatting, his head down, wiggling his hands under his feet to bring his arms in front of him.

"Chris!" she screamed as Olaf raised the weapon.

Again, Chris stunned both her and his opponent with flash reflexes. In what seemed one smooth, controlled move, he surged to his feet, ramming the crown of his head against the man's pistol grip. Olaf's arm was knocked upward. The gun fired, but the bullet whizzed harmlessly into the ceiling.

As Olaf stepped back to take aim again, Chris swung his chained hands into Olaf's chin and followed with a downward swipe across the thug's gun hand. The gun clattered to the floor, and before Olaf could stoop to pick it up, Chris kicked it. To Brianna.

Her breath hitched as she scrambled to gather the gun with her cinched hands. Awkward as it was, she grabbed the weapon but couldn't get a grip that allowed her to aim or fire.

She glanced toward Hunter just in time to see him raise his knee into the bald man's groin. Axel had dragged the senator's limp body outside onto the deck and rushed back into the cabin, sending an assessing gaze around the confined space. His gaze went to the cabinet where the bomb ticked down.

Brianna glanced that direction, as well—7:39 and counting. A spurt of fear slithered through her. If she, Hunter and Chris didn't get free, didn't stop the timer, it wouldn't matter if they'd overpowered the senator's thugs. Olaf shook off Chris's last strike and turned, storming toward her. Her pulse scampered. There was no way she could keep Olaf from overpowering her and wrenching the weapon from her.

"Chris!" She flung the gun back to Chris, over Olaf's head, in a deadly game of keep-away. Ben's father stretched his chained hands out but fumbled the weapon. It fired as it bumped to the floor, and Chris howled in pain.

As Olaf lunged for the weapon on the floor, Chris snagged the gun up and fired. Olaf clutched his chest. Fell. A crimson stain spread on his chest.

Chris re-aimed the gun toward Axel, who flung himself back out the cabin door. Chris's shot pocked the doorframe, splintering the wood. The gunfire so close to his head drew the attention of the bald man, who was taking Hunter on fist to fist. In the split second of his opponent's distraction, Hunter drove his elbow into the bald man's ribs and reared back so that his head smashed the man's nose.

Staggering back, the bald man picked up a large, jagged-edged shard of wood from the door. Hunter was bent at the waist, gasping for a breath, when the bald man surged toward him with the sharp shard of wood raised.

"Hunter, look out!" Brianna screamed.

Hunter twisted, ducked.

And another ear-shattering gun blast echoed in the small cabin. The bald man's head snapped back, a large hole in his face.

Brianna whipped her head toward Chris, who still held the smoking pistol.

From out on deck, she heard the voices of the other men coming back. Reinforcements. Damn it!

But in a surprise move, Axel shouted something in a foreign language and fled. The sound of the speedboat motor revving filtered up from the water, then faded as the surviving henchmen saved themselves. And why not retreat? she thought glumly, glancing at the bomb timer.

5:01. And they were still chained to the yacht.

Chapter 18

Hunter groaned and slid to the floor, holding his aching ribs. His entire body hurt, but at least he was alive. "Brianna?" he croaked. "Are you all right?"

"Y-yes," she said, her voice full of tears.

He glanced at the dead man at his feet, then to Chris. "Nice shot. Thanks."

The prince bobbed a nod, then slumped to the floor as well, clutching his foot, which bled profusely.

"Hunter."

He turned his gaze back to Brianna, and she pointed across the room. "The C-4!"

Damn it. How could he have forgotten *that*? The timer said they had just under five minutes to get free and get off the boat. Or defuse the bomb. His army training gave him the know-how but...

He raised his chained hands, which were bloodied, shaking and starting to swell and stiffen. With his fine motor skills compromised, he was as likely to set the bomb off as defuse it. "We have to get off the boat," he said, thinking aloud.

Cristoff snorted wryly. "Good idea." He raised his chained hands. "How?"

Hunter's feet were free even if his hands weren't. He was Brianna's and Chris's best chance of getting free. He tried to push to his feet, but as his adrenaline level receded, his level of hurt grew. Baldy and Axel had done a number on him. As he shifted to stand, an agonizing pain shot through his ribs. He dropped back to the floor, harder than he intended, and fresh lightning bolts cracked in his skull. He bit out a curse and ground his teeth together. A sheen of sweat rose on his skin. He hurt so badly he thought he might vomit.

"Hunter?"

Brianna's worried voice reached him through his fog of misery. He had to marshal his strength, block the pain somehow, at least until he could get Bri safely away from the yacht. He peered across the cabin, squinting as pain blurred his vision. The bomb timer read 3:47.

Hunter's injuries were worse than Brianna had feared. He didn't even appear fully coherent. If they were going to survive, she needed to shove her fear aside and think. Swallowing the taste of bile that rose in her throat, she forced her brain to settle, to focus. Her first task was to get her hands free. She bit harder on the plastic strips, desperate to get the bindings off.

"Brianna, pull your arms against your chest…as hard as you can."

She glanced across the room at Chris, who was watching her vain attempts to gnaw free.

"What?"

"You have to break the straps. Pull both arms straight back, and jerk your wrists apart. You can snap the ties."

"No...she's not strong enough." Hunter held out a set of keys. "Saw them off. With these."

"We don't have time for that!" Chris argued. "One quick thrust, and they'll be off. Trust me, Brianna!"

She glanced at Hunter, wavering. What did she do? Could she even reach the keys Hunter was offering?

"At least try my way," Chris pleaded. "We're running out of time!"

His reminder of the literal ticking time bomb sent a spurt of tingling fear through her. Gritting her teeth and using the fear-induced adrenaline, Brianna held her bent arms in front of her as Chris demonstrated, then pulled her wrists to her chest in a quick, hard yank. Though the motion hurt like hell for a second, the ties snapped, freeing her hands. She gave a glad cry and rubbed feeling into her numb hands. "It worked!"

The joy over her small victory was short-lived. After all, her feet were still chained to the wall.

"Any thoughts on getting out of the chains?" she asked, sharing a look between Chris and Hunter.

Hunter gave her a bleary-eyed look, then rolled to his hands and knees and threw up. Her pulse spiked seeing that he had blood in his vomit.

Chris held his bleeding foot and grimaced. "Find the key?"

She huffed. "Brilliant."

Taking another calming breath, she closed her eyes. When Olaf had chained her feet, what had he done with the key? She exhaled slowly, conjuring the memory. *His pants pocket.*

Olaf's dead body lay sprawled and leaking blood in the space between her and Chris. Again she stretched out on the floor and reached as far as she could. She could touch Olaf's shoe, the cuff of his pants…

She strained against the metal shackle on her ankle, ignoring the bite as it dug into her skin. Her fingers inched closer to his pocket as she tugged on the leg of his pants. Finally she hooked a finger into his pocket, then another, until she had a better grip on the pants. Tugging with every ounce of her strength, she pulled at the pocket. If she couldn't drag Olaf's body closer, maybe she could rip the pants. In the end, she managed a combination. She dragged Olaf's legs a couple of inches closer, but the seam of the pocket also tore. With a clink, a small silver key tumbled out onto the floor. Tears of relief filled her eyes, and she had to blink them back as she fumbled to grab the key.

"I got it!" she cried when her fingers closed around the means of their escape. She cut a glance to the timer on the bomb as she shimmied back across the floor. 2:28.

Please, God, help me work fast! Help me get Hunter and Chris away from the boat!

With trembling fingers, she keyed open the cuffs around her ankles. Kicking them off, she clambered to her feet. Knowing she'd likely need Chris's help to drag Hunter to safety, she raced to him first and unlocked the cuffs on his wrists. The chains fell away and dangled from the hasp on the counter.

"Can you walk?" she asked, turning her attention to his injured foot.

"If not, I'll hop. Go!"

Glancing at the bomb timer—now down to 1:55—

she said, "You be our clock. Keep a countdown in your head."

He nodded and started limping toward the door as she hurried over to Hunter.

Her gut knotted. Hunter was barely conscious. The senator's henchmen had beaten him severely, and the blood he'd thrown up suggested internal injuries. When they jumped into the ocean, how was Hunter supposed to tread water, much less swim? And swim they must to get far enough from the yacht when it blew up.

"Come on, Hunter. I've got you. Can you get your legs under you?" She shoved a shoulder under his armpit and lifted.

When he tried to stand, his face blanched, and he moaned in agony. He waved her off and slumped back onto the floor. "Save yourself. Leave me."

"Like hell I will." She turned to Chris as he hobbled by. "Get his other arm. We need to get him up."

Chris looked skeptical but moved into place. "One twenty-seven, one twenty-six…" he counted aloud.

With Chris under Hunter's other arm and bracing his weight on his good foot and Brianna channeling the adrenaline swirling through her, they hoisted Hunter to his feet. He swayed but stayed upright with Chris and Brianna's help. Taking small, shuffling steps, she guided Hunter from the yacht's cabin out to the deck.

As they inched toward the railing, one painstaking step at a time, she put her brain on fast-forward. What else would they need in the water? How would they be rescued? Was there anything she'd need before the boat blew sky-high?

Some floatation device. A way to call help. Maybe a

gun, in case Axel and the others returned to finish the job they'd started. Did she have time to get those things?

She cast her gaze around the deck in a sweeping glance as they staggered along, and she spotted the life-preserver ring mounted on the outside wall of the cabin. Below it in a box was a fire extinguisher and a flare gun. Bingo.

They reached the side of the yacht and helped Hunter sit on the bench seat along the railing. Until she could be in the water with Hunter to help buoy him, he needed to stay on the deck. Chris was another matter. "Time?"

"Forty-three seconds."

A shudder raced through her. "Go! Get in the water!"

"But you—"

"We're coming. But you have a country to lead. And if I don't make it, our son will need you." She pointed to the water, her face pleading, and shouted, "Go!"

Clearly the idea of leaving her, saving himself before her, bothered Chris, but to his credit, he didn't waste precious time arguing. Frowning, he gave a tight nod, then kissed her mouth quick and hard. "Thirty-six seconds. Hurry!"

With that he climbed on the bench seat, swung a leg over the side of the yacht and dived into the water.

"Wait here," she told Hunter, realizing how stupid it sounded as she dashed back across the deck. Where would he go?

She grabbed the life preserver and attached rope, then fumbled the glass box below it open. The fire extinguisher was no help she could imagine at this point, but she grabbed the flare gun.

Loading a flare, she fired it into the air as she rushed back to the other side of the deck. Already Hunter was struggling to crawl over the railing, grunting and gritting his teeth, clearly in tremendous pain.

"Twenty-five seconds!" Chris called from the water.

She tossed the life preserver into the water, then stuck her shoulder under Hunter's arm again. "I know this will hurt. I'm sorry."

"Do it," he said through clenched teeth.

She shoved him up, and he struggled to swing his legs over the rail. Pushing off, he flopped more than dived into the water.

Nineteen...eighteen...seventeen, she counted in her head as she climbed up and clambered over the railing.

Chris had swum a good distance away from the yacht already and watched her with a tense face. "Hurry, Brianna!"

Gulping a deep breath, she jumped into the water. The cold Atlantic jolted her system, and she barely managed *not* to suck in a gasp of shock and a lungful of salt water with it. As she broke the surface, she quickly scanned the waves around her. Hunter was a few feet to her left, struggling to keep his head above the waves. "Hunter!"

She spotted the life preserver, bobbing a few yards in the opposite direction, and swam toward it. She snagged the rope and turned to swim the other way.

"Bri, get away from the yacht! Twelve seconds!" Chris yelled.

Her chest clenched. Her dunk in the frigid water sent a renewed spurt of energy through her. "Not without Hunter!"

She dug her arms into the water and pulled against the waves. Kicking as hard as she could, she glided through the water to Hunter in a few strokes.

In her head she heard a gruff male voice shouting at

her, *No wasted strokes, Coleman! Pull the water! Kick harder!*

When she reached Hunter, he'd fought his aches and injuries enough to break the surface and gasp for a breath.

"Grab hold and don't let go!" She flipped the life preserver over his head, then wrapped the rope under his arms and threaded the end through the center of the life preserver.

"Brianna!" Chris sounded panicked. "Six, five…"

She pulled hard on the water and poured every ounce of her strength into kicking her legs and swimming away from the yacht. She took up the count in her head as she tugged Hunter with her. Four…stroke, kick. Three… stroke, kick…

Suddenly Chris was beside her, tugging on the life-preserver ring, as well. His powerful arms helped propel Hunter and the life preserver faster, allowed Brianna's efforts to go farther.

Two…

"Under!" Chris shouted.

Brianna released the ropes she clung to and dived under the waves. As she sank, she fisted her hand in Hunter's shirt and tugged him down, beneath the surface.

Boom!

Even beneath the ocean water, the concussion, the noise, the shock of the explosion rocked Brianna to the core. The pressure waves reverberated in her chest and made her ears pop.

Around them, chunks of fiery debris splashed into the ocean and sizzled as they were extinguished. When she thought the worst of the fallout was over, she kicked hard, pulling Hunter to the surface with her.

He shouted in agony as he fought his pain to grab the life preserver again and loop his arm through it.

Brianna searched the area around her, waiting for Chris to resurface. Chunks of splintered fiberglass, smoldering wood and broken furniture bobbed around her. But not Chris. Her heart lurched. "Chris!" She coughed as she took in a mouthful of seawater.

The sound of splashing called her attention to a large piece of wood decking to her right. A hand floundered toward the wood, then Chris's head appeared, and as he seized the floating debris, he gasped for a breath. "Bri?"

"Over here! Are you all right?"

He swiped water from his face and winced. "Yes. It's difficult to tread water with my injured foot, but…I'm making it. You?"

She grabbed a nondescript scrap of fiberglass, probably a piece of the destroyed yacht's hull, as it floated by and threw her arm over it. "Shaken, but safe. I'm worried about Hunter, though."

"I'm…okay," Hunter rasped, coughing on some water after he spoke.

"Bull. You're in pain, and the movement required to stay afloat has to be torture." Clinging to her debris, she kicked to stay close to Hunter. She wrapped the rope from the life preserver around her hand so he wouldn't drift too far.

"Better than…blowing up." He tried to smile, but it was more of a grimace. "The cold water…is helping numb…the pain."

Working as gently as she could, she fed the rope under his arms again, wrapped it through the life preserver, then knotted the ends. If Hunter did pass out, she prayed the rope would keep him from sinking.

Chris had paddled closer and panted for a breath as he turned his gaze toward the remains of the yacht. A tall plume of smoke billowed into the air even as the shards of the ravaged hull took on water and sank into the Atlantic. "Hopefully, if the authorities didn't see your flare, they'll come investigate the explosion and smoke."

Brianna's teeth chattered. "How long do we have… b-before hypothermia sets in?"

"Good question," Chris said. "And will the rescue teams get here before sharks smell the blood I'm trailing?"

Brianna's pulse skipped. She'd almost forgotten Chris's gaping wound. In the water, it wouldn't clot. He could bleed out if help didn't arrive soon.

Had they escaped Viktor's henchmen and the C-4 explosion only to drown in the icy Atlantic? She could tread water and cling to the floating debris for as long as it took, but Hunter and Chris were losing blood, their strength fading. They'd fought valiantly to save her life, and now she had to find a way to keep the men she loved alive until help came.

Chapter 19

Feeling a warm hand on his cheek, Hunter cracked his eyes open and blinked away the blur of sleep to focus on the lovely face beside him. "Bri?"

He frowned as the strange room came into focus, and he needed a moment for the events of the past hour—or had it been longer?—to come back to him. Pain. Cold. An explosion. Then a Coast Guard patrol, ambulance ride, warming blankets and CT scans. The muted sounds of the hospital emergency room drifted in from the hallway, confirming the foggy memories.

"Sorry to wake you," Brianna said, "but I have someone on the phone who is quite worried about you and just wants to hear your voice."

She held a cell phone to his ear, and he angled his head toward it. "H'lo."

"Hunter! Sweetheart, are you okay?" his mother said. "Don't lie to me! What did the doctors say?"

"I'm all right. Sore as hell. Tired." His head swam, even though he hadn't moved, and he closed his eyes for a moment. "Haven't talked to the doctor."

"Oh, honey…your dad and I are coming up there tonight."

"No, Mom, you don't—"

"We're coming. Don't argue. And put Brianna back on the line. I want to know what the doctor said."

He opened one eye to look at Bri. She wore a hospital gown, as he did, and had a blanket draped around her shoulders. "She wants you now."

Brianna nodded and, clutching the blanket closed at her neck with one hand, put the phone to her ear. "Yes, ma'am? I did."

Hunter fought the pull of whatever painkiller was being fed into his body through the IV line, trying to stay awake long enough to hear what Brianna told his mother.

"He has a couple of cracked ribs, but the CT scan didn't show any serious internal injuries. The doctor said the blood I saw him throw up was likely some he'd swallowed because of his broken nose. We all had mild hypothermia, but the Coast Guard saw the explosion and got to us pretty quickly." She paused to listen for a moment. "Chris is in surgery to repair the damage to his foot. He lost a lot of blood from the gunshot wound, and they'll have to keep him for a few days to monitor him." Brianna nodded. "Yes, ma'am, I gave a statement to the police, and Hunter will have to do the same later, when he's up to it. I think someone at the Cape Cod P.D. called the U.S. State Department, because I was told officials, including a security detail, are en route from Meridan, even now."

A nurse stuck her head in the room and hesitated when she saw Brianna on the phone.

"Yes, they're keeping Hunter for a day or so for observation. Just to be sure they didn't miss something." Brianna sent the nurse a quizzical glance, and the woman in pink scrubs pointed to the hall, indicating someone was outside. "Yes, ma'am. I need to go. The nurse needs to talk to me."

When Brianna lowered the phone, the nurse said, "You asked to be told when Chris Hamill got out of surgery? He's done, and they'll be taking him upstairs to a room soon if you want to see him."

Brianna cast a guilty-looking side glance to Hunter. "I—"

"Go," he croaked. "I'm 'kay. Gonna sleep."

Furrowing her brow, Brianna bent to kiss his cheek. "I'll check on you again in a bit."

She turned and followed the nurse out, leaving Hunter alone in the stark exam room. He sighed. His ribs ached, his muscles were stiff, his nose throbbed and he felt cold to the bone. But his worst pain had nothing to do with his physical ailments and everything to do with the choice he knew Brianna would make in the next couple of days.

Back in her own clothes after one of the E.R. nurses had them dried in the hospital laundry, Brianna hustled upstairs to see Chris. She got to spend only a couple of minutes with Chris before he, too, was drifting off to sleep, the remnant anesthesia tugging at him. She and Chris had a lot to talk about, but the conversation was one that should wait until he had all his faculties back.

As she left Chris's hospital room, a man in a dark suit approached her. "Miss Coleman?"

The man's foreign accent sent a hair-trigger shot of anxiety through her. She took a step back, prepared to run, to scream for help. The man held up a badge, then stowed it in the breast pocket of his jacket. "My name is Jorge Locke. I'm head of security for the Meridanian embassy in Washington."

She remained leery but shook his hand when he offered it.

"I have permission from the local authorities to interview you regarding what happened today with Senator Viktor."

She sighed. "I'm rather tired. Can't you just get a copy of the transcript of my statement to the local police?"

"I will. But I have questions of my own." He smiled and put his hands in his pockets. "They will keep until you are better rested."

She nodded. "Good. Thank you."

He took a few steps toward Chris's room, and a prickle of alarm and protectiveness spun through her. The local police, in cooperation with the FBI, had posted guards at Chris's door to protect him until his personal entourage from Meridan arrived. Jorge Locke flashed his credentials to the guards and received permission to enter Chris's room.

Brianna hesitated. How did she know she could trust this man? What if he—

"By the way," Locke said, turning back to her, "based on the description you gave the police of the men with the senator, we were able to identify them and flag their passports with Interpol."

She straightened, her pulse picking up.

"I just talked to our ambassador," he continued, "who said the FBI detained the three men who escaped the explosion earlier today when they tried to board a plane at Logan International Airport. They are in FBI custody and will face multiple felony charges both here in the United States and in Meridan."

She released the breath she held, feeling a coil of tension in her loosen. "That's a relief."

He stepped close to her again and touched her arm. "This has been an upsetting and difficult time for you, I'm sure."

She grunted. "You could say that."

"But it's over. With Senator Viktor dead and the last of his accomplices in custody, King Cristoff recovered safely and returning to the throne, the danger to you and your son has passed."

Hope fluttered in her chest. She wanted to believe that. "You're sure? The coup against the royal family—"

"Was never as widespread as the media portrayed it to be. Senator Viktor was behind the reports given to the media to incite fear and doubt among the people of Meridan. So that he could appear all the more the hero for quelling the threat when he took power."

"But with Chris…King Cristoff," she corrected herself, "taking the throne, peace is restored and all is well?"

Locke flattened a hand against his chest. "Meridan is not without naysayers, but on the whole, yes. When Cristoff is able to travel, he will be safe to return home."

Which meant Ben was safe, as well.

She released the knot of breath in her lungs. Finally some good news after weeks of worry and looking over her shoulder. She could finally move forward. But to what?

With both Hunter and Chris sleeping off their painkillers and hypothermia, she had time to think. She had decisions to make.

She spent some time outside, where the sun was setting and the moon crept higher in a clear sky. Her stomach rumbled, and she realized it had been hours since she'd eaten her blueberry muffin.

As she walked down the hall toward the cafeteria, a directional sign caught her attention. Chapel.

If ever she needed guidance and direction, it was now. She followed the arrow until she found the room with stained glass and religious decor, and she took a seat on one of the pews near the front. Bowing her head, she said a few thank-yous that she, Hunter and Chris were safe. She asked for healing for Hunter and Chris and protection for Ben. Taking a deep breath, she added, "Help me know what to do. I loved Chris once. I still do in many ways. He's Ben's father. But I love Hunter, too."

She heard the door at the back of the chapel open and glanced over her shoulder. Then blinked her surprise. "Mrs. Mansfield?"

Julia Mansfield glanced in her direction, and a smile brightened her face. "Brianna. Hi!"

Brianna rose to greet Hunter's mother with a hug. "How long have you been here?"

"About five minutes. We were on our way to the elevator when I saw the chapel. Seeing as God saw fit to spare my baby boy's life today, I thought I'd stop long enough to say thank-you."

Brianna nodded. "Same here. That and…well, I have important decisions to make, and I thought maybe I'd see things more clearly if I prayed about it."

Julia smiled and touched the cross charm on her necklace. "It's always worked for me." She tipped her head.

"Would these decisions you're making have anything to do with my son?"

Brianna glanced down at her hands briefly. "Yes. And my son. And my son's father."

Julia raised her brow and nodded. "I see." She squeezed Brianna's arm and added, "Speaking of your son, he's right outside with Stan."

Brianna gasped her delight. "He is?"

"We knew you'd be eager to see him, so…"

Brianna gave Julia another quick hug, then hurried toward the door.

"And, Brianna?"

She stopped and glanced back at Hunter's mother. "Once you cut through all the clutter of guilt and worry and other people's expectations, God will speak to your heart, and you'll know exactly what you need to do."

Warmth filled her chest, an appreciation for the motherly concern and advice. Having lost her own mother so early in her life, she hadn't had anyone there to comfort her and advise her in matters of the heart.

The delegation from Meridan had arrived. That was more than obvious as Brianna stepped off the elevator and was greeted immediately by armed guards. Jorge Locke spotted her and waved her past the guards. The man gave Ben a curious look, then a smile as she passed, and she wondered what, if anything, Chris had told him about Ben.

She knocked on Chris's door and waited to be invited in. She held Ben close to her chest, her heart beating a nervous rhythm against her ribs as she approached Chris's bedside.

His gaze went immediately to the bundle in her arms, and he sat straighter in his bed, his expression eager.

Brianna placed Ben in his father's arms, her throat catching as she said, "Ben, this is your daddy. Chris, this is our son. I named him Benjamin."

Chris's eyes were wet as he stared at his son, traced the baby's nose with a finger and unwrapped him to look at Ben's feet and tiny hands. When he glanced up at her, he smiled in awe. "He's beautiful. Perfect."

She laughed and nodded. "I know. Right?"

"Why Benjamin? Not that I don't like it…" he added quickly. "I do. I just wondered. Is it a family name?"

She bit her bottom lip. "It's Hunter's middle name."

Chris's face sobered. "Hunter's?"

She nodded.

He studied her face, his brow beetling. "So, what is his story? Who is he to you?"

A sweetness filled her chest when she thought of all Hunter had done for her, all he'd come to mean to her. She explained to Chris how Hunter had helped her at the car accident, how he'd stood by her through Ben's birth and the days since. The sacrifices he'd made, the risks he'd taken, the love he'd shown Ben.

When she was finished, Chris was silent. He stared at Ben, stroking his son's cheek and ruminating over all she'd said. Finally he sighed, and without looking at her he asked, "Are you in love with him?"

Her pulse quickened. How did she express her feelings toward Hunter? She owed Chris the truth, but she hated the idea that either he or Hunter would be hurt going forward. She was caught between two men she cared for. What was more, she had a son to consider. What was best for Ben?

Chris was staring at her, waiting for an answer. She swallowed hard. "Chris, try to understand. I didn't have any memory of us. Not until a couple of days ago. He's been so good to me, so helpful with Ben, and he's a good man with a good heart who—"

"Is that a yes?"

Her chest ached. "It is." He frowned, and she hastened to add, "But I know I loved you once, too. I still do in many ways. And I want to do what's right for our son."

"And what is that?"

She sighed and shook her head. "You tell me. What do the laws of Meridan say about Ben's future? What will be required of him as your heir?"

Chris's face hardened, his eyes troubled. "Forget the law for a moment. I want you, both of you, in my life. But what do you want?"

At that moment, Ben yawned and stretched his tiny arms over his head. The lines in Chris's face eased as he beamed at their son, chuckled at the sweetness of his heir's sleepy wiggling, smacking lips and birdlike peeps. The awe and love in Chris's face both warmed Brianna's heart and broke it. How could she deny a father the place in his son's life he deserved? How could she steal Ben's chance to live a privileged life, to rule the country of his forefathers?

She cared for Chris, had loved him once. In time, she could love him again....

Hunter pushed his IV stand down the hall, moving slowly, gritting his teeth against the ache of his ribs. He'd urged his parents to go get dinner, told them he wanted to nap, when in truth he wanted a chance to talk to Cristoff alone. Man to man. He had to know Brianna would be in good hands with the prince before he could walk away.

He was stopped at the end of the corridor of the wing where Cristoff was recovering from his surgery. He told the guards who he was, was frisked and then waved through by a man who checked his name against a list on a clipboard. The door to Cristoff's room was flanked by two more guards, who eyed him darkly as he pushed open the door that stood slightly ajar.

The tinkle of Brianna's laugh stopped him. The happy sound twined with a lower chuckle, a soft murmur. Silently, Hunter peered around the door to the bed where Cristoff and Brianna sat. The prince had Ben in his arms, and the man's face glowed with affection the way his brothers' had when they held their daughters. Parental love.

But it was the warm smile on Brianna's face that stopped him, that made his heart contract and a knot of loss tie his gut. She beamed as she watched Cristoff with their son. The three of them were a family. A unit. And when Ben squawked and his parents laughed together, Hunter saw the truth like handwriting on the wall. Brianna had a destiny that didn't involve a construction foreman from Lagniappe, Louisiana.

She had the chance to live the fairy tale every little girl dreamed. A handsome prince. A castle in a foreign kingdom. A happy family. Children. Wealth. Power.

Who was he to stand in the way of all of that? With a heavy, searing pain in his chest that had nothing to do with his cracked ribs, Hunter backed quietly out into the corridor and headed back to his room. In the morning he would be discharged, and he'd go back home with his

parents, back to the family business, back to his bachelor life. And begin healing his broken heart.

Muscles aching, Brianna woke the next morning on
the fold-out chair next to Chris's hospital bed. His staff
had used their sway to have a bassinet from the newborn nursery and a supply of diapers brought into Chris's
room so that Ben could stay with his parents.

Hearing softly whispered endearments, she sat up,
rubbing her eyes, and smiled when she spotted Chris,
sitting on the edge of his bed and leaning over Ben's
bassinet, cooing to his son.

Chris's love for Ben was obvious, and as more and
more memories of the time she'd spent with the Meridanian prince last winter came back to her, she was more
certain he'd be a good father to Ben.

She and Chris had stayed up late talking about the
past, about Meridan, about what would happen between
them going forward. About how they would raise Ben.
And she'd made the tough choice about her own future.

She'd gone to Hunter's room as soon as she'd made
her decision, to tell him what she'd realized when she'd
searched her heart. But he'd been asleep. After the trau-
matic and draining day he'd endured, she'd chosen to
let him sleep.

Knowing he was being discharged this morning, that
he'd be leaving for Lagniappe soon with his parents,
however, Brianna felt an urgency now to try again to
see him before he left. Leaving Ben with his father and
the royal guards, she hurried down the hall to the wing
where Hunter's room was. She arrived just as Hunter
was moving stiffly from his bed into a wheelchair to
leave the hospital.

"Brianna! Good morning," Julia Mansfield said brightly when she noticed Brianna standing in the door. "We were just on our way down to see you and say goodbye."

Hunter glanced up, his expression inscrutable. He flicked her a tight smile that didn't reach his eyes, and Brianna's stomach swirled anxiously.

"We're on the eleven-o'clock flight back to Louisiana," Julia said. "I'm sure you could still get a ticket if you wanted to come with us."

Brianna heard the hope, the unspoken question in Julia's voice. The same query was in Hunter's eyes as the family awaited her response.

"Oh, um…no. I'm staying here. I…" She wiped her sweaty palms on her pants. "Can I have a minute alone with Hunter before you go?"

Julia cast her son a worried glance, and Hunter's jaw tightened.

"It's okay, Mom. I'll be there in a minute." He sat straighter in the wheelchair and waited until the nurse and his parents had left before raising his gaze to Brianna. "So you've decided to stay with Chris." A statement, not a question.

"Once he's discharged, we'll go to my parents' beach house for a couple of weeks. He deserves some time out of the public eye to get to know his son before returning to Meridan."

Hunter nodded, his mouth grim. "Sure. Good idea." He took a deep breath, his nose flaring as he turned his face toward the window. "It's what's best for Ben… and you."

Brianna's pulse tapped an anxious rhythm, uneasy with Hunter's dark mood. "Are you all right? You seem…upset."

He scoffed and sent her another forced tight smile. "I'll be fine. I knew, deep down, it would come to this."

"Come to what?" She sat on the bed and tipped her head, her heart drumming a staccato beat.

"You and the prince. Ben. You belong together. You're a family. I understand."

She swallowed hard and took his hand. "I don't think you do. When Chris goes back to Meridan…I'm not going with him. Ben and I are going home to Louisiana."

Hunter jerked his head around, his gaze crashing into hers. "What?"

She turned his hand over and laced her fingers with his. "Chris and I spent a long time last night talking. About Ben. About where our relationship stood, where it might go." She squeezed his hand. "About you."

His eyebrows rose. "Me?"

"Yes, you. He wanted to know what kind of man you were. He wanted to know more about the man who'd helped protect his son."

A little of the darkness lifted from his expression. "What did you tell him?"

"I told him that you were a man of integrity, of courage and of compassion. I said that you'd been there when Ben needed you, that you'd sacrificed for Ben and shown him love, that you'd put his needs over your own and had protected him from all kinds of peril. Just as you did for me."

She stroked his stubble-dusted face and fought the lump swelling in her throat. "I've felt alone most of my life, Hunter. I've lost people I loved and counted on, had to take a backseat to the demands of my aunt's career…

and Chris's. He left me last February because of his duty to his throne. He may have loved me, but not with his whole heart. I don't want to be second with the man in my life. I want unconditional love and loyalty. I didn't have that with Chris."

Hunter blinked as if he wasn't sure he'd heard her correctly. "What are you saying?"

"I'm saying I told Chris I couldn't marry him."

"But what about Ben? His right to the throne in Meridan?"

She nodded. "The throne will still be there when Ben's older. He'll still be Chris's legal heir. Chris has agreed to keep Ben's identity a secret until Ben, at age eighteen, can decide for himself what he wants to do with his life."

Hunter narrowed his eyes. "And what happens until Ben is eighteen?"

"I'll raise him, with financial support from Chris, and Chris will have liberal visitation rights with his son. Ben will spend time, maybe summers, in Meridan, learning the culture and history. We want him to make an informed choice when the time comes."

Hunter stared at her, his gaze stunned and his eyes searching hers. "So...where does that leave us?"

She bit her lip and took a deep breath. "I guess that's up to you. Since the day we met, you've stood by me, even when you thought you might lose me to another man. I know you've felt like someone's second choice before, like you've always had to settle for other people's hand-me-downs. I'm sorry if my situation made you feel pushed aside or less than completely cherished and appreciated for who you are."

He shook his head. "It's okay."

She cupped his face between her hands. "No, it's not. Because you aren't second to me. I love your courage and conviction, and I treasure the warmth and compassion you show everyone in your life. I see your integrity and values in every choice you make, and you inspire me to be a better person. I love your sense of humor, your patience, your love for your family…even your stubbornness. I want to wake up to your sexy smile and beautiful eyes, and when my doctor's six-week moratorium is over, I want to make love to you until we're both too weak to do anything but sleep in each other's arms. When I look at all you've come to mean to me and my son, I can't imagine putting you anywhere but first in my life. Just the way you've put me first these past weeks. When I think about the future, I don't want the *life* of royalty, I want a *love* that makes me feel royal to one special man. I want what I've found with you. I love you, Hunter. *You're* my future."

His eyes grew damp, and he threaded his fingers through her hair. "Me, too. You're an amazing woman, Bri." Wincing, he leaned forward and kissed her nose. "I guess the reason none of my other relationships fit right was because I was meant to be with you." He sat back in the wheelchair, holding his ribs. "I want to grow old with you, Bri."

A release swept through her, relief that she hadn't misread his feelings for her, joy for the days ahead. "That sounds wonderful." This time, she leaned closer to kiss him, but pulled back at the last second. "And you're okay with raising another man's son? Sharing custody with Chris?"

Hunter captured her nape and tugged her forward,

completing the kiss. "As long as I'm not sharing you, your heart."

She bit her lip and shook her head. "No, that is entirely yours. Always."

His expression warmed, and his eyes lit with his smile. "Then I'd be honored to help raise your young prince."

"*Our* young prince. You have every right to claim him."

He cocked his head. "Do you think Chris would be all right with me adopting Ben?"

"I know he would. He wants what's best for Ben, and he knows you've gone the extra mile already for his son. In fact, Chris said when he got back to Meridan, he'd see that you were duly recognized for your heroism. He mentioned you being knighted." She sent him a lopsided grin. "How does *Sir* Hunter Mansfield sound to you?"

He gave a short laugh. "Not as good as making you Mrs. Hunter Mansfield."

She raised a startled gaze. "Is that a proposal?"

"No," he said, then struggled, grimacing, to get out of the wheelchair and down on one knee. "Brianna Coleman, the day you nearly ran over me was the luckiest day of my life. I pretended that day to be your husband, and the role felt right. I'd like to apply for a permanent gig. Will you let me have the honor of being your real husband?"

She slid off the bed so that she knelt in front of him and gently looped her arms around his neck. "The wife of a knight. That sounds a bit like a fairy tale, too."

"As long as we get the happily-ever-after, that's all that matters to me." He framed her face with his hands and drilled her with his intense blue gaze. "So is that a yes? Will you marry me?"

She laughed and kissed his bruised cheek. "Oh, did I forget to answer?"

"Not funny, Bri." He gave her a mock scowl. "Will you answer already? My ribs are killing me."

She chuckled and kissed him deeply. "Yes, Sir Hunter. Of course, yes!"

* * * * *

A sneaky peek at next month...

INTRIGUE...

A SEDUCTIVE COMBINATION OF DANGER AND DESIRE

My wish list for next month's titles...

In stores from 20th June 2014:

❏ Wedding at Cardwell Ranch — BJ Daniels

& Stranded — Alice Sharpe

❏ Explosive Engagement — Lisa Childs

& Undercover Warrior — Aimée Thurlo

❏ Hard Ride to Dry Gulch — Joanna Wayne

& Sanctuary in Chef Voleur — Mallory Kane

Romantic Suspense

❏ Lone Wolf Standing — Carla Cassidy

Available at WHSmith, Tesco, Asda, Eason, Amazon and Apple

Just can't wait?

Join our *EXCLUSIVE* eBook club

FROM JUST £1.99 A MONTH!

Never miss a book again with our hassle-free eBook subscription.

★ Pick how many titles you want from each series with our flexible subscription

★ Your titles are delivered to your device on the first of every month

★ Zero risk, zero obligation!

There really is nothing standing in the way of you and your favourite books!

Start your eBook subscription today at www.millsandboon.co.uk/subscribe

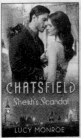

Join the Mills & Boon Book Club

Want to read more **Intrigue** books?
We're offering you **2 more** absolutely **FREE!**

We'll also treat you to these fabulous extras:

- Exclusive offers and much more!
- FREE home delivery
- FREE books and gifts with our special rewards scheme

Get your free books now!

visit **www.millsandboon.co.uk/bookclub**
or call Customer Relations on **020 8288 2888**